A WITCH'S LAMENT

THE SALEM WITCHES - BOOK ONE

Cathy Walker
Author

BOOKS BY CATHY WALKER

A Witch's Lament – The Salem Witches Book 1

A Witch's Legacy – The Salem Witches Book 2

A Witch's Light – The Salem Witches Book 3

The Witch of Endor – The Witch Tree Book 1

The Daughters of Endor – The Witch Tree Book 2
Coming in 2024

The Book of Endor – The Witch Tree Book 3
Coming in 2024

Sword Across Time

The Crystal of Light

Solitary Cove

Pandora's Quest

CHAPTER ONE

People whisper tales behind quivering hands and murmur behind doors closed against prying ears. These tales bespeak of an age-old darkness that creeps into the fiber of a person's soul and uses them to lie, steal, rape, and murder. Ancient woes of entire civilizations disappearing and people turning on their own in an unexplained rampage are laid at the feet of this darkness that no one understands.

Gaining strength and a need for more—more hate, more lust, more death—this darkness appeared most recently in a small village called Salem, Massachusetts in the year 1692. After a brief but horrifying reign of fear and death, it was defeated. So people think. With an innate sense of survival, it burrowed into a soul weak with greed and there bides its time until circumstances allow a reappearance and a chance to feed upon man's fear.

For any who read this entry be warned, do not let judgments and narrow-mindedness rule. Only one's commitment to goodness and pure love-energy can defeat, possibly even destroy, this phantom of hell.

Excerpt from *Faerie Enchantments and Sorcerer Magick*

A sliver of moon cut through the night sky like a scythe. Its rays cast a low glow across the land, barely enough light to illume the frantic scampering of a rodent intent on escaping the needle sharp claws of a rapacious owl. But nightfall lent cover to more than just nature's cycle of life. The light of day ebbing to the dark of night gave other creatures freedom to act on their baser instincts. Or, as in the case of the person in a darkened cellar, the freedom to act on a soulless promise given centuries before.

Hidden from the moon's rays, locked from even the most intent of night crawlers, the tiny room thrummed with feverish expectancy. Hot wax sizzled from the array of strategically placed candles, while flickering flames danced shadows on roughly hewn walls. Purple silk cloth lay across the dirt floor like a mantle and a crudely carved stone altar provided the only furnishing in the room. Upon the altar rested an oval-shaped silver bowl beside an ornate knife of Celtic design.

And a terrified young woman.

Rustling cloth signaled the movement of someone from the darkest shadow into the dim glow of candlelight. Shrouded in a black hooded robe, the figure moved toward the altar.

Eyes bulging in terror, the woman kicked her bound feet in a feeble movement of defense, but only managed to twist her body partly off the altar stone. None too gently, her captor hunched over and swung her back into place. Keeping a tight grip on her arm, the robed figure knelt before the altar and reached for the knife. Low chanting began, and with care and precision, the perpetrator of the ritual thrust the knife into the woman and sliced her from throat to belly. The pain-filled scream, hardly able to be credited to a human, lasted only a second and the struggling ceased. Blood ran everywhere as the killer's incessant chanting continued.

Finally, the chanting ceased and silence fell.

Intently filling the altar bowl with blood, no thought was spared for the corpse that had been a living, breathing person until a moment ago. Grasping fingers plunged into the bowl and smeared blood on the wall; an action repeated until each one bore the symbol of a pentagram. However, the person had drawn the symbol upside down in an insulting manner directed against the benign beliefs of Wicca. With each point to signify a different meaning, fire, earth, water, air, and spirit. The figure took silent pleasure in twisting the pentagram's position to oppose the very roots of the symbol's meaning.

The room was prepared. The time was here. A verse memorized so long ago, a lifetime ago, was recited with focused intent. The vengeful voice pulsed through the room and the words spoken brought forth ancestral powers and forces of darkness.

Upon this eve, I bid you here
A pact long ago spoken
Now shall be woken
My life exchanged for a knife
The essence of many souls given
For mine own soul's eternal power

With each word, the figure seemed to grow and pulsate. Uneven breathing rasped within the breeze that suddenly twisted through the room. With certainty lighting empty eyes, the speaker folded to the floor in exhaustion and choked out two words before succumbing to a faint.

"She comes."

Skye Temple eyed the sign in the window and breathed a frustrated sigh. *Out to Lunch. Be back at 1:00.* She'd pushed the speed limit for the last 3 ½ hours, only to have to wait anyway. Figures. Tamping down her excitement, she ran her fingers through her hair and surveyed the street. Tingles fluttered in her stomach. She was really here. Salem, Massachusetts; a town with a chaotic history of blood lust, witchery, and Puritanism.

Strangely empty, the street conveyed an eerie, muffled stillness broken only by a dry leaf blowing across the cobbled sidewalk and the honk of a distant horn. She shivered as her blood thrummed, swirling and searching for the fulfillment of something primal. Ancient. Unknown. Present within her was a deep surety that she was where she needed to be, though her purpose remained unclear. Salem's atmosphere awoke a longing for something she hadn't even known was missing in her life until her visit two weeks ago. Strange as it seemed, the town now welcomed her back like a lost daughter or a sheep returning to the fold.

A moment of unexpected panic seized her. What had she done? Had she made a mistake? Her heart thudded fiercely in her chest and stole her breath. If it was a mistake, it was too late to do anything about it now. Giving herself a mental shake, not even wanting to consider what problems her hasty decision might herald, she glanced at the real estate office where she'd come to pick up the keys to her new house. The house she'd bought on impulse.

Looking for a way to pass the time, her gaze came to rest on a store across the cobbled pedestrian walkway of Essex St. The store's uniqueness piqued her curiosity with its curtained windows, lack of any obvious advertising, and a huge front door of elaborately knurled dark wood. The only statement the store made that attested to retail was the ornate gold lettering carved into a plaque of wood that hung above the doors.

Witches Haven.

Unease rasped down her spine. But why? Witch stores abounded in a town like Salem, and nothing about this one seemed threatening. Intrigued and wary, Skye stepped carefully over the uneven cobblestones of the narrow street and placed her hand on the cool handle of the door. She hesitated. The urge to go back and wait in the Jeep hit her, but it was so brief that it must have been her imagination. Her mother always cautioned that her impulsiveness overrode her common sense. Skye took a deep breath and tried to mind-sense what waited on the other side of the door, but nothing jumped out at her. No sense of impending doom or danger.

A feeling of warmth brushed across her arm, and a whisper tickled her ear.

You've come too far. There is no turning back.

She snatched her hand back from the door. When had she started hearing voices? And there was no turning back for sure, as she'd already bought the house. Skye shook her head to clear the uneasy thoughts, and then, with an assertive yank, opened the door, and stepped into the store.

It took a moment to adjust to the subdued light, but then her gaze swept the store, mainly to reassure that no danger hovered in the shadows. Bookshelves stretched the full length of the wall on one side of the store, while glass showcases laid claim to the opposing wall. Floors shone with the look of freshly polished wood, and a few antique wooden tables dotted the store. Crystal figurines, candles, and jewelry filled the display cases.

The perfection of it all struck Skye as odd. Books lined the bookshelves in order of height from shortest to tallest, each table possessed its own color theme with nothing allowed that didn't fall within that specific color, whether it be purple, green, yellow, or blue, and even the items in the showcases had a certain order of size and color.

A couple of customers browsed the shelves, while a woman argued with a deliveryman in the farthest corner of the store. The woman's voice, subdued as it was, swelled with anger and frustration, while the man just shrugged and gestured toward the boxes.

"Excuse me, could I just reach past you."

Skye started, her attention redirected from the arguing couple, although their discordant voices buzzed her subconscious. "Oh, I'm sorry." She stepped aside to let a young girl take a deck of tarot cards off the shelf.

"No problem. If it's your first time in here, I can understand your zoned-out state. Impressive place, isn't it?"

She nodded and smiled. "Oh, yeah. Although..."

"I know. It lacks feeling."

"Exactly. How did you know what I was thinking?" Skye looked at the young, blond girl whose face radiated friendliness.

The girl shrugged. "I sense things." The girl quickly added, "Are you from around here? I know most local people, but haven't seen you around. Are you visiting? If you are, I can recommend some great places to see. There's the Salem Witch Museum, Peabody Essex Museum, the Witches Dungeon. Oh, the best place to see is the Witch House. It's the only place still standing that goes back to the trials, and it belonged to one judge who condemned all those innocent people to death. You might also want to see..."

"Okay, enough." Skye laughed and raised her hands in protest. "I'm not a tourist. As soon as I sign some papers, I become an official Salem resident."

"Oh, how cool. Too bad I won't be around long enough for us to get to know each other." The girl rolled her baby blue eyes. "I'm enrolled at Boston University in the fall, you know. I can't wait to get away from here."

"You don't enjoy living in Salem?"

"It's all right, I guess, but..." she took a quick look around and whispered, "...all the witch wannabes kind of irritate me."

"Witch wannabes. I haven't heard that term before."

"Yeah, and my mom is the worst. Always trying to talk me into doing some ritual or other." She flashed the tarot cards in her hands. "Hence the cards. Mom figures that no self-respecting witch should be without at least one deck. She never inherited grandma's powers, but I did, so Mom tries to live her magic through me. Does that make sense?"

"I guess." Although the concept of a mother actually encouraging her daughter to practice magic was a difficult concept for Skye to grasp, especially when her own mother discouraged that very thing. Not always successfully. "But I'm sure she only wants what's best for you. At least she's willing to give you some guidance. Maybe you shouldn't shrug off her advice."

"Maybe." The girl extended her hand. "By the way, my name's Chastity."

"I'm Skye." She took Chastity's hand and instantly wished she hadn't.

A vision of blackness thrust itself onto Skye, along with a sense of warped intent. Chastity's face glowed briefly in Skye's mind's eye only to split in two when a knife slashed across the younger woman's features. Streams of blood shot through darkness and turned blond hair to red. Skye's breath caught in her chest as she struggled to regain her senses. A scream of pain and fear echoed through Skye and she watched helplessly as Chastity drifted into the darkness, leaving Skye with one last shimmer of blue from lifeless eyes.

With a sob, Skye pulled her hand from Chastity's and managed to disconnect herself from the vision. It took a moment to regain her breath and become aware of her surroundings. Unfortunately, the icy stare of the woman in the corner and Chastity's frown let Skye know that her vision hadn't gone undetected.

"What did you see?" Chastity whispered, her blue eyes round and glowing. "I knew it. I knew you had powers the moment I saw you. I felt you before you even entered the store."

Skye struggled to act normal. That was the first time a vision had intruded so fiercely, and with no warning. It left her weak and more than a little scared. Sure, she'd experienced the occasional wavering of reality or a flash of light signaling the presence of a sprite or spirit, but never to the degree she'd just felt. She'd always consciously instigated any wanderings into another realm or altered state of consciousness with her mom's firm supervision.

So how had such a vivid vision struck her so unexpectedly and with such power? More importantly, what should she tell Chastity? The vision showed the young woman in some kind of danger. Serious danger. Should Skye attempt another vision? No. She didn't know enough about guiding her own visions to attempt one of her own accord. Besides, she had barely kept control over that vision. An attempt at another one without being prepared might prove disastrous.

"Skye?" Chastity laid her hand on Skye's arm. Warmth and comfort flowed between them and Skye realized that Chastity was using her own energy to settle Skye's. She smiled.

"I'm okay." She looked into blue eyes filled with concern and saw the shimmer of a knife reflected. She gasped and stepped back, fighting the urge to flee. "Chastity, I..."

"No, don't tell me." Chastity took a step back as well. Her voice wavered slightly when she spoke. "I've always felt that once voice is given to thought, it becomes a reality. Whatever you saw, keep it to yourself. Please." She pleaded. "Besides, visions are private. I understand if you don't want to tell me what you saw." Her gaze darted to the woman in the corner who'd abandoned her argument with the delivery man and was speaking vehemently into a cell phone. "You know, sometimes I feel my powers are dangerous. I've told no one that before. It probably sounds silly."

Torn between sharing her vision and keeping such a repulsive scene to herself, Skye tried to comfort Chastity. "It's not silly; it's just a fear of the unknown. The more you develop your powers, the more comfortable you'll feel with them." Was she trying to comfort herself more than Chastity? "Look, if you need anyone to talk to, I bought a house on Winter Island Road and you're welcome to visit anytime."

Chastity frowned. "Far as I know, only one house over there was up for sale, and I can't believe you had the nerve to buy it. It's haunted, you know."

"Haunted?" A finger of cold drew a line down Skye's spine.

She hadn't considered that possibility when she'd bought an old house in a town full of witches. "I'm sure it's just local hype. You know, for the tourists."

"No. It's really haunted." Chastity leaned closer and whispered, "Rumors are that something horrible happened there about thirty years ago and the ghosts of the past will possess anyone who dares enter the house."

An ominous weight settled over Skye, and she gave herself a mental shake. Why did she suddenly have a sense of the inevitable creeping up on her? As if her path had been set the instant she'd laid eyes on the house and an unseen force had directed everything she'd done from then on. Crap. How did she get herself into these situations?

Not wanting Chastity to see how much her words had upset her, Skye smiled. "Give me a couple of days to settle in, and then I'd love to have you over to regale me with ghostly tales of Salem." She hoped Chastity would accept and not be scared off by Skye's unusual behavior. Besides, after her vivid, disturbed vision, Skye felt some responsibility to keep an eye on her new friend.

Chastity studied Skye as if weighing the wisdom of pursuing a friendship. She shrugged. "Sure, I'd like that."

"Great. Why don't you give me your phone number and I'll call you."

While Chastity wrote her number on a piece of paper, Skye considered her vision and pondered the wisdom of at least giving Chastity the gist of what she'd see, even if the girl didn't want to know. The thing was that visions couldn't be interpreted literally, and she didn't want to come off sounding like some lunatic and scare Chastity more than she already had.

"Here you go."

Skye took the paper and shoved it in her jean jacket pocket.

"Look." Skye placed her hand on Chastity's arm. "Be careful."

An awareness of the inevitability of fate flashed across Chastity's face. In a deliberate gesture, she placed the tarot cards back on the shelf and left the store. Her departure left Skye drained and wondering what force of fate had led her to Salem. What more did that same fate hold in store for her? Well, she'd bought a haunted house that couldn't help but stir things up.

Only barely aware of the woman approaching her from the back of the store, Skye realized that Mr. Lambert should be back in his office by now. The urge to reassure herself she'd made the right decision drove her out of the store and across the street to claim the keys to her home.

Fierce anger tore through Jerome Phips when he looked down at the mutilated body of another young girl. A couple of kids on a bike hike had found the ritual setting of the girl's final resting place just outside of town. Jerome could only hope that the naked, bloody condition of the body wouldn't haunt them for too long.

His radio crackled, and Chief Wilder's voice breaking over the airwaves interrupted Jerome's roiling emotions.

"Hold tight, Jerome, C.I.D's on their way and I've called the D.A's office, so the usual teams will be there to investigate."

Jerome clenched his teeth when he replied, "They won't find a damn thing. They never do." Futility whipped through him at the memory of two other sites just like this one. Young girls, locally born and well known around town, had disappeared, only to reappear shortly after—dead and sacrificially dismembered. "Whoever's doing this has to make a mistake sometime."

"I'm sure you realize..."

"I know. The time between murders is getting shorter. Just do your job and keep your head."

"Yeah, sure." Jerome disconnected his boss and life-long friend with a deliberate snort. As much as he hated to admit it, Samson was right. He needed to control himself because he didn't want to be responsible for what would happen if he let loose. The emotions welling up inside almost choked him with their ferocity. And he didn't have enough control over what powers he had to lend reality to the ones he wasn't sure about.

While he waited, he paced. But he avoided the murder scene. It was up to the forensics experts now. Besides, the visions of white flesh torn ragged with streaks of red and the contorted features of the body would haunt him forever. Or at least until he saw the bastard who'd performed such a sick ritual brought to justice. Or dead.

Without thought, memories of his past intruded on the more recent murder, and he cursed them for the thousandth time. His senses nagged him with the surety of a connection between past and present circumstances. Pacing the hard packed ground and keeping his eyes off the gruesome sight of death, he breathed a sigh of relief when the sound of tires crunching on gravel announced someone's arrival. That meant he could leave the scene.

He needed a shower. He also needed to talk with Eldon.

CHAPTER TWO

Skye opened the finely etched glass door and stepped inside. The jingle of a bell and the clack of her cowboy boots on the hardwood floor announcing her presence. It was a nice enough office with dark mahogany furniture, pastel-colored paintings of flowers dancing in a field, and muted shades of lavender wallpaper. Skye waited for a moment, the silence of the room echoing the earlier silence that had greeted her when she arrived in Salem.

"Hello. Anyone here?"

Though she'd spoken quietly enough, her voice blasted like a cannon shot, but garnered no answer. Skye shifted her feet and tugged at the hem of her jean jacket. Truth was, she'd sent the movers yesterday with instructions to pick up the key at the realtors and return it after unpacking, but as far as Mr. Eldon Lambert knew, she wasn't arriving in town until tomorrow. She chewed her lip and wondered about exploring the shadowed hallway at the back of the room when footsteps sounded in the hall and Eldon appeared. A frown creased his forehead and added wrinkles to an already wrinkled face. The furrows deepened when he caught sight of Skye.

"Miss Temple. I wasn't expecting you until tomorrow."

"Sorry, Mr. Lambert, but I finished last-minute details sooner than expected. Did the movers pick up the key as planned?"

"Yes. Yes, of course." He motioned her to take a seat by his desk. "Sit. There are a few papers for you to sign before I hand over the keys. And please, call me Eldon."

Eldon shuffled the papers across the desk, clearing his throat and looking as if he wanted to speak. Unease gave Skye pause, and she held the pen poised over the papers.

"Is everything all right? I mean, I hope that showing up early hasn't caused any problems."

"No. No, of course not." His avoidance of direct eye contact belied the truth of his denial.

Anxiety licked up Skye's spine. He was hiding something. But for the life of her, Skye had no idea what it could be or how it could have anything to do with her. Eldon's strange behavior coupled with lingering uneasiness from her vision almost sent her racing for her Jeep and home, except she remembered she'd given up her apartment in Camden. Home was here, in Salem. Knowing she'd come too far to back out now, she sent Eldon a tremulous smile and, ignoring her inner thoughts of flight, signed the final papers with a flourish.

Eldon cleared his throat. "Well, it's too late to back out now."

Skye stared at the realtor. Had he read her mind? "Why would I want to back out?"

Eldon smiled. "Just a little real estate humor."

"Oh." Skye didn't see the humor, but refrained from remarking. Instead, she picked up her keys and pensively weighed them in her hand.

"I bet you would never have guessed that a writing assignment about a local bed & breakfast would result in you becoming a homeowner." Eldon's intent gaze bore into her as if he expected some explanation for her impulsive act.

"No. It's the last thing I would have imagined." The last thing her mother would expect either, but that was a situation to confront after she'd settled into her new house. After she'd worked up the nerve to approach her mother with the news that would most definitely send the woman into a tirade.

"You're sure you've never been here before? Maybe you have family who used to live here or something?"

"No. As I told you, I've never been to Salem, and neither has anyone in my family." Eldon's probe for information made Skye uncomfortable because she remembered how he'd subtly drilled her when she'd originally shown interest in the house. Some questions he'd asked her had seemed strange, and slightly out of character for a real estate agent to ask a potential buyer.

Do you know anything about the witch trials? Does your family have ancestors from this area? What drew you to this house in particular? How old are you? Did your mother live in the area about thirty years ago?

Of course, he'd peppered the questions in amongst regular conversation, and it wasn't until Skye had left town that she started putting them together as a strange combination of probing questions that had nothing to do with her buying the house. She'd chalked it up to curiosity.

Now she thought differently. Skye was sure that Eldon's probing had a purpose. But what could he possibly be looking for? Whatever it was, she didn't have it. Or did she? An irritating niggle in her mind warned her that all was not as it seemed and that maybe some deep fragment of her did hold some secrets. The same secrets Eldon seemed so intent on drawing from her. None of this made sense, and as long as she was in the dark, she felt vulnerable. Maybe it was time to go on the offensive and ask some questions herself.

"So tell me, why did the house sit empty for so long? It's a gorgeous lot, the house doesn't need that much work, and the price was more than reasonable. I just don't understand how someone hasn't snatched it up long before now."

A flush rose from Eldon's neck to color his face and he clenched the papers until his knuckles turned white. When he cleared his throat and spoke, his voice was a whisper. "It's supposed to be..."

"Haunted? I've heard." Skye almost laughed, but Eldon looked so serious she was afraid to offend him.

Her acceptance of his statement seemed to release a flow of information from Eldon. "It was built about twenty-five years after the witch trials, you know, the Salem witch trials. It belonged to Dorcas Good, the daughter of Sarah Good, one of the first three. First three accused, that is." He stopped and looked at her as if waiting for her to comment. When she didn't, he shrugged and continued. "Dorcas lived there for five or six years, but, from what I understand, the townspeople never let her forget her mother had been hanged as a witch. One family in particular, the Putnam family, harassed her until she couldn't leave her own home for fear of being stoned or threatened. Even staying home wasn't a solution, because they'd throw rocks through her windows or set fire to her garden. She finally moved out of town and never returned."

"But that doesn't explain the house being haunted."

Eldon shrugged. "No one knows for sure, but some say that the ghost of Sarah Good vowed vengeance for her daughter's unjust harassment. Others say that when Dorcas died some thirty years later, she didn't want anyone else living in the house she'd been driven from, so her spirit came back to haunt it."

Although a place like Salem must be rampant with rumors of hauntings and ghosts, something about this tale, in particular, made Skye feel queasy. "You couldn't have told me this before I bought the house?" She tried to infuse her voice with humor but failed miserably.

Eldon frowned and stared at her. "I thought you would have known the stories."

"How would I know?"

"Because...well, I just figured you would have heard, you know, being in town and writing the article and all."

"It was a travel article on a bed-and-breakfast."

"Oh, well. You've signed the papers, so you can't back out now." Flustered, he walked toward the door and waited for Skye.

She followed pensively, unable to understand the undercurrents that filled everything Eldon said. She didn't care if the house was purported to be haunted. Heck, it made her purchase more interesting, if somewhat disconcerting. What she didn't understand was Eldon's assumption that she should know about its history, and, even though he hadn't said anything, the sense that he thought she was hiding something from him.

She absent-mindedly climbed into her Jeep and pulled away from the curb. The fact that the house was haunted didn't surprise her. The house had compelled her from the start, while Salem prodded the deepest part of herself that Skye had kept buried all these years. And being a firm believer in fate, Skye knew that the house was meant for her. Breaking free from her mother's constant attention, even if well-intended, was partly why she'd moved to a town rampant with magic. But mainly, her blood sang with the need to understand her own abilities and move beyond the simple rituals she'd done until then, and that was why she'd bought the house and moved to Salem.

Following Eldon's directions, Skye easily found Winter Island Rd. It followed a stretch of the Atlantic Ocean and then circled around and back onto itself. Butterfly wings tickled her stomach as she drove past the few homes gracing the street and considered herself fortunate to have found a house so reasonably priced in the area. She slowed down and practically drooled over one of the houses, a grand one that boasted three steep gables, a deep porch, and triple casement windows. Painted dark gray, almost black, the house also included two stone chimneys that speared to the sky.

The next house, she couldn't see because it rested too far back on the winding drive amidst a grove of gigantic oak and maple trees. The third house was hers. A narrow gravel drive curved through a copse of black cherry trees that gave shade to a ground cover of white cushion moss. Skye drove under the umbrella of leaves and her pulse quickened upon approaching the house.

She was a homeowner. It was hard to believe after ten years of giving in to the wanderlust that carried her across the country, building a name for herself as a travel writer. More precisely, a writer for connoisseurs of the perfect bed-and-breakfast. When she'd told her boss at *Wandering Minstrel* magazine that she was quitting, he'd almost had an apoplectic fit, even going so far as offering her a raise which Skye had been tempted to accept just to make the tightwad part with some of the money he hoarded so much. But the memory of the house and the feelings it had instilled within her at first sight kept her from accepting his offer.

Gravel crunched under the tires, and she maneuvered the Jeep around the last curve of the winding drive. Just like the first time, the sight of the house greeted her with a familiar sense of returning home. Haunted or not, the house was hers. Tears welled in her eyes as she appreciated the fading beauty and grace of the Colonial structure. Georgian Colonial, according to Eldon. An overgrown pathway led through a garden to a sweep of wooden stairs that climbed to a front door topped with decorative crown molding. Columns rose on either side of the door and windows ran the length of the building, each one with nine panes of glass streaked with weather and dust. The overall effect accentuated the square, symmetrical shape of the house.

Skye stepped into the house for the first time as its owner, and tingled with the awareness of her surroundings. A faint musty smell tickled her nose and mingled with a waft of disturbed dust, making her want to sneeze, but the shrill ringing of her cell phone shattered the stillness and stopped the sneeze. With a gesture of impatience, not bothering to check the call display, she answered the phone.

"Skye, where have you been? I've been trying to get a hold of you for days. Every time I try to call your apartment, some droning machine tells me your service is disconnected. What is going on?"

She rolled her eyes and cursed whatever had made her answer the phone without checking to see who was calling.

Jerome arrived home and gulped a deep breath of air into his lungs. He reveled in the salty crispness of the nearby sea air and let its freshness wash over him as he strode through his front yard. Weaving through and around the many carved tree stumps that dotted his yard, he affectionately patted the head of his favorite; a wolf he'd carved from a tree stump so huge that he hadn't been able to span it with both his arms.

Taking the back stairs two at a time, he headed directly to the phone just inside the sliding glass door and punched in Eldon's number. Not even giving the realtor a chance to say hello, Jerome harangued him with questions. "Eldon, we need to talk. Has that woman picked up her keys yet? Did you find out anything more about who she is?

"Slow down, Jerome. Yes, she picked up her keys. As far as I can tell, her name is Skye Temple, and she has no connection to anyone or anything."

Jerome removed his hat and ran a hand through his hair, making a mental note that it needed cutting. He liked to keep it short, almost a buzz cut. Tossing the hat, he watched it settle on the counter, its well-known witch on a broomstick crest blazing bright blue, black, and yellow against the white countertop. He paced the kitchen floor. "I don't believe it. She has to be a Good, or she wouldn't have bought that house. That damn house only appeals to descendants of the Goods and you said that she bought that particular house because it drew her inexplicably."

"Yes, I said that, and if she is who we think, you need to get control over your impatience. This could get dangerous if we're not careful."

"It already has gotten dangerous for three murdered girls."

"Three?" A veil of silence grated through the phone line.

"Jerome, I'm so sorry. No wonder you're upset."

"Dammit, Eldon, sorry doesn't cut it." Taking a shuddering breath, he counted to ten. "Sorry. We both know what's at stake. Is she a descendant of the Goods? Is she Flora's daughter? Has she developed her powers? Has she turned to the darker side of witchcraft, like her mother? Does she have anything to do with the murders?"

"Jerome, we don't know for sure Flora had anything to do with your mother's disappearance. Heck, even if Flora is Skye's mother, I don't see how she can have anything to do with the current murders. Please don't do anything you might regret. There are too many unknowns and everyone is innocent until proven guilty."

"My mother didn't disappear. Someone murdered her, and I'm going to find the killer, whatever it takes. Until then, no one who was there that night is innocent."

"Including me?" Eldon spoke softly, but the hurt was apparent.

Feeling guilty for making such a blanket statement, Jerome was about to apologize, but choked on the words. Christ, all these years of friendship and he couldn't tell Eldon that he trusted him. Shock at the sudden realization left Jerome speechless until the jingling of a bell in the background signaled the arrival of someone at Eldon's office. With a reticent goodbye, the realtor hung up, leaving Jerome alone with the silence of his home and a feeling that things were bad and about to get worse. Even worse than the memories of a time long ago when terror had ruled the night.

Skye took a deep breath and wondered what had prompted her mother to call from a cruise ship in the middle of the Caribbean. Her parents, Walter Adams and Flora Temple, had sailed two weeks ago, which meant they still had four weeks before returning home. The secret was to keep the conversation light. No need to break the news over the phone, even though the prospect of avoiding a face-to-face confrontation made it tempting. But she didn't want to ruin her parent's vacation. Yeah, that was it. She'd tell them later.

"Hi, Mom. How's the cruise? Have you and Dad survived without killing each other?" She did her best to keep her voice even though her pulse raced.

"The cruise is fine. Your father and I would never stoop to murder. What are you trying to hide from me?"

In an attempt to still her nervousness, Skye strode to a pile of boxes covered by a blue tarp and tugged at the corner.

"Skyyyee."

"What?"

"Don't what me, young lady, I know you too well." The deep blast of a ship's horn sounded through the phone and mingled with sounds of laughter and splashing.

She imagined her mother lounging by the pool, most likely sipping some fancy drink decorated with an umbrella. She'd be dressed in one of her caftans, probably gold or burgundy, her silver-gray hair pulled back into a long braid. Her father would be close by as well, because the two rarely left each other's side. Skye did not know how they made it through thirty-five years of living together without a major blow-up. Most couples she knew couldn't spend a full day in each other's company without arguing about something.

"Sounds like you're by the pool." She tugged harder at the end of the tarp. "Must be nice to laze around while the rest of us are working."

Her mother whispered to someone at the other end. "Dear, your father wants to say hi, but we're not done talking yet."

One last tug, and Skye managed to remove the tarp from her stuff and start a mental check to account for everything.

"Hey, baby doll, how's it going? Her father's voice boomed loudly enough through the phone that she had to move it away from her ear.

"Everything's fine." Damn, she'd tried to keep her voice even, but, as usual, her father picked up on her mood. The sounds of revelry faded, and Skye assumed he was moving away from the pool. And her mother.

"Really. Now try telling me the truth."

"Everything is fine. It's just that I've done something I know is going to upset Mom. A lot."

"She knows."

Skye gasped. "How can she know? I only just got here."

"Got where? She doesn't know what you've done, sweets, only that you've done something." He heaved an exaggerated sigh. "Maybe you should enlighten me so I can ease the way for you." The 'as usual' went unspoken.

She chewed her lower lip, pushed a box out of the way, and plopped down on her couch to consider the situation. When her magic abilities had made an appearance, back to the very first time she'd ever lit a candle without a match, her mother had insisted that Skye never practice magic alone. At first, Skye had thought all witches had a partner or a coven when practicing their craft, but as she grew older, she realized many people were solitary practitioners. When she confronted her mother with this knowledge, her mother had grabbed her arm and made her swear an oath never to practice alone. She'd even gone so far as to prick both their fingers with a boline, her mother's ritual knife, and swear a blood oath. Skye never knew why her mother was so adamant, but she'd always kept her word.

Until now. For some reason, the Fates had forced her into taking a stand and making a change. And it seemed as if being here, in Salem, presented an atmosphere conducive to her powers. The longer she spent here, the harder it was to deny what she felt bubbling up inside, like a boiling volcano. But she couldn't tell her parents that. They didn't need to worry. Besides, this was something she needed to do on her own.

She whispered to her father, almost afraid to speak the truth. "I sold everything, used my savings, and bought a house in Salem." She grimaced. So much for waiting to tell them. She waited for the bellow of anger. Nothing.

"Dad." The whispered word barely made a ripple over the phone.

Still nothing. The distant sound of splashing reassured her she still had a connection. "Dad, say something. Please."

"There's nothing to say. What's done is done." Resignation gave his voice a heavy quality, and guilt stabbed her. She hated disappointing her father.

"But, you're not even going to yell at me. After all, it was a totally irresponsible thing to do."

"It was bound to happen sometime."

"Bound to happen? I'm confused. Mom's always preaching about not using magic, so what do I do? Move to a town with one of the most vivid histories of witchcraft, and most likely the highest population of actual witches. You should be furious with me."

"Your mom warns you about using your craft alone, not that you shouldn't practice. She worries about you."

"Yes, and that's what I don't understand. There are witches all over who practice solitary craft with no danger. Why should I be any different?"

"You are different." His voice faded into an echo, and Skye almost jumped from the couch when her mother's voice blasted over the phone.

"Tell me you aren't doing your magic without me."

"No, Mom, I'm not." She thought about the vivid vision she'd experienced only a short while ago and added silently, *Not intentionally.*

"Then what are you hiding from me?"

"Mom, Dad has something to tell you. Talk to you later." With a flick of her wrist, Skye snapped her phone shut. "Chicken shit," she muttered. She couldn't face her mother's anger. Her father would smooth the way for her, and when they returned from their cruise, her mother would be more rational and easily reasoned with.

Sighing, she gazed around her new home, and fingers of excitement mixed with a dawning feeling of dread. Eldon and Chastity had said the house was haunted. What if it was? And if Dorcas Good's ghost did roam within these walls, what circumstances had led to her restless spirit not finding peace? She shivered as a cloud passed over the sun, darkening the room and cooling the surrounding air. A flickering movement by the window drew her attention, but when she looked, she saw nothing more than a curtain fluttering in the breeze.

Except there was no breeze. And something was different. The atmosphere had shifted since her first time here, and she had the distinct impression that the house was trying to communicate with her. Maybe even warn her. Goosebumps crept up her arms and gut-felt fear took root. All sound ceased and the room around her receded into a blur, darkening into an abyss. It swallowed her like a giant beast. Dizziness, or more a sense of wavering, came over her as her vision cleared and she found that her surroundings no longer resembled her new home. Instead, finely carved wood furniture and damask drapes replaced the cardboard boxes and created a refined vision of times gone past.

Tentatively, she reached out, ran her fingers over the gilt carvings of a dark walnut chair and came to rest on the needlework embroidery that depicted water lilies. Awed by the delicate designs of Queen Anne furnishings, Skye wanted to explore her vision further, but movement drew her attention. No more than two feet in front of her, a wisp of mist wafted about the floor and grew into an almost distinguishable human shape. A woman. Dressed in an ankle-length gray skirt, darker gray blouse that buttoned down the front, and white apron, the woman gestured urgently for Skye to follow.

Still stunned at her second vision of the day, Skye could only stand and try to grasp what was happening. By the time her senses returned, the vague figure disappeared—driven away by the echo of a distant voice that brought Skye's vision to a squelching halt.

"Hello. Anyone around?"

She jerked back to awareness of the present, once again surrounded by boxes and half-empty rooms. A woman strolled into the room, the measured stride and silken blue pantsuit that shifted and hugged to a lithe form screamed culture and refinement. When the woman stepped from shadow into sunlight, Skye saw that she was about fifty-five years of age with blond hair that was probably bottle produced. Self-conscious and feeling awkward, Skye tugged at the hem of her jean jacket and noticed how the woman's eyes swept across the room. Glints of steel-like emotion flashed deep in eyes of deep-water blue.

"The door was open, and I called out, but no one answered, so I let myself in. I'm guessing you're the new owner of the house." The woman reached out to brush her fingers across Skye's in a poor imitation of a handshake.

"Yes. I'm Skye Temple." She hated weak-wrist, fingertip handshakes.

"Skye Temple, what an absolutely delicious name. I'm Verity Parker. I own *Witches Haven*, a quaint little store in town that offers tarot cards, tools of divination and other witchy objects to the hordes of tourists that find their way to our little city." Her voice was smooth, and she drew each word from her lips in an overly affectatious manner.

"Oh. Of course." Skye recognized her now. "I was just in there." And she certainly wouldn't describe it as a quaint little store.

"I know. I meant to talk with you, but that blasted delivery person. You can't trust those people with the blue-collar mentality to do the job unless you're standing right over them. The stories

I could tell you about some of them." She lowered her voice and leaned forward. "Lately, I've even noticed that there are more, you know, Mexicans and dark-skinned people being hired to deliver."

Skye almost choked on her own spit. It had been a long time since she'd heard such blatant bigotry, not to mention the fact that she had friends who delivered for Fed Ex or UPS. None of whom she'd classify as having a blue-collar mentality. Before she could make any kind of reply, Verity's gaze swept over the boxes.

"We can't have our newest resident tied up unpacking. I'll send my son, Matthew, over to help you move some of the heavy things. He's busy today, but can be here first thing tomorrow to help. That way you'll be ready in time for the summer solstice and not have to miss the ritual because you haven't had time to set up your altar."

"I...but how do you know that I even practice the craft?"

A ripple of subdued laughter crossed perfectly glossed lips.

"You wouldn't have bought this house unless you had magic in your blood." Her eyelids lowered, a motion that gave her eyes a hooded, considering look. She ran a red-tipped finger across Skye's cheek hard enough to make Skye flinch. "The question is, how aware are you of what runs deep within? And what will it take to bring you to the full bloom of your power?"

A stifling weight settled on Skye's chest, while her ears rang with the sound of rolling waves. She struggled to keep her focus on the present, but it wasn't easy. "I'm in no hurry to set up." Her voice sounded shaky even to her own ears, and the shocked look on Verity's face prompted her to offer an explanation. "It's just that my Mom and I always do ritual together and she's on a cruise for the next few weeks."

Verity raised an eyebrow. "But you have to rejoice and pay tribute to the sun and cycle of birth. I know, you can join us. Wouldn't that be fun?" Without waiting for Skye's answer, Verity gave a wriggle of her fingertips and walked away. Skye could only stand open-mouthed and try to muster up an answer when Verity's voice echoed from the driveway. "See you tomorrow night." The Vroom of a powerful car engine accentuated the declaration.

"I'll think about it," she shouted after the retreating car. Even knowing that Verity couldn't possibly have heard her, Skye felt better for the effort of standing up for herself.

She felt as if a whirlwind had blown into her life, and she didn't like the feeling. She'd been enjoying her short taste of freedom and looking forward to discovering her own way without her mother's interference, and then this stranger sweeps in to take over as if she had a right to interfere. Granted, Verity was trying to be helpful, but the last thing Skye needed was another domineering woman in her life. And she definitely hadn't enjoyed the sense of being overwhelmed when that woman had touched her. She shrugged. The solution was simple. She just wouldn't go to the summer solstice ritual. After all, no one could force her.

Chapter Three

I f Skye had known what the first night in her house held in store for her, she might have tucked her tail and run back to Camden, Maine, as fast as possible. As it was, she blithely set about lugging boxes and shifting furniture, hoping to get it done so that when Verity's son showed up tomorrow, she could smile, thank him for his time, and send him on his way. Placing a rug under one end of the couch, she lifted, pulled, and maneuvered it into place. The chairs and tables were easy for one person and she needed to empty some of the boxes before she could carry them, but other than that, she was able to get every item in its intended room.

The grumbling of her stomach alerted her to the passage of time. When she checked her watch, she couldn't believe that it was after eleven. She'd been unpacking for over seven hours without stopping for food. No wonder her stomach was protesting. Kicking empty boxes out of her way and shoving newspaper into a garbage bag, she cleared the kitchen counters. She heated some vegetable soup, fixed a lettuce and tomato sandwich, and sat at the kitchen table with a sigh of relief.

Tired and sore, she ate her food while considering tomorrow's plan of action. Thankfully, she didn't own a lot, and she'd managed the worst of the moving, so it was just a matter of unpacking the smaller boxes and arranging things where she wanted them. The distant roll of thunder drew Skye's attention to the window, and she watched the tree branches sway back and forth in the rising wind. Occasionally, a branch swept in close enough to brush the window, an action that mimicked a cat scratching its claws on glass.

The rumbling thunder came closer and gave way to veins of lightning slashing across the dark horizon. Skye stood and moved to the window for a better view of the coming storm. Across her backyard and through the trees, the ocean was barely visible, but she could see the swelling of the waves and a glimpse of whitecaps breaking and rolling back into the ocean. Storm clouds obliterated her view of the sky as they crept ever closer to Winter Island Rd. and Salem.

When a crack of thunder caused the kitchen lights to flicker, Skye did a quick mental inventory of still packed boxes, trying to remember which one held her candles. The deluge of rain slapping outside sent her sprinting upstairs to retrieve some candles before the increasingly flickering lights finally gave out for good. Thunder and lightning now cracked and flashed at regular intervals while the rain beat fiercely on the roof and against the side of the house.

In her bedroom, Skye found the box she was looking for and dug frantically for candles and matches just as the lights gave a last flicker and went out altogether. Tree shadows danced in the storm outside her window. The sound of a window slamming against the wall downstairs let Skye know that the wind had blown one open. Probably the library window, because it hung on side hinges that opened inward and she'd noticed earlier that the latch was loose.

With shaking hands, she set a candle on her nightstand, struck a match, and lit the wick. The candle flame illuminated her room enough to ease her jumpiness. Another banging crash sounded from downstairs, and she steeled herself to make the trek down the dark stairway with only a candle for light. Leaving a couple of candles burning in the bedroom, she took another and stepped into the hallway. Eerie shadows greeted her as they wavered and jumped in response to the candle flame. Carefully, she made her way down the stairs to the library door.

She reached for the door handle, but a sudden fear stilled her hand. Hesitating, Skye noticed the absence of all sound. Warning whispers brushed her mind, but she shook them off and forced herself to open the door. A survey of the room showed nothing out of the ordinary except for the shutter swinging on its hinges. Shelves packed haphazardly with books lined three walls of the room, while a large desk and chair sat at the far end of the room in front of a full wall of windows and a patio door that led outside. Skye breathed in relief until a gust of wind blew into the room and slammed the shutter against the wall, making her jump and spill hot wax on her hand.

"Damn." She placed the candle on the nearby desk and picked the wax from her skin. Shaking her stinging hand, she crossed the room, yanked the shutter closed, and latched it securely. An inspection of the wall showed a couple of dents and ripped wallpaper, but it didn't matter, as Skye had already decided to peel the existing paper and re-paper with something that would brighten the dark room. She'd have to make a point of going through the multitude of books piled everywhere as well, just to bring a semblance of order to the messy space.

While Skye imagined what the room could look like with some manual labor and redecorating, an insistent urge drew her toward one of the bookshelves. Hardly aware of moving, she walked across the dingy orange carpet that she meant to rip up and stood in front of a shelf. Directed by an unexplained force, she lifted her hand and pushed at a knurl of wood that decorated the edging around the bookcase. Nothing happened. She tried again and felt something move, so she pushed harder.

Wood on wood let out a wrenching screech, and the entire bookcase swung out into the room and let loose a horrid musty smell. Tangled with the disturbed cobwebs and dust came the culmination of Skye's worst nightmares as grasping, bony fingers fell forward and raked through her hair. Panic flared as she shoved her attacker away, only to realize she was shoving at a skeleton.

Fresh terror wound itself through her stomach as she realized what she'd uncovered.

With a single wrenching scream, she freed her hair from the bony fingers and threw the skeleton back into the hole from where it had fallen. A sharp crack of thunder jolted her frayed nerves, while lightning streaked through the sky. The flash of light lit the room briefly. Enough to highlight the macabre grin of the now still skeleton. Jesus. Skye shivered and prayed that her cell phone was working. Racing to the kitchen where she'd left it, she dialed the police with shaking fingers. No way was she spending the night in this house with a skeleton.

Jerome's shift at the Salem Police Station had just started when the call came through. He'd brought his coffee and case files on the murdered girls to the command center near the front of the station because Jaks, the night shift 911 officer wanted some company. Thumbing through a case file and adding the occasional, *mmmhmm*, Jerome listened to Jaks drone on about his newest relationship. Jerome was only barely aware when the phone rang, its sound cutting through the glassed in area that constituted the heart of the station with its bank of phones and monitors. Officer Jackson answered the phone, his usual monotone voice abruptly shifting to disbelief as the conversation advanced. The change in tone grabbed Jerome's attention, but it was Jaks's pale face and shifting gaze looking anywhere except at Jerome that worried him. This was obviously more than a call about the power being out in various parts of the city.

Jaks's voice rose excitedly. "We'll send someone out right away. Don't touch a thing." Jaks disconnected the call and turned to Jerome, his face fraught with wariness and uncertainty. He cleared his throat. "Seems this woman, the one who moved into the old

Good house, just found a skeleton behind some kind of secret bookcase."

His words triggered a wave of old memories, dark shadows, and rampant fear. A flame of nausea licked Jerome's stomach and clenched his throat into a tight ball. A skeleton hidden in the very house that had haunted his dreams for thirty years. Possibilities bounded through his mind, but he discarded each of them until there was only one explanation left. After all these years, he was about to find answers to what happened on that night.

"Jerome?" Jaks frowned at him. "Will you be all right? You know, because..."

"I'll be fine." Although he had no idea how he'd react when he saw the skeleton. Keeping the memories of that night at bay was hard enough, but to face the solid truth of a thirty-year-old mystery might be too much for him.

"You better get going. The woman sounded a little unwound. Although, who wouldn't be after finding a skeleton, in the middle of a storm and blackout no less." The shrill ringing of the phone cut through the room and Jaks spun his chair back around to answer the call.

Jerome cursed under his breath, left the command center, grabbed his jacket and a flashlight, and stepped from the safety of the police station to begin a journey that could quite possibly put an end to past ghosts and help shape the future.

His intestines twisted into knots at an increasing rate as he turned onto Winter Island Rd. and drove past his own home. He noted the darkened windows and hoped that his dog, Second Chance, was okay. The poor guy was afraid of the dark, and although Jerome was tempted to stop and check on him, the need to see the skeleton gnawed at him and forced him to continue up the street to the old Good house.

Dipping and diving, tree branches reached out and scraped along Jerome's car as he wheeled into the winding drive. The resulting sound sent shivers down his spine. Darkness shrouded the house, a sure sign that the power hadn't come back on yet.

Jerome shifted into park, swallowed the fear that rose in his throat, and dashed for the front door. A gust of wind sent a deluge of water from the trees above and he grabbed his raincoat close to stay dry. Cursing the weather and the circumstances that brought him here, he rapped on the door and listened as the sound echoed into the recesses of the house.

Almost immediately, the door swung open. A brief break in the clouds released a ray of moonlight and revealed a woman with blue eyes, a beautiful face creased with uncertainty and distrust, and a tangled mass of hair that fell past her shoulders in a raven dark wave. In light of his attraction, Jerome found it difficult to remember that this woman could be very dangerous. He cleared his throat and reined in his emotions.

Seeing her expectant gaze, he pulled out his badge and shoved it under her nose. "Officer Phips of the Salem police, Miss Temple, I'm here about the alleged skeleton."

Rivulets of rain fell from his badge, distorting it. Skye hesitated and then opened the door. Candles lit the hallway with a soft glow and accentuated the rain sluicing down the windows.

"Alleged? Look, I'm not imagining things and I'm not overreacting because of the storm." Her eyes darted from his face to the floor and back again.

"Fine. Let's see what you've found." His voice came out harsher than intended, but his focus at that moment was on the skeleton and its identity. He didn't have time or patience for niceties.

"Of course." Her lips pressed together, and she strode down the hallway.

The library was dark, almost seeming to want to hide the secrets of its past. Skye reached over and lit a candle, which she held out to Jerome, but he ignored her offer and pulled his flashlight from his pocket. With a shrug, Skye set the candle back on the small marble top desk and waved toward the bookcases. "You'll find it over there." She hugged herself and stepped back. "I'll wait here."

Jerome didn't care. His focus was on the bookcase that sat askew, its corner jutting into the room at an odd angle. The harsh white beam of his flashlight cut through the dark as Jerome aimed the light across the room. His heart beat fiercely. Each step formed an eternal moment, but finally, he reached the bookcase. With a shaking hand, he touched the worn leather cover of one of the books, almost afraid to look into the slash of black that was the secret place behind the bookcase.

"Is everything all right?" Spoken quietly through the dark, the words still shrieked through the room.

"Yes." A single word forced through clenched teeth and aching jaw. Jerome couldn't delay the inevitable. He had to know. He grasped the corner of the bookcase and swung it fully open to reveal the contents of the secret room. What he saw sent him to his knees with a gasp. A beam of light from the flashlight reflected the expected skeleton, but it also highlighted the luminescent glow of a pearl necklace. Jerome's last shred of hope crumbled to dust. Suddenly, he was six years old and caught in a situation beyond his control. Memories of flickering candles and chanting melded with the soft sound of his mother's reassuring voice. Then hell had broken loose. That was when he'd run. That was the last time he'd ever seen his mother.

Until now.

CHAPTER FOUR

A crash from the far side of the library caused Skye to jump, and the sweeping arc of light rolling up the wall and across the ceiling made her realize the sound must have been the flashlight hitting the floor. A strangled gasp cut through the room, and Officer Phips knelt, his powerful, sinewy form outlined in the muted beam of the now still flashlight. Skye moved toward him, but the sound of someone calling from the front door stopped her. What should she do? Was Officer Phips all right? She couldn't tell, and she didn't want to leave him alone, but if something was wrong, she needed to get help. Spinning on her heels, she ran into the hallway, almost knocking over two police officers. Or rather, almost found herself knocked over.

One of the officers was of average height. Heck, he possessed average looks as well. But the other officer—Skye had to turn her face up to look into his and swallowed at the fierce look of intent that set his square jaw into a solid rock and sent shards of light snapping from his eyes. His shoulders spanned half the width of the average guys and the way he filled out his uniform made it obvious that he was in amazing condition.

"We're here about the skeleton." The average guy flashed a badge.

Without looking at her, the big guy snapped out a question. "What happened?"

Intimidated by his abruptness and size, Skye choked on her answer, "I...You..." But when he turned to look at her, the candles in the hallway revealed gentleness in his blueberry colored eyes.

34

"It's okay, just tell me what happened." He must have realized he'd scared the crap out of her, because this time his voice was calm and reassuring, even though his body was taut with readiness.

"I don't know. He went over to the bookcase. I heard him gasp and then drop his flashlight. That was when you guys arrived. Please hurry, he didn't sound good at all."

Her plea spurred the two men forward, both of them reaching for their guns. One of the men pulled her behind him while the other officer stood by the side of the library door, his gun now drawn.

"Is there a chance that anyone else is in there?"

"I don't see how. Unless they snuck in the window."

A look of agreement passed between the two men and the one with his gun drawn slid it back into his holster. "I have a feeling I know what's wrong. Stubborn jackass should never have answered this call alone. Brent, you stay with her. I'll go see to Jerome."

Resignation wove deep through his voice and he stepped into the room, his dark hair reflected in the hallway candles before he disappeared into the darkness. Confused, Skye turned to the other officer, who shrugged. "He's the boss. I do what he says. What about you? Are you all right?"

Skye snorted. "Let me see—first night in my new home and a storm hits and knocks out my power and then I find a skeleton in a secret hiding place. I'd say I'm holding up under the circumstances."

"Sorry, Miss Temple. It's not always like this in Salem, I swear."

Skye managed a short laugh. "I hope not."

"By the way, I'm Sergeant Maynard, and the big guy is Chief Wilder."

"Nice to meet you." Skye wondered why the police chief was coming to the scene of an old crime. She was sure his position would put him above doing such things. The sound of whispered voices drifted from the library and she looked toward the open door. "What did Chief Wilder mean about having an idea what's going on in there?"

"It's not my place to say, Miss Temple, but if it's what I think, I sure don't envy Officer Phips about now. He's in good hands, though, he and Chief Wilder have been friends for years." He stepped between her and the doorway as if guarding the secrets within.

Friends for years. Hmm, that might explain what the police chief was doing here, but it didn't explain anything else. Everyone except her seemed to have some knowledge of what was going on, even though it was her house. She had a right to know, but one look at Sergeant Maynard's unwavering expression, and she didn't even bother asking for answers. The next couple of minutes passed agonizingly slow, but the two men finally stepped from the room and Chief Wilder gave a brief nod as if confirming something.

"Brent, if you'd take Miss Temple to the kitchen and get her statement, I'll handle things here."

Frustrated with feeling like an outsider in her own home and ready to collapse with fatigue, Skye shrugged Sergeant Maynard's hand off her shoulder. "No, I won't go into the kitchen like a good little woman. This is my home and if something is going on that's a danger to me, I have the right to know. Do you know who the skeleton is...was? Does any of this have to do with why the house was empty for so long? Could the murderer still be around? What have I gotten myself into?"

"Miss Temple, calm down." Chief Wilder's voice brooked no argument, and his gaze bore into her with all the intensity of a high-powered laser beam. "This is not the time or place."

Skye was about to ask what better time or place there could be when she noticed Officer Phips staring into the shadows of the library, his gaze never wavering. His teeth clenched in a way that the muscles in his jaw bulged and his eyes reflected the darkest jade green in the candlelight's glow. Waves of anger and grief emanated from him to such a degree that Skye had to set up a border of white light protection against his pain. What could have caused such pain?

Silence settled in the hallway as she looked from one man to the other in an attempt to understand the undercurrents scraping her own emotions. No one met her gaze. One more look at Officer Phips and the quivering of his lower lip convinced her to keep silent. With a nod of acquiescence, she made a move to follow Sergeant Maynard into the kitchen, but before she could leave, Officer Phips spoke.

"It's my mother." Three words filled with pain and loss.

Officer Phips glared at her, his eyes reflecting a myriad of emotions. Accusation? Hate? Skye couldn't understand the reasoning behind his silent recriminations. She'd only moved in. How could he blame her for a skeleton obviously hidden for years? She tried to wrap her mind around the situation, but all she could do was offer an inadequate response.

"I'm sorry. I had no idea."

Officer Phips's nostrils flared, and he clenched a fist. Skye had a distinct feeling that he wanted to hit her, and her own anger heightened. She was tempted to blast him for his silent accusation, and probably would have if he hadn't just suffered such a terrible revelation. Instead, she turned to Sergeant Maynard. "I'm ready to give my statement."

Without waiting, Skye strode for the safety of the kitchen, all the while feeling Officer Phips's gaze burning into her. She shivered and wondered what events her discovery that night had set in motion.

It was after 3:00 a.m. before Skye was alone. The storm had subdued to a distant rumble with only the steady drip, drip rhythm of water from the trees to disrupt the night. She sat at the library desk and watched the candlelight throw shadows on the walls. Exhausted, stressed, and hungry, Skye's anticipation drove her to touch the old book she'd found in the hidden spot with the skeleton. Strange, with all their poking around and collecting of evidence, no one else had discovered these two books.

In the evening's aftermath of excitement, Skye had felt drawn to investigate the now empty spot behind the bookcase. Hesitatingly, she'd ducked under the police tape surrounding the scene. She figured that she'd deal later with whatever repercussions came from tampering with a scene. Right then, she needed to follow her instincts. As she'd stepped into the dark hole, she'd almost choked on the dry dust and the feeling of encroaching walls. With a shallow breath, she'd run her hand down the dirt wall until she felt an indentation.

Excitement rose as the quiet voice echoing in her mind moved her to claw at the loose dirt until it gave way to the crumbling rattle of rock and dirt hitting the floor. She'd opened a crevasse in the wall and uncovered something wrapped in heavy canvas. The two books that now rested on her desk.

A twinge of guilt prodded her as she considered the books, but she ignored it, deciding that she'd been led to the hiding place to find them as much as the skeleton. Besides, it was her house, so technically they belonged to her. A flimsy excuse, but it assuaged the guilt. If she found anything in them that would lead to how that poor woman ended up locked in that cubbyhole, she'd pass it on to the police.

She imagined the shock that poor guy must have had, coming here and finding his mother's skeleton. How long had she been missing? Had he any idea it might have been her when he came here tonight? Had her death been accidental or murder? If so, who was her killer? Why had Officer Phips glared at her with such accusation, as if finding the skeleton somehow made his mother's death her fault? And why had she shivered when he fixed his gaze on her? A shiver of fear or desire?

Skye remembered his eyes, as green as the darkest jade, his cropped, dirty blond hair and how his uniform melded to a powerful body. She'd been impressed at how even under such emotional circumstances, he hadn't lost control of himself. Skye usually rolled her eyes at that masculine drive to remain staid and silent in the face of adversity, but any other reaction wouldn't have fit with Officer Phips. He oozed strength and an aura of ability that would make a person feel able to rely on him. She found the masculine trait a very sexy one.

But then she recalled the threat that had laced his voice and the shot of hate that had drilled through her when he'd pinned her with his gaze. Fear rivaled desire, and Skye decided to avoid Officer Phips and the conflicting feelings he evoked.

She shook herself out of the thoughts of confusion evoked by a stranger and turned her attention to the books. Had they been what the misty figure had been trying to lead her to earlier? She picked up the nearest book and held it closer to the candle. Finely detailed stitching accented the frayed leather edges, while dark cherry coloring had faded to almost pink in some spots and the gold lettering had flaked away over the years. Peering in the flickering candlelight, she read the words and gasped. It couldn't be. Stunned and breathless, she traced the words with her forefinger, hardly daring to believe what her mind already knew to be true. Faint but definite letters spelled out a name.

Dorcas Good.

Grabbing the other book, Skye brought it close to the candle-light. More difficult to read than the first book, but discernible nonetheless.

Sarah Good.

Sweet Jesus.

Skye expelled the breath she'd been holding and leaned back in the chair. What an amazing find. Diaries—not only of mother and daughter—but a mother and daughter both accused of witchcraft during the infamous trials of 1692. In her possession, she held a part of history that had enchanted, enthralled, disgusted, terrified, and fascinated people for generations. What truths did these diaries tell about such a horrendous time when an entire town had gone mad with vengeance and secret imaginings of evil witches and devil worship?

With heart pounding and thoughts racing, Skye wondered if this was her purpose. What measure of Fate had led her to purchase this house and then led her to the library and secret cubbyhole? Why had she been the one to find books that had remained hidden for centuries?

Cripes, she felt the ache of longing for her mother. She'd know better what to do with the weight of such responsibility. Heck, not even being a fully initiated witch yet, Skye's powers were weak, her spells unpredictable, and her confidence bordered on non-existent.

Reverently, she lifted one book. Maybe it was nothing more than simple ramblings about daily life in Salem or the childish musing of a young girl. Her hand tingled with a rush of energy, and Skye knew she was hoping for the impossible. These books held power and knowledge. Magic and truth. No doubt about it, she had to call her mom.

Frantically, she searched for her cell phone, only to realize that she'd forgotten the number for the cruise ship. In the living room, she dug through a pile of work folders stuffed with research information and magazines until she found her address book. Thumbing through the pages, she found the phone number, punched it in, and stood there tapping her foot while it rang and rang. No answer and no answering service. Someone needed to complain to the cruise line. Sure, it was late at night—here anyway, but who knew what time it was wherever the ship happened to be. But what if there was an emergency? Frustration prompted her to throw the phone to the couch.

Okay, no problem. She'd just keep calling until she got through to her mom. As the meaning of that thought registered in Skye's mind, she stopped cold. Expelling a frustrated breath, she plopped her butt onto the couch and considered the situation. She'd spent the last while making plans, changing her life, and enjoying being out from under her mother's constant attention. And then what does she do at the first sign of trouble? Calls her mom like a little girl who got in trouble at school.

For years, her mom had cautioned Skye against practicing the craft on her own, warned her about strangers, pleaded with her to give up the job that kept her traveling from town to town, and generally ruled Skye's every move. Skye had acquiesced most of the time because it was the easiest thing to do. She'd always shied away from confrontation, knowing her mom would inevitably have a valid reason for her warnings. A fact born out by Skye's failed attempts at any kind of rebellion and her mom's *I told you so* look. Well, maybe she needed to start handling her own problems without her mother's help. Wasn't that part of the reason she'd bought the house without telling her parents?

So, she'd handle this situation on her own. It shouldn't be too difficult. After all, the only real problem was that she'd bought a house purported to be haunted, experienced a vivid vision of death and blood, uncovered a thirty-year-old skeleton who turned out to be the missing mother of a man who hated her for no apparent reason. Not to mention discovering two diaries written by women accused of witchcraft, one executed, the other to disappear and never to be heard from again.

No problem. Skye wearily wiped the back of her hand over her eyes. She wasn't thinking clearly, so now was not the time to make decisions. She needed food and sleep. Tomorrow, she'd think about whether or not to call her mom. Tomorrow, she'd start reading the diaries. It would be interesting to take a step back into history. After all, what harm could come from just reading them?

CHAPTER FIVE

Against Samson's advice, Jerome had stayed well past the end of his shift. Of course, he hadn't gotten much work done, as he was too busy trying to keep his sanity, but the familiar routine of the police station and its somewhat military ordered atmosphere forced him to stay in control. Besides, he wouldn't be satisfied until he confronted one of the people he considered responsible for his mother's death, and *Witches Haven* didn't open until 9:00 a.m.. He glanced at his watch and cursed. It was 8:30, only five minutes past the time he last looked.

"Damn it, Jerome, I'm your commanding officer. You really should listen to me when I give a direct order."

Jerome had almost forgotten that Samson was standing over his desk, and given the fact that Samson was usually more subtle than to give a direct order for anything, Jerome figured he'd better answer his boss. He shrugged. "I know."

Samson had been the one who had suggested that Jerome apply to join the police force. They'd been friends since childhood, the difference being that Jerome had left town and only returned a few years ago, while Samson had always lived in Salem. He'd worked his way up from patrolman to sergeant to lieutenant, then captain and finally police chief, all the while building and maintaining the respect of every man in the department. He was fair, but expected a lot from any man who wore the uniform, holding them to a rigid set of principles that had everything to do with honor, loyalty, and respect. If Samson ever found a dirty cop under his authority, it was a safe bet that he'd rout out the man and prosecute him with no leniency. Jerome happened to agree with his philosophy. That was one reason they got along so well.

Another reason was the bond between them that had been cemented the night Jerome ran from the Good house so many years earlier. When searchers had found him the next morning, shivering in the cold, Samson's parents had taken him in and cared for him in the weeks that followed. Until his aunt had come and taken him to live in Boston.

More than friends. More like brothers. Jerome knew Samson's concern was personal as well as official, and he appreciated that. Nonetheless, he tried to ignore Samson's presence at his desk. It didn't work.

Samson shook his head and plunked a mug of steaming coffee on Jerome's desk. "At least fortify yourself before you go off like some avenging crusader." Samson leaned on the desk and folded his arms across his chest. He pinned his gaze on Jerome, the blueberry-colored eyes that Jerome constantly teased him about, warm with sympathy.

"You know nothing for sure. Maybe you should wait until you've calmed down and the evidence from the crime lab has come back."

Jerome slammed his fist on the desk and sent splatters of coffee all over the reports he'd been staring at. Grabbing the papers, he wiped them with a tissue, his hands shaking. "I know. I was there, remember."

"Your memory of the night is from a six-year-old child's point of view, and if I remember correctly, when you ran from the room, your mother was still alive. You didn't see anything. You can't go making accusations, Jerome. Especially in your present state of mind."

He looked at his watch and stood, deliberately avoiding Samson's gaze. "My present state of mind has no bearing on my ability to do my job. And since I'm not getting any..." He paused and shot a quick glance at Samson, whose gaze had narrowed while he unfolded his arms and straightened to his full 6'6". Jerome didn't need to look up at his friend to know that he hadn't fooled him one bit.

"Since you're not getting any help from me. Right?"

"That's not what I was going to say."

"Don't lie to me, Jerome, we've known each other too long. Christ. If I could put more men on it, I would, but you know the situation. I'm afraid that three murdered girls in less than eighteen months, takes priority over a thirty-year-old death."

"Murder. A thirty-year-old murder." His gaze burned into Samson, daring him to deny the statement. Of course, Samson hadn't gotten to be police chief by being shy or soft. He shot a steely gaze right back at Jerome.

"Unexplained death, until we have proof to the contrary." He spoke each word firmly, but softened them with a touch of compassion.

Jerome clenched his teeth to keep from lashing out. Samson was right, but that didn't make it any easier to bear. Hissing a release of breath through his teeth, he turned. "Time to go."

Samson gripped his arm and considering his size and strength, it wasn't a light grip. "Jerome..."

"Don't worry. I understand."

The gleam of pity shone from Samson's eyes. "Don't do anything foolish. Okay?"

"I won't. I just want to let her know what we've found, that's all." He stared into Samson's blue eyes and put all his thoughts into convincing his friend to let him go. "Trust me."

Samson snorted and let go. "Of course, I trust you, but I also worry about you."

"Good, that's what friends are for."

"Yeah, well, I'm your boss as well, so I'd appreciate it if you don't do anything stupid enough that I have to arrest you, fire you, or worse."

"I'll behave."

Jerome meant what he said, but each step he took closer to *Witches Haven* set his heart to pounding. Flashes of that night assailed him, and he struggled to keep the horrendous memories at bay. He took a deep, calming breath and quickened his pace. With an effort, he pushed open the heavy wooden door and entered.

Once his survey of the store assured him it was empty of other customers, his main reason for coming so early, he flicked the lock on the front door. The snapping sound echoed sharply into the far corners, and then silence fell.

Voices drifted from the back room. It sounded like Verity and Matthew. Their voices rose in anger, and then quieted to a whisper. All was obviously not well between mother and son. Jerome waited. The approaching click of heels on wood signaled the end of the argument and Jerome waited, still not sure what he was going to say.

The back office door opened and anger whipped through Jerome. Anger that must have shown on his face because when Verity saw him standing there, her hand flew to her throat and she stepped back. Jerome stepped closer, wanting to see her eyes, wanting to see the truth there when he told her. She hesitated and then forced a smile to her lips.

"How nice to see you. I don't believe that you've ever been in my quaint little shop." Her words were rushed, her tone rose and fell unevenly, and she brushed at a strand of blond hair that had escaped its hair-sprayed position. "Are you looking for a gift for someone? Something for yourself? We have a wonderful new shipment of tarot cards and crystals. Maybe I could show you something from there. I'll just have to go to the stockroom and pull out a couple of things."

Before she could leave, Jerome spoke three words that meant everything. "We found her."

Verity froze as still as one of the figurines on her shelves. Cold fear crossed her face, but she covered it with a smile and a shake of her head. "Found who, dear?"

Jerome banged his fist onto the top of a nearby table, an action that sent figurines and statues bouncing about as if to fall to the floor in shattering pieces. "No more games. I know you had a part in her murder and I'm one step closer to proving it, so enjoy your freedom while you can, because it won't last much longer."

Rather than scare Verity, Jerome's threat seemed to inflame her. "You know nothing, and I'll thank you to keep your threats to yourself. If you insist on digging into a thirty-year-old mystery, you might not like what you find. You were six years old, for God's sake. Do you really think that you can rely on the memory of a child?" She thrust her finger toward the door. "Now, get out of my store."

"I'll find out what happened that night." He turned to leave, but hesitated. "By the way, the new woman in town, Skye Temple, I'm not sure whether or not she's with you, but I'm watching."

He unlocked the door and stepped into the welcome heat of the morning sun, apprehensive, yet relieved, that events had finally been set in motion. Setting a pace back to the station to retrieve his car and go home for some much-needed sleep, he couldn't help but ponder Verity's statement about his memories. It bothered him that the sentiment echoed Samson's earlier words. Was it possible that his memory of events that night was unreliable? Thirty years had passed, and he had been only six.

No!

He beat down the doubt before it could creep in and weaken his resolve. He'd been right about his mother being dead, despite the well-intentioned cajoling of people who'd tried to convince him there was a chance she was still alive. With a surety fired by an innate bond between mother and child, he'd hung on to the truth that she'd never leave him alone. He'd been right. And he was right that someone attending the ceremony that night was responsible for her murder. Nothing that happened that night had been an accident.

Unlocking his car, he climbed in with a weary sigh and started the engine. Until he solved her murder, his own life existed in limbo. Until he avenged her death, he wasn't free to live his life.

CHAPTER SIX

The blaze of the morning sun warmed her face and woke Skye long before she'd planned on waking. She pulled a pillow over her head, tossed and turned for a few minutes, but couldn't settle back to sleep. With a sigh, she kicked off the blankets and swung her legs to the floor.

"Curtains. Gotta put up curtains today." She shuffled over to the window and peered out, her eyes still blurry with sleep. Facing east, the window framed the perfect portrait of nature. The ocean waves sparkled between the trees that scattered her backyard, while dawn's pink still colored the sky. Far above the water, a lone bird rode the wind on high. With a blackish-brown back and breast, white head, neck, and tail, and massive wingspan, Skye had no doubt it was a rare bald eagle. She watched the impressive raptor weave a circular pattern, coming ever closer to the shore until descending to the rocky hills and disappearing.

"Wow. Tell me that wasn't worth getting up early for." All weariness gone, Skye realized that despite yesterday's events, she was looking forward to today. The first full day in her new home. It didn't take long to run a brush through her hair, a toothbrush over her teeth, pull on jeans, a peach colored T-shirt, moccasins, and bound down the stairs two at a time. Her plan for the day was simple; eat breakfast, finish unpacking, and then read the diaries.

Things went according to plan and within a few hours she'd unpacked all the boxes and arranged most things in their intended place. Fortunately, she didn't own much. With the lure of the diaries tugging at her, Skye mulled over the dilemma of whether or not to call her mom. Combining all that she'd experienced in the last 24 hours with the sense that her presence in Salem was not a coincidence, and she wavered in her resolve to remain independent. She'd come this far on her own and hated to give in and call her mom for help, but the facts of her situation demanded more experienced and wise counsel. Her mom. With a sigh, she picked up the phone and dialed the now memorized number. The operator answered with a cheery hello and forwarded the call through to her parent's room, where the hollow, insistent ring of an unanswered phone echoed. Skye hung up before the ship's operator cut in. What Skye needed to say couldn't be said in a message.

Relieved at the reprieve to her independence, she fixed a pitcher of ice tea and a plate of cheese and crackers and set up one of the lounge chairs on the back deck to settle in for an afternoon of reading. She took a moment to appreciate the profusion of flowers in a slightly overgrown garden surrounding the deck and made a vow to do some weeding as soon as possible. With fragrances of bluebells, lilac, and lavender tickling her nose, Skye picked up Sarah's diary and opened it to the first page. The faded handwriting was bold and sprawled in a looping manner across the pages. But even with the fading effects of time, Skye had no trouble reading the words.

Each entry was brief and touched on the daily routine of life in the late 1600s, including the food. It seemed that they had eaten an abundance of boiled meats, salted pork, casseroles, and puddings. Heavy, filling food to sustain a person, yet wouldn't be offensive to Puritan beliefs by being overly decadent. Sarah stated her preference for a lighter diet of berries, corn, beans, and the use of maple syrup to flavor her food. She detested the ever-present cod, which was salted for the winter, as well as shellfish and lobster, but tended to lean toward venison, goose, turkey, and pheasant.

Great, but where's the good stuff? Skye stretched and sipped her ice tea. She'd been hoping for something that referenced the witch trials or Sarah's own powers—if, in fact, she had any powers. Skye flipped to the middle of the diary.

Always sneaking around, throwing stones and garbage at me. Those vain young girls, Mercy and Ann. They whisper snide words about evil, but they only repeat what they hear from the mouth of Thomas Putnam, and he only seeks to discredit me because I claim he stole our property in a vile and dishonest manner. Forcing us to live on the streets. What manner man of God be he? He decries my lack of attendance at church, where he preaches honesty and faith, yet he steals from us. No coercion from him shall ever return me to the house of God. My strength feeds on nature and the bounty of the earth. Threaten me, he may do, but I need do nothing to Mister Putnam, as his actions will set his own fate.

Wow. This was more like it. Sarah's reference to her strength feeding on nature sounded similar to the nature-based belief of modern-day Wicca. Munching on a cracker slathered in peanut butter, Skye scanned the pages and waded through the mundane entries of daily life, trying to find more good stuff. She read about the abuse heaped upon Sarah by the girls, Mercy Lewis and Ann Putnam, as well as the escalating harassment by Thomas Putnam trying to force her to drop a complaint she'd filed against him for various business proceedings that had ended in the Goods losing their property and possessions.

Then she found what she was looking for.

Chapter Seven

*T*hey came for me today. Dragging me from my husband and child, allowing me only meager belongings, they charged me with suspicion of witchcraft and doing much injury to Eliz Parris, Abigail Williams, Ann Putnam and Elizabeth Hubert of Salem Village, sundry times within this two months past. Ne'er have I sought to harm anyone. More likely 'tis a result of these same girls comin' upon me one night in the glen north of town. Pray they did not understand the meaning of the ritual and the knife. Pray also that the ritual completed the cycle before interruption or I dismay at what might follow. The next day, Ann, with her servant Mercy, belayed me in the street and demanded I teach them the ways of the witch. I spoke no, but they persisted until I had to force my arm from Ann's hand and tell her that no witch would beat upon animals the way she did, no witch would tease the younger children to tears, or smack a servant for no reason at all. Neither of them held the disposition most necessary for a witch of pure magic. The snap of the devil played in Ann's eyes and she grabbed Mercy's arm and dragged her away, muttering of revenge and evening the insult.

Five days now, I have shivered on hard-packed dirt in a damp, dark cell with one candle for light and fare of cold beans and oatmeal. I fear the girl and her father have found revenge. But how

far will they play the game? I am charged with healing by way of the Devil's hand, yet today the pinched-face wife of Samuel Parris gave ministrations to poor Sarah Osburn, who acquired a hacking cough, probably due to the harsh conditions of this Salem prison. I clearly detected the aroma of marshmallow root, a mixture I gave Mrs. Parris to prevent her own chilblains, and useful for cough and colds. She also made a visit to Bridget Bishop's cell, I heard their voices through the walls, and smelled sarsparilla. No doubt Bridget's arthritis pains her. But how can this woman administer with the same herbs I am accused of being a witch for using?

I hear other voices in the dark of the night and the shuffling scrape of feet, heavy with the weight of intolerant imprisonment. Oh, fates above, protect me from the narrow, judgmental denizens seeking to pad their own pockets with the hard-earned property of others. So many dark days and endless nights gone, I have no idea.

Questions. Too many to be able to answer them all. Their sly manner of weaving about the truth, demanding of me more answers.
Sarah Good what evil spirit have you familiarity with? Have you made no contract with the devil?
Why doe you hurt these children?
Why did you go away muttering from Mr. Parris, his house?
Sarah Good, doe you not see now what you have done? Why doe you not tell us the truth, why doe you thus torment these poor children?

My head aches and I hear the snicker from the girls who pretend to fear me. They cringe when I enter the court, as if in fear, yet doe I see the truth in the sharpness of their eyes, the twist of their lips as they spill another lie.

I must admit to no charge, no matter my weariness, even if it means my death. I only pray fervently that the girls had no understanding of the ritual performed in the glen that night. The night that started this. Such power in unseasoned hands could bring about a downfall of the many good followers of the way. Intended only for the benefit of all, the knife used in that ritual could be turned to evil purpose.

All eyes condemn me. My death approaches, no longer stealthy or uncertain. Dear Goddess and earth-born powers, please carry me on the winds to a place of love and caring and keep my daughter, Dorcas, safe. Young as she is, I am left with no choice, but to whisper the secret of the ritual to her and bind her with the responsibility of this diary and knife. I hope that they'll allow her to visit. If not, I'll burn this diary to keep secret forever the ritual to ignite the power of the knife.

Oh, Goddess. My poor child. Last night, youthful screams echoed from within this hell and I right away knew them to belong to my

sweet Dorcas. Whispers flew from cell to cell and it is said that she stands accused of witchcraft.

What is the nature of these citizens of Salem to accuse a child of witchcraft? How I would give my own life to ease her plight. No greater pain can they inflict on me now than knowing the child of my womb shivers in a dark cell. Even now, I hear her calling for me, terror shredding her voice into a screeching plea.

Skye turned the page, only to see it was blank. As was the rest of the book. A breath of ocean breeze ruffled her hair and cooled the single tear that traced a path down her cheek. She closed the book gently, giving a thought of respect for the condemned woman. That poor woman. To be imprisoned on the word of a snotty teenager intent on getting her way and then to have her young daughter imprisoned and accused. Skye couldn't fathom the frustration and terror that must have haunted Sarah for the last days of her life. Although the diary entries ended, Skye remembered her history and knew that Sarah had hung for her supposed crimes while Dorcas had been set free.

Had Sarah known about her daughter's freedom or had she gone to the gallows thinking that her daughter's death was inevitable? And what was the reference to a powerful knife? Had Sarah passed the ritual on to Dorcas? If so, had Dorcas passed it on to her descendants? What kind of power did the knife have? Too many questions and not nearly enough answers. But Skye had a feeling that the questions and the answers were extremely important—possibly even part of what had drawn her to Salem.

A flicker of movement on the beach drew her attention toward the ocean. Outlined against the backdrop of sparkling blue, a man and a dog ran in unison across the sand. As fluid as the waves, legs pumping, muscles rippling, they presented a picture of strength and a testament to the bond between a man and his dog. Clad in shorts with his T-shirt stuck in the waistband, the man's tanned, bare chest gleamed with sweat while his abs rippled with muscles. Her gaze moved upwards and Skye realized the jogger was Officer Phips. Her face flamed in remembrance of his pointed dislike and distrust of her last evening, and while she considered going down to the beach and offering her condolences, she wasn't sure if it was appropriate considering that his mother's skeleton had been found in her house. She couldn't shake the impression that he somehow blamed her for his mother's death. A ridiculous notion to be sure, but one he seemed to have.

He picked up a stick and threw it for the dog. Reddish gold fur shone in the sun as the dog jumped for the stick and ran back to drop it at his owner's feet. The occasional excited bark drifting across the sand brought to mind memories of Skye's own childhood and her black lab, Ranger. He'd been a Christmas present one year, just a puppy, all squirming and cute, and he'd lived a full fourteen years as her faithful friend. Thinking of the day when they'd taken him to the vet and had him euthanized still brought tears to her eyes. Her one regret with the constant traveling her job entailed was that she couldn't own a dog.

She straightened up in her lounge chair. Nothing said she couldn't buy a puppy now. Heck, she owned her home and had no travel plans in the near future. Hmm, maybe Officer Phips could give her advice on where to look for a puppy. Yes, she'd promised herself last night to avoid the man at all costs, but she found the attraction of a tanned, bare-chested man playing on the beach with his dog too hard to ignore.

The dog noticed her first and, in a whirlwind of flashing red, flying sand, and flopping ears, ran toward her and slid to a grinding halt by her feet, where he proceeded to sniff her voraciously. Skye laughed and knelt down on the sandy beach to scratch his ears, which he enjoyed enough to stop sniffing, melt into a sitting position, and look up at her with adoring eyes.

The crunch of sand signaled Officer Phips's approach. Intimidated by his presence towering over her, Skye squared her shoulders and met his gaze while continuing to play with his dog. As impressive as he'd looked in his uniform, he looked amazing in his shorts, and she barely stifled a moan of disappointment that he'd put on his T-shirt. He wore his dark blond hair cropped close to his scalp, his shoulders had breadth, while his well-defined chest gave way to a tapered waist, strong looking hips, and muscled, tanned legs that were currently set shoulder width in a defensive stance. Skye realized she was staring. What was wrong with her, anyway? She lifted her eyes to his face, only to have his hostile glare slam into her. His wide mouth formed a grim line, and he worked his jaw back and forth in a grinding motion.

Skye wondered briefly if she'd made a mistake confronting an obviously emotional, slightly pissed-off looking man on a deserted beach. In an effort to break the tension, she stood and busied herself brushing sand off her knees. Taking the moment of distraction to collect her traitorous emotions, she then did something her mother had taught her never to do without permission and sent a single searching thread from her mind to his. She thought she'd be able to find the source of his obvious dislike of her.

At first, she encountered a wall of resistance and should have pulled back to leave him his right of privacy. But she persisted. And wished she hadn't. The crack was a small one, merely a wavering of thought that gave way to the inner recesses of his mind, and Skye's probe honed in with an intent that surprised her. It's not as if she did this kind of thing every day. It should have taken more thought, more of a push.

Passing through the crack had the sensation of pulling the cork out of a bottle of wine and when she popped to the other side, the coldness and mass of conflicting thoughts shook her to her very core. Shivers cut deep in her belly and worked their way to her extremities. She needed to pull out fast before she became lost in his mind. She didn't have experience enough to try to weave through his thoughts to find the ones that concerned her, and she silently cursed herself for trying. With a slight gasp, she withdrew, but not before feeling a rush of warmth that blew over her from the furthest corners of his mind. So the man wasn't a complete ice man. There was hope for light and warmth.

"Are you all right?" His tone suggested he wouldn't care much if she wasn't.

"Yes." No. But she wasn't about to tell him that her mind feeler had found such a seething tangle of conflicting thoughts that she'd been afraid to burrow deeper in case she burst the tightly controlled emotions. She realized he was staring and felt the need to fill in the uncomfortable silence.

"Officer Phips, I just wanted to say how sorry I am about your mother. I can't imagine what you must have gone through last night...you know, being the officer to answer the call." Could she have sounded any more trite? But what else could she have said? Maybe she could put more feeling into her words, or try a different approach.

"Jerome."

She shook her head, trying to understand. "What?"

"My name is Jerome."

"Oh." Tears pricked behind her eyelids and she shrugged. "Jerome, I'm so sorry."

His gaze wavered and then returned to her face. Was it her imagination, or had his jaw loosened ever so slightly? "Why are you here?"

Skye motioned to her back deck, which was visible through the trees. "I was sitting on my back deck and saw you, so I thought I'd come down and say hi."

"No. I mean, why are you here in Salem?"

"I saw a house I liked and bought it." She shrugged. "So, here I am."

He stared her down. Waiting. He seemed to want something specific from her, and his gaze was making her very uncomfortable. Before either of them could say anything more, someone called a greeting from the pathway leading up to Skye's home.

"Hello."

A man waved and approached at a jog. With pale blue eyes, black hair and an open, welcoming look, he presented a sharp contrast to Jerome's guarded look and sharp green eyes. The stranger thrust his hand forward and smiled.

"Hi. I'm Matthew Putnam and I'm guessing you're Skye."

Skye took the proffered hand. "Yes, but how..."

"Sorry. Verity Parker is my mom. She described you to me, although I must say, she didn't do you justice." His gaze ran the length of her body and settled on her bare legs long enough that Skye felt uncomfortable. She flushed. Jerome snorted.

Matthew's eyes flamed as he turned to Jerome and nodded. His welcoming smile changing to a forced grimace. "Jerome."

Jerome ignored him and whistled for his dog, who'd wandered off in search of interesting smells. With a bark, the dog bounded back from the edge of the water, and Jerome shot Skye a hooded glare. "We'll talk again." Still not acknowledging Matthew, Jerome broke into a light jog, his dog following at his heels.

"Is he always so..." Skye couldn't think of the right word to describe the man who frustrated and excited her.

"Rude?" Matthew's laugh broke the tension. "Jerome likes to think of himself as the brooding artist type."

"Artist?"

"Sure. He works as a police officer to pay the bills, but plays at being an artist. He carves wood or something."

"He doesn't seem to like you." Skye ventured the comment only because the animosity between the two men had been so obvious it would be strange for her not to comment.

Matthew shrugged. "Who knows?" He watched Jerome's retreating figure. His eyes changed to the blue-gray of the ocean just before a storm, then returned to pale blue when he looked at Skye.

"Hey, I'm here to help you unpack. Mom said you could use some muscle power." He flexed his arms and posed like a body-builder, except he didn't have the muscles to carry it off. His mouth quirked into a teasing smile, and he mimicked the guttural sound of an ape grunting.

Skye liked Matthew's easy manner of making fun of himself. "Actually, I've been up since seven and everything's done."

"You're kidding. Heck, I figured you'd sleep in after last night's excitement, otherwise, I would have come earlier."

"How could you possibly know about what happened last night?"

"Salem's still small enough that word gets around. Especially if you know the right people."

Skye doubted it got around that quickly. After all, Salem wasn't that small of a town, but before she could ask questions, Matthew spoke. "Mom said that you're joining us for the solstice celebration tonight. That's great. It's always nice to have new people interested in joining the coven."

"I told her I'd think about it. Besides, I usually do ritual with my mom and she's on a cruise right now, so I'll probably pass on celebrating the solstice tonight."

"No. You can't do that." Matthew's carefree rose a pitch, and he looked upset. He gave a quick laugh, as if to cover his reaction. "Look, you're new around here, and this is a great way to get to know some new people. If you're not comfortable taking part, just come and watch."

Skye hesitated. She would like to meet some people, and as long as she didn't have to participate in the ritual, she wouldn't be breaking her promise to her mom. But that wasn't the only cause of her hesitation. Subtle energies whirled beneath the surface of each person she'd met so far. And even though it wasn't her intent, Skye felt as if she were part of whatever was brewing. Problem was, she was a reluctant participant. Matthew must have sensed her wavering, so he cajoled her with a nudge.

"Come on. You know you want to."

Skye laughed. He seemed harmless enough, even though his mom had been kind of out there. "Okay, okay. Just tell me when and where and I'll be there."

"That a girl. 8:30 tonight at the store. Come around to the back garden."

"Is there anything I need to bring?"

"Just yourself." He motioned toward her house. "Are you sure you don't need any help?"

"Nope, it's all done. Sorry you made the trip from town."

"Hey, I don't begrudge the trip. I met a beautiful woman. Come on, I'll walk you up the trail."

They exchanged light banter for the few minutes it took to walk to where the pathway split into a fork. "I saw you on the beach, so I parked there rather than in your driveway." Matthew pointed toward the road. "I'll see you later tonight."

She waited while he walked up the trail and wasn't surprised when he turned back with an easy salute before he climbed into his red convertible, revved the engine, and took off up Winter Island Road. Conflicting thoughts prodded Skye as she crossed her yard and climbed the steps to the deck. As open and carefree as Matthew was, Skye's mind returned to Jerome and his brooding magnetism. Being close to him had sent tingles up her spine, and she wondered what it would be like to have him make love to her.

Jeez, where had that thought come from? She didn't usually think in terms of making love. Her few experiences comprised a few forgettable one-night stands with no commitments. Feeling a desire for someone who obviously disliked her was a strange new experience. Definitely not a normal reaction. Probably not even a sane one.

Absent-mindedly, she plopped into the lounge chair and tried to decipher the undercurrents emanating from Jerome. He seemed to expect something from her, something she wasn't sure how to give. Damn, she'd forgotten to ask him about where to look for a pup. That had been her reason for going down to the beach. Oh, well, there was always tomorrow.

With a sigh, Skye reached over to the diary, her fingertips brushing across a thick parchment page. She jolted to awareness. She'd closed the book before going to the beach, but now it sat open to the last page. Who had invaded her privacy? Matthew could easily have been here before coming to the beach, but Jerome had plenty of time to sneak up here after he'd sprinted off with his dog? She shivered and realized that she couldn't trust either of them.

Another realization struck her, and she wondered what had taken her brain so long to kick into gear. Jerome Phips. A Phips had been governor of Salem during the witch trials. Could Jerome be his descendant? If so, did he have some special interest in the diaries? Damn, she couldn't remember her history well enough to know what role the governor had played and how it might affect Jerome's actions or color his thoughts during present times. Time spent at her laptop doing some research was definitely in order.

Her gaze fell to the diaries that laid bare the truth of a condemned woman's tragic life, and Skye sensed that her presence in Salem had ignited the revival of long-buried secrets. With that in mind, she wondered if she should go to the summer solstice ritual that night, and decided it wouldn't do any harm just to watch. Nothing said she had to participate.

Skye felt overwhelmed, and realized that she needed some advice. She grabbed her cell phone and tried the ship again, only to hear the insistent ring of an unanswered phone. Skye snapped the phone closed, her heart beating in time with the rhythm of the surf pounding against the shore.

CHAPTER EIGHT

C hanting voices melded into a mellow hum. There were fifteen people in attendance, not including Skye, and according to Matthew, only eleven belonged to the coven, while the others were vying for the two empty places that would make the coveted thirteen. Enclosed by a high wooden fence, the garden behind *Witches Haven* reflected Verity's personality with its precisely laid flowerbed split into four sections by two stone pathways running north to south, and west to east. Each area of garden boasted a single color of flower and a statue on a raised dais. Peach, purple, yellow, and blue, each color represented in turn by a unicorn, dragon, lion, and hawk statue. In the center of the garden, an altar of black onyx rested on a huge slab of pink granite.

The coven and hopefuls formed a circle around the altar, their ritual preparations tuning the small garden with spikes of power and weaving into a palette of slender threads that wrapped around the surroundings. Skye sat in the shadowed recess of the back door where she'd been directed after her refusal to join the circle had earned a raised eyebrow and a dismissive shrug from Verity. Feeling somewhat alienated and having second thoughts about keeping a promise made to her mom so many years ago, Skye sipped the herbal tea that someone had handed her and watched the ritual with interest. She had nothing to compare it to except for the same old rituals she practiced with her mother, which never varied, never stretched the extent of the power she often felt bubbling inside.

Verity lit the red candles that adorned the altar and handed one to each person in the group. She then turned to the east and proclaimed, "Breath of the Goddess, blow the fierce-some power of the wind to fill our souls. Join us here to celebrate this awakening."

Turning to the south, she raised her arms and formed her hands to fists. "Empower us with passion and heat. Soften our limbs in the ancient dance of life and fertility."

Most witches, whether solitary or practicing in a coven, molded certain rites and verses in a way that resonated within themselves. But the verse Verity spoke resembled nothing that Skye had ever heard or read. She made an effort to remember the words exactly as spoken so she could ask her mother about them later. She recited the words silently until her mind buzzed and warmth spread through her body in a wave of passion. Her vision wavered while the scene before her shifted into a group of people in hooded cloaks who spoke a language familiar, yet unfamiliar. The moon rode high in a darkened sky and she wondered how daylight had passed without her noticing. She was unable to make out the fence that a moment ago had surrounded the perfectly manicured garden, and she could have sworn that the coven now stood amid a bank of misty darkness.

With heavily accented words and a deeper tone of voice, Verity continued speaking as she turned to the west, arms raised and hands cupped. "Oh, ye vital waters, blood o' the earth, flo with'n us all an' gie us our life desirous."

One last time the cloaked figure turned to face north and Skye could have sworn the earth shook beneath her feet. The mist rose from the ground and unreasoning panic sparked through her as she tried to move and couldn't. The bubbling feeling increased beyond comfort to a state of pain, and heat now raced through her veins to such a degree that she feared she'd ignite into flames. No one noticed her plight. Her vision wavered again, and she could have sworn that the coven now stood naked before her. The flickering candle flames reflected on flushed skin, giving light to the erotic scene of naked flesh performing sexual acts.

The woman spoke again. "Mother Earth, our foundation, giver o' life. Plead we with you on this night to fertilize our wombs, enrich our powers, and lend us your essence."

Passion flared as a naked figure advanced on her. Smoke and mist obscured his face, but his penis stood rigid with expectation. Urges beyond her understanding tore through her and she ached to be naked beneath this man. She throbbed with need and somehow thought that if she could mate with him, she could release the powers that had raged within her for so long with no relief. The need to give freedom to the core of her being suddenly seemed the most important thing in the world.

She moaned as he brushed a finger across her naked breast. Not even stopping to wonder what had happened to her clothes, Skye arched toward his touch. Thrumming mingled with chanting. She felt all-powerful and wondered in amazement that she'd denied herself for so long. The summer solstice was not meant to be an innocent gesture of laying offerings for the nature faeries, or meditating in a garden to show respect. No. It was meant to be the powerful union of man and woman. A testament to the cycle of birth, life, and death. What could be more natural? She craved the soul-searing touch of his hands on her body. She ached for the fulfillment of her powers that only the act of sex could offer her.

Suddenly, her world shattered.

The distant slam of a door and the sound of an angry voice drifted from within the store. With a jolt, Skye came to a hazy awareness of her surroundings and saw the garden and coven as they had been before her erotic vision. Her face flushed hot with shame and confusion. She stumbled to her feet, trying to squelch her tingling blood and whirling energy. Approaching footsteps drowned out the hushed whispers of the coven members and

Matthew stepped toward her, only to have Verity grab his arm and shoot him a warning glance.

The back door flew open, banging against the brick building as a shadow filled the doorway. It wasn't until the shadow stepped into the candle-lit garden that Skye realized it was a furious Jerome. His glance swept the garden, across the altar, and burned through each person as if trying to memorize each face. His gaze found Skye, and his cheek twitched while he clenched his jaw in anger.

"What the hell have you done to her?"

Skye tried to tell him she was fine, but her tongue wouldn't move.

Jerome brushed a wisp of hair from her cheek and took her chin between thumb and forefinger. He searched her face and obviously didn't like what he saw, because a spark of anger flared deep in his eyes.

"Jerome, darling, you're overreacting. As usual." Verity's voice sliced the tension, the sly undertones hinting at something beyond Skye's understanding.

Jerome stiffened. Without a word, he took Skye's arm and dragged her to the back gate. His hand burned her arm, and she tried to pull away, but his grip was too tight. Dizziness overcame her, causing her stomach to heave. With a yank, she freed herself from his grasp, sank to her knees, and promptly threw up all over Verity's peach colored flowers.

"Goddamn," Jerome swore softly.

"Sorry, but I couldn't help it." Skye pushed to her feet and stood on unsteady legs.

"I wasn't swearing at you."

She ignored his words because she was too busy watching his bottom lip move at twice the speed as his top lip and his rubbery face shift into that of a misshapen animal. Skye giggled as his nose protruded into one that would have set Pinocchio's to shame. Jerome frowned and reached out to her. Skye's last thought was that she hoped he was close enough to catch her, because she was about to faint.

CHAPTER NINE

S omeone was washing her face with sandpaper. Skye moved her head, trying to shake off the wet, scratchy sensation on her cheek, only to feel the warm breath of an unpleasant aroma tickle her nose. Yuck. Where was she? Uneven lumps dug into her back and she realized that she was laying down, but not in her own bed. Her head throbbed, her teeth felt as if they'd grown a fur coat, and her stomach roiled in waves of nausea.

A hangover? No way. She hadn't been drunk since her parents, aunt, uncle, and cousins had taken her on a drinking binge the day she'd turned twenty-one. The memory of throwing up in the car on the way home, waking up to the bright flash of her aunt snapping a photo the morning after, and then racing to the bathroom to throw up again, was enough to set off her inner alarm whenever she got close to her limit of alcohol.

With an effort, she opened her eyes and came face to face with a beast whose huge teeth were only inches away. She gasped and sat up. The beast gave a joyful bark, ran in a circle, jumped up on the couch, and tugged at her arm with his paw.

Recognizing Jerome's dog, Skye gave a laugh of relief and reached out to scratch behind his ears. Moaning with undisguised ecstasy, the dog rolled over on his back for a belly rub. Shameless, but adorable. She rubbed his belly while looking around what she assumed was Jerome's living room. What was she doing here?

She remembered arriving at *Witches Haven* and sitting in the backyard watching the solstice ritual. Everything after that was blank. She wracked her brain trying to remember what events had brought her here, but all she could recall was a vague sense of embarrassment and then some kind of a threat. Flashes of skin and memories of sexual passion taunted her with the wavering face of a naked man. Her heart pounded as bits of last night returned to her and she remembered warmth when Jerome engulfed her in his arms and carried her to safety. At least that's what she thought. What if he'd been the naked man? Had he done something to her while she was unconscious?

Feeling vulnerable, she stood and took a tentative step. Although her legs wobbled, she was able to move. She looked around the spacious room. An open-concept design that consisted of a living room, kitchen, dining room combination surrounded by floor to ceiling windows and a sliding glass door that led outside to a wrap-around deck. Furniture was sparse, but the few chairs, as well as the couch, were invitingly large with a bustle-back design and plush pillow top arms that created a sense of cradling comfort. In the far corner by the sliding doors, a beautiful, rustic pine curio cabinet displayed a collection of carved figures. In fact, the entire room seemed alive with carved figures of owls, wolves, rabbits, eagles and more. The woodcarvings ranged in size from the smallest in the curio cabinet to a full-size rendition of a bear that towered above everything else in the room.

Mesmerized by the sheer perfection and lifelike features of the carvings, Skye moved to the nearest one, a small barn owl perched on a tree limb. She ran her fingers over the feathers and beak, amazed at the minute detail of even the most delicate feather. And Matthew had said that Jerome played at being an artist. Huh, she knew jealousy when she heard it.

"You're awake. How're you feeling?"

Jerome's voice startled her enough that she almost knocked the owl off its perch. She spun around to see him standing by the open patio door, droplets of water beading in his short hair and his chest dripping with water as if he'd been swimming. Running her gaze lower, she swallowed and took a calming breath when she saw that his only attire was a short, boxer style bathing suit. Green, just like his eyes.

When she didn't answer, he moved into the room and snapped his fingers to call his dog. The traitor deserted her immediately and ran to his master, flopping to the ground and presenting his belly for scratching. With a grin that softened his features, Jerome knelt down and obliged.

Great, now she'd get some answers. She cleared her throat.

"What exactly is going on here?"

"I'm petting my dog." He didn't even bother to look at her, just continued scratching.

"That's not what I meant. How did I get here? What happened to me? Why do I feel so sick? What have you done to me?"

The last sentence obviously touched a nerve and with a deceptive calm, Jerome rose and faced her, his brow furrowed. "What have I done to you?" He snorted, grabbed a T-shirt off the back of a chair, and pulled it over his head. Striding to the kitchen, he grabbed eggs, cheese, butter, and milk from the fridge. Jerking a frying pan from its hanging place above the center island, he slammed it to the stovetop and threw in a slab of butter, and then put four slices of bread into the toaster.

Uncertain, and not liking being ignored, Skye followed him and stood with hands on hips. "Answer me. What's going on?"

A muscle tightened in Jerome's jaw, but he didn't look up, just continued making an omelet. "I should be asking the questions. What were you doing there last night?"

She tried to understand why he was angry with her. She hadn't done anything wrong. Or had she? "You mean at *Witches Haven*?"

She watched him pour the omelet mixture into the now hot pan. The enticing sizzle made her mouth water. "Of course I mean *Witches Haven*."

With the omelet frying a merry tune on the stove, Jerome turned the full force of his gaze to Skye. "The only reason I didn't leave you to suffer whatever fate they had in store for you is the fact that you weren't actually participating in the ritual. That makes me wonder how much a part of this thing you really are."

"What *thing*? What are you talking about?"

Distrust swirled in his eyes as they swept over her, measuring her in ways that made her feel invaded. She crossed her arms over her chest and snapped, "Stop staring at me like that."

With a shake of his head, Jerome turned away and proceeded to flip the omelet. The toaster buzzed and popped the toast up. Furious at unspoken accusations, confused over her loss of memory, and starving, Skye grabbed the tub of butter and buttered the crispy bread. No one spoke. With coffee brewed, omelet, toast, and jam on the table, they sat. Still, no one spoke. Overcome by her hunger, she picked up her fork and ate. The food was delicious, and the coffee hit her belly with a welcome warmth.

"I don't remember much of last night, you know."

"That's because you were drugged."

Simple words that held a depth of meaning. Skye's fork clattered to her plate. "What?"

"It was in the herbal tea you were drinking. Didn't you notice a strange taste or even a smell that seemed off just a little bit?"

She remembered the slightly bitter taste of her tea. "I just thought it was an unusual herbal tea that I'd never had before."

He snorted. "Well, you were right about that. It was probably maca root, yohimbe bark, kava kava, or even horny goat weed."

Skye laughed. "You had me up until the horny goat weed."

He stared, his fork halfway to his mouth.

"You're not kidding, are you?"

"Whatever they used would have stimulated you sexually, but it wouldn't have been enough to do whatever they intended, so it would have been mixed with some kind of hallucinogenic drug."

"Oh. My. God. I can't believe it. Why would someone drug me like that?" Her face flamed at the remembered sexual fantasy and aching throb that had flared when her dream man had brushed a finger across her breast.

Jerome pushed his plate away and leaned back, arms crossed across his chest. "You tell me."

She threw her hands in the air. "I don't know. I only moved into town two days ago. You know that. How could I possibly have any idea what's going on?" She shot him an accusing glare. "How do I know it wasn't you who drugged me?"

"Right. What possible reason could I have for drugging you?"

Skye's mind raced, grasping for some sense of logic in the situation. Finally, she shrugged. "I have no idea, but I do know that your ancestor was some kind of witch-executioner, so maybe you're carrying on an age-old vendetta against witches."

"He was not a witch-executioner, as you so thoughtlessly put it. He was governor and oversaw the trials. It so happens he pardoned some people who stood accused after the initial rush of the trials and he was instrumental in bringing an end to the aggression and abuse of the Court of that time."

"Well, la de da. From what I understand, it was his proclamation that resulted in prisoners being thrown into irons, and he put some zealot in charge of the trials who actually allowed—what did they call it—spectral evidence, to count against the poor, innocent accused. How barbaric can you get?" Skye threw out the information that she'd read off the internet only yesterday. "He probably only pardoned those accused people to make up for his huge blunder in getting all those other innocent people hung."

Jerome's eyes turned that familiar dark jade. Cold and hard. Skye knew she'd hit a nerve and felt a second of compassion for the descendant of a man responsible for the deaths of innocent people. She'd deliberately played up Governor Phips's original misjudgment of the situation and downplayed the positive actions the man had taken once he realized his mistakes. But she wouldn't give him the benefit of admitting that. He'd called her clueless.

"Fine. You're entitled to your opinion. Now let's concentrate on the present situation?"

"Sure. My question was, how do you know it was Verity or Matthew who drugged me?"

"Oh, it was them all right, and I'd like to know their reason."

"I don't know Matthew or his mother well enough to guess at their motives."

"If you don't know them very well, then why were you there last night?"

"They invited me. I'm trying to make friends in my new hometown. Why wouldn't I go?"

"For God's sake, woman, have you no sense?"

Jerome shoved back from the table, picked up the empty plates, and carried them to the kitchen. Skye's face turned hot with anger and embarrassment. He chastised her like one would a child for doing something wrong. In fact, her mother had said almost the exact thing to her when she was about 10 years old and set a section of the garden on fire. She'd been trying to set up her own altar and stocking it with some of the essentials; a small wooden bowl she'd carved out of a piece of oak, a pewter statue of her favorite mythical creature, Pegasus, a chunk of amethyst stone, a forked branch from a nearby willow tree she could use as her divining rod, and a couple of candles. Once she had all the items assembled to her satisfaction, she had tried to light one of the candles—without a match. Why not? After all, she'd felt the tendrils of power swirling within for a long time, so she knew she had power. Maybe even more than her mother, who she loved to watch perform her magic.

Lighting the candle had been easy. A mere thought sent out with a vision of a flame and the wick ignited. Unfortunately, so did the willow branch, the other candles, the wooden bowl, and everything else on or around the altar. Her screams had brought her parents running from the house, and her mother had managed to douse the flames with her own magic. After slapping her soundly on the butt, her parents had sent her to her room, where she could hear them talking for most of the afternoon. When they'd finally called her down, her mother had pricked both their fingers, mingled their blood, and made her swear a blood oath never to practice her magic alone. Skye had kept that promise. Although, lately, it had been a struggle.

Last night had been her first step toward any kind of ritual without her mother, and look what had happened. She'd been drugged, experienced some sort of sexual fantasy, and woken up on the couch of a man she'd only known for a day. Yikes, her mother would have a heart attack.

She suddenly missed her mother. Flora would understand what was going on.

"Well, your mother's not here."

She could have sworn she hadn't said that out loud. Skye frowned at Jerome's intimidating back, noting how his T-shirt molded so nicely to his body and outlined some impressive muscles. She must have spoken her thoughts. How else would Jerome know what she'd thought? She cleared her suddenly parched throat and felt it necessary to defend her need for her mother.

"We're close, and she always seems to know how to make things right." She shrugged. "I mess up a lot."

Jerome closed the dishwasher and turned to her with a considering frown. "Are you really as innocent in this whole thing as you let on?"

"What whole thing?" She slammed her open palm onto the table and winced inwardly at the stinging sensation. "You keep talking about some conspiracy or something that I don't know anything about. I think your imagination is working overtime."

"Oh, and I suppose that my mother's skeleton in your house is my imagination."

Skye had almost forgotten about that. "You can't think I had anything to do with her death." She softened her tone. "Look, I'm sorry about your mother, but I keep telling you I have no idea what happened—either to your mom or at last night's ritual."

The tension must have bothered the dog because he came up and nudged her hand with his wet nose, as if offering comfort. She smiled and reached down to scratch his ears. "It's okay, bud."

"His name is Second Chance. Chance, for short."

Hearing his name, Chance trotted to Jerome for more attention. "Three years ago, I found him tied in a garbage bag along with five of his siblings." His voice mixed affection with anger. "He was the only one still alive, and only barely at that. I brought him home, hand-fed him, and kept a constant eye on him until I was sure he was going to live, then I started my own investigation into who would have done such a thing."

Silence followed, and thinking he wouldn't finish telling the story, Skye prompted him. "And did you find out who did it?"

"Yes."

Jeesh, getting this man to talk was like pouring molasses in winter. "So, what did you do?"

"I didn't do anything. But I figured anyone who would do something like that probably wasn't a shining example of humanity in other aspects of his life, so I set some of our guys to digging into his affairs. They found enough to send him to jail for a few years. I paid him a visit, just a friendly visit to ease his mind and let him know that Chance was in good hands."

Skye chuckled. She would have loved to have seen that visit.

"Enough. Chance. Go find a bone to chew." Jerome stood and leaned against the counter, his gaze resting on her in a less belligerent manner than earlier. "You haven't answered my question yet."

"Which one?"

"Why did you move to Salem? That house in particular."

"Oh, we're back to that, are we?" She shifted her butt on the chair and considered the man asking the question. She was having a hard time keeping up with this conversation, with all its hidden meanings and veiled accusations. She pinned her version of an intense gaze on Jerome, but he didn't waver. With a sigh, she realized she'd never win a staring contest with this man.

"Fine. I was in town doing a travel story on a local bed-and-breakfast and saw the house one day while driving around. It was early morning. Mist wafted from the ground and muffled all sound as it wound around the house and faded into the distance. I sat in my car and watched a hint of pink spread across the sky as the sun rose over the water. I waited while the sun rose higher, burning the mist away to reveal the forlorn beauty of a once great house."

Skye grinned at his raised eyebrow. "Sorry, I tend to get carried away sometimes. The overblown verbiage of a travel writer, you know."

The corner of Jerome's mouth lifted in a half-smile, and she relaxed enough to realize that she was actually enjoying his company. She sensed a solid quality about him, a hint of steel that promised strength and fairness, even if he was stubborn and harbored an unfounded distrust of her.

"Myths and legends say that descendants of Dorcas Good are drawn to that house and are the only ones who can live there without Dorcas's ghost haunting them mercilessly. The last family who lived there reported floating objects, ear wrenching screams and howling in the middle of the night, as well as voices during the day. They left about fifteen years ago and no one's lived there since."

"Well, I haven't experienced anything like that." But even as she spoke, Skye remembered the vision she'd had on her first day, as well as the urge that had drawn her into the library and guided her hand to open the secret panel. Not only that, but the diaries. Some unseen, unexplainable force had definitely drawn her to them. But that wouldn't qualify as being haunted. She'd felt no animosity or desire to drive her from the house. In fact, she'd felt safe and comforted in a strange way.

"Maybe you're safe because you're a descendant of Dorcas Good."

Skye frowned. She was sure she hadn't spoken that statement out loud. It was probably an after effect of the drugs, but it was a disconcerting sensation that he seemed to pluck her thoughts right from her mind. "Sorry to disappoint, but you're the only one with such illustrious ancestors."

"Are you sure of that?" He moved to stand in front of her and brushed a fingertip down her cheek to her lips. Her heart pounded, and she leaned closer, her body aching for more of his touch. Taking her movement as an invitation, he kissed her.

It wasn't just any kiss.

And it left no doubt that he was as attracted to her as she to him.

Demanding, intense, almost primal in its execution, the kiss caused her senses to soar to a level beyond the physical. Each thrust of his tongue, every grind of his hips into hers, moved them further into an ethereal plane, where mundane matters of the world ceased to matter. Heat seared her body as Jerome ran his hands down her back, grabbed her butt and, with an aching moan, pulled her to him. She swore she was floating; teased with unexplored promises of fulfillment beyond her wildest imaginings. The physical ceased to exist. It was a melding of two souls. A completeness of two halves.

Then the phone rang.

Its shrill sound sliced through the mystical center they'd created and brought them back to awareness. He swore, his ragged breath warming her ear and neck. With an effort, they stepped away from each other, and Skye suddenly felt alone and cold. While Jerome answered the phone, she absent-mindedly scratched Chance and tried to bring herself under some semblance of control. Was she insane? How could she have let a stranger kiss her like that? How could she not have? Never had she experienced anything as overwhelming. Heck, she'd never even imagined that kind of a kiss in her various nighttime fantasies. She'd no idea a kiss could feel like that.

"Goddamn." He slammed the phone in place, his face tight and drained of color. Without a word, he strode into another room and returned a minute later, zipping a pair of jeans and buttoning a shirt. "Come on. I'll drive you home. I've got to report to the station."

Crap. Typical male, going from intense passion to distant stranger in the span of a moment. She was still shaking from their encounter. How could he turn it off so easily? Jerk. "I'll find my own way home. I'll take a taxi or something."

Jerome's answer was to grab her arm and drag her out the door with him. If Skye hadn't sensed his anger and genuine distress, she would have at least tried to free herself. As it was, she let him thrust her into the car and she sat quietly while he climbed behind the wheel and started the engine.

She was afraid to say anything in case he turned his anger on her. She hoped it was a quick trip to her house because she didn't think she could shield herself from such intense feelings for long. Jerome backed the car up and drove a short way up the road before Skye realized where they were.

"We're neighbors. Why didn't you say anything?"

Without answering, he pulled into her driveway and came to an abrupt stop in front of her house. He shot her with a blazing gaze, all signs of the softer, nicer Jerome gone, and thrust a finger under her nose. "If I find out you had anything to do with that phone call, or that you really are part of Verity and Matthew's coven, you'll be sorry."

Skye sat in stunned silence while he leaned across her, opened the door, and pushed her out. She had to move back to avoid being hit by bits of gravel from the spinning tires. What the hell? Had the kiss never happened? Who did he think he was to treat her like that? And why did he assume she had anything to do with whatever that phone call had been about?

Tired, confused, and ticked off, she spun around and strode to her front door. At that moment, she remembered Jerome's comment about the possibility of her being a descendant of Dorcas Good. That would explain the gut-deep urge that had drawn her to Winter Island Road, this house especially, and the sense of belonging that she felt for the first time in her life. The house seemed as alive as the black cherry and willow trees that surrounded it, its windows staring over the yard like sentries, the paired chimneys reaching to the sky, and front door beckoning her. She shivered.

She needed to read Dorcas's diary.

CHAPTER TEN

*A*s time passed into forgotten ages, the darkness bided its time in otherworldly realms. Growling impatiently, it threw out tentacles of energy to test the time of return. Over the centuries, the physical world of man continued obliviously, explaining earthquakes and other such disasters as natural phenomenon. Now, ignited by promises given and feeding upon greed and revenge of a blighted soul, the darkness has returned. Whispers of the past mingle with present reality and bind a woman with ancient powers to her birth-task.

Excerpt from *Faerie Enchantments and Sorcerer Magick*

I cannot abide the nightmares any longer. My mother's presence haunts me, drives me from bed to pace the cold floor, my mind reaching for understanding of why she persists. Sometimes, her voice shakes with the screams of her death and I think that maybe my own screams of terror answer her as they did so many years past when the bastards of Salem dragged her to an unwarranted death. My head bursts with the knowledge of something undone, something so vital that it prevents her from reaching the peace she so deserves, which means I find no peace either.

Skye shifted in her lounge chair and gazed out over the ocean to give her eyes a break. She'd been reading for over an hour and most of the diary entries spoke of how Dorcas had been haunted by memories of her mother's death and then driven half crazy by her ghost. Poor Dorcas—haunted in her own home, and by her own mother, no less.

She wondered if she'd been too rash in buying this house with its history of ghosts and death. She didn't belong here. But she was here, and the house had led her to the skeleton and the diaries. Therefore, the responsibility for anything that happened because of her discovery was hers.

Skye was uncomfortable with such responsibility, not sure how to handle it. Under her mother's careful watch, she had spent her life reining in her powers, keeping them under a firm hand and never really letting free what she felt beating at her deep within, but now she was being led by a force beyond her understanding; a force intent on placing her in situations that required her to use her power.

Hesitantly, knowing she was about to be rash again, she reached out and ran her hand across the wooden railing of the back deck. She cleared her mind of any extraneous thoughts or emotions, especially hard after the kiss she'd shared with Jerome, and tried to open her senses.

Ever since childhood, she'd been able to communicate with the nymphs and elves of nature. The unseen faeries who flitted about meadows and gardens. She'd never told anyone about the ability upon which she'd stumbled quite by accident, especially her mother, and because she'd kept her dabbling with nature creatures a secret, her glimpses into the otherworldly realm had been occasional and fleeting. She didn't consider her communication as a ritual, so she'd never considered that she was breaking the promise to her mom. Semantics, probably, but it worked for her.

Now, circumstances dictated she stretch her usual boundaries and try for a dimension beyond the usual. She needed to find a way to the dimension that held the souls of the dead.

She consciously relaxed her muscles one by one and concentrated on the breeze that brushed her face and the nature scents that surrounded her. It was so easy. A weightless feeling intertwined with a tingle that signaled a connection, and Skye became aware of a circle of faeries surrounding her ethereal self. The faerie creatures sang a song of longing. Their voices echoed with rhymes of ancient battles fought, magic, enchantments, and times forgotten, yet not gone. With a smile, she passed them by, offering her thoughts of goodwill in allowing her to pass across their land. The place she searched for was beyond, and the further she wandered from her own time and place, the more she felt drawn by urgency. An opal mist hovered ahead. Warm and soft, it invited her forward, and instinctively she knew that was her destination. She would find answers beyond the mist.

She hesitated, sensing more. Something that didn't belong. A darker portal opened beside the light, and it beckoned to her. Whispering of rewards and brighter places it teased her with pulses of sexual pleasure and ultimate fulfillment. Intermittent tendrils of dark reached beyond the portal, looking like arms grasping for a way out, or maybe grasping to draw her in. Knowing it was wrong, yet unable to fight, Skye moved toward the dark until one of the tendrils brushed her arm and drew her closer. Panic flared as she struggled, knowing that she no longer had control over her own movement. She was trapped.

A rush of cold air swept over her and broke the grip that held her. A screech rent the air, its timbre shriveling the portal to a mere sliver and releasing Skye, who came to her senses with a gasp. It took a moment to tune to her surroundings, and she realized she'd returned to her lounge chair and the diary still rested in her lap. She wasn't sure what had happened, or where the dark portal had come from, but she knew that the very last thing she'd seen before returning was a woman dressed in old-fashioned, puritanical clothing. A woman whose eyes reflected pain and suffering, yet whose longing smile bespoke a timeless bond.

A fierce howl accompanied the frustrated trashing of the altar. To be thwarted so close to culmination—again. The cursed woman had come so close to stepping into the portal where her powers would have been sapped from her body and given to someone more deserving. She was so naive and untrained. How had she been able to avoid the trap? Something had interfered, both last night and today, and an answer was needed before another attempt. The third time would be the last. The forces of dark magic held little tolerance, and each failure increased the danger tenfold. Another failure would yield certain torturous death, and it wouldn't be Skye's.

Robes swished across the dirt floor as the distraught person paced, attempting to understand what prevented success. The only reasonable conclusion was that the legends were true. The knife hidden by Dorcas Good was an instrument of transference and was needed to drain the power of any Good. A booted foot struck out and kicked a nearby empty box, hurtling it across the floor to smash into the stone wall. Detesting the dingy basement altar room, the shadowy figure's stomach roiled with the need to steal the powers of the Goods and take the rightful place as the most powerful witch of all time. At any cost.

A cloud passed over the sun as Skye settled back into her chair after a short walk on the beach. She'd needed to bring herself back to a sense of reality after her strange experience, but the diary beckoned to her relentlessly. With a sigh and an aching desire for her mother's guidance, Skye opened the diary and began to read.

Sometimes, I am nothing more than the little girl locked in the darkest, dampest room in Ipswich prison, that morbid prison where the "guilty" were held so many years past. Fear is my constant companion, just as those months when I was a prisoner. Being but a child, I had understood nothing of the questions asked by the inquisitors. I thought maybe it was a game of make-belief, and if I played along, I would waken to find myself in my own bed again. So, in the dark of fear, I spoke the words that would condemn my own mother to her death.

Torment is my life-mate. I suffered greatly at the hands of my father, who held me in low-esteem upon my release from prison. Whether it be that he blamed me for my mother's death, or he wanted no reminder of that time, I know not, but his abuse continued until I left his house. I suffer daily agonies of guilt for speaking against my mother and being that much responsible for her death. Now, many years later, I suffer at the hands of those who hold bitter memories of a time best forgotten.

Though I practice only the ways of the earth and show respect for the nature that abounds, I only use my heightened abilities and senses to help others, never to harm. Where is the evil in that? If I am a witch because I harvest the herbs that lend ease to the sick, or give reverent gestures for the change of seasons that bring life, then so be it. I am a witch. I show more caring and respect for life than the pinch-faced Puritans who assemble each Sunday to whisper behind their hands and point out the shortcomings of those who they smile and socialize with on other days.

I have remembered. Praise the Goddess and kiss the earth. My mother has not been haunting me for vengeance, she has been trying vainly to make me remember that last day in her cell when they allowed us our time together before they hanged her. She spoke most urgently and swore me to secrecy and memory. Of course, being so young and overburdened, I forgot everything she said that day. Almost as if that would enable me to forget everything else. It didn't. Now, the constant battering of night terrors and her whispering voice have finally prodded me to remember. Though, I wish that maybe I hadn't. Responsibility now weighs heavy on my weary shoulders. I love my home and suffer little abuse as it sits so far from town. I am a recluse and am enjoying the freedom to wander unharassed. This new knowledge means that I must act. I must return to my childhood house and find the diary and knife that she entrusted to my keeping. If anyone else should find these items, danger would follow for many.

So close to death. I barely have time to scribble my last words as I scramble to flee from my home. 'Twas easy to sneak into the house where I'd suffered such abuse. Twilight always brings the snoring slumber of my drunken father, who could sleep through a cavalry attack. Memory served me well, as I dug up the diary and ceremonial knife entrusted to me these many years. As I gripped the canvas wrapped knife in my hand, a piercing warmth shot through me and I gasped. That single sound almost became my undoing as I woke my father. Cursing me for a witch and declaring I came to end his life, the now unwrapped knife his

85

proof, he shouted down the roof. *Distant voices and clattering footsteps answered his drunken calls, his own voice must have carried enough fear to make them listen in spite of his nightly drinking rants.*

Able to make my way home, I know they will follow shortly and I fear that hanging trials will pale in comparison to what they will do to me for attempted murder with a witch's knife. With the power over us that this knife lends to others, I must protect any descendant's of our bloodline. I must hide the knife where it can never be found and used against us. How such an object came into being is beyond my knowledge, I only know of the verse that crossed my mother's cracked lips and the fear instilled within me.

Shaped from the truest of earth's steel
Forged in fire blessed by the fire Goddess, Brigid
Cooled by the water of the sacred Chalice Well
And breath-blown for purity by Arianrhod, Goddess of air
This knife shall contain the magic of the craft
Perfected by the Goods and passed to each in their line
But beware, Goods from ancient to new
Guard this knife, ritual-bind it and keep it near
For this same magic may be turned for evil purpose
With mere intent and a sacrifice of human blood
This knife of divine creation will instill the wielder
With the powers of the sorrowful witch sacrificed

I've assembled my belongings and will leave this house forever to disappear from the sphere, if not the memories, of anyone involved in the witchcraft of Salem. When I die my spirit will return and protect the sanctity of this place and only those withe the blood of the Goods will be drawn and find welcome here. Any others shall be driven out by the force of my very spirit.

Before I leave, I'll hide the diaries behind the bookshelf, but I must hide the knife in a better place in case the townspeople ransack or burn my house out of spite. I'll not write it here, but will pass the location on to kin once the knife has been secreted.

As a precaution, I'll change my appearance as well as my name. In homage to nature's bounty and a deliberate slight to the stagnant buildings declared as churches, I shall henceforth be referred to as Rose Temple.

Skye bolted straight up in her chair, almost choking on her ice tea. Jerome's words from earlier that day flew through her mind. Maybe you're safe because you're a descendant of Dorcas Good. Now Dorcas's own words revealed how the house would draw those of Good blood, and that she had changed her last name to Temple before fleeing for her life.

Sweet Heaven, she needed to talk to her mother now more than ever. If any of this was true—and she had no reason to doubt that it was—what did it mean? What purpose had she been drawn here for? First, the skeleton in her home, and then her exposure to a ritual thick with references to darker times and rampant with sexual hallucinations that awoke primal longings within. Magic and intrigue whirled around her, ever quickening in its hold, and Skye had no idea what to do. Her mother had never prepared her to face a power of the magnitude she sensed in Salem. Then another thought struck her cold. Did her mother know they could trace their bloodline back to the bitter carnage of the Salem witch trials?

She rose from the deck chair and paced, her bare feet slapping lightly against the wood. Was that the reason she insisted that Skye not practice her craft alone? But what could one have to do with the other? Her mother knew. With bone-deep certainty, she knew her mother was in possession of the truth, and it was time to find out what was going on.

With determination, she strode into the house, picked up the phone, and dialed the ship's number. This time, she wouldn't give up until she reached her parents. A cheery voice greeted her, and she asked for room #1921, only to hear the distant ringing of an unanswered phone. Damn.

Instead of hanging up, Skye remained on the phone until the cheery voice came back on the line to take a message. She explained her concern for her parents, as she hadn't been able to get a hold of them for days. It took five minutes of foot tapping while on hold before she finally found out that her parents had left the ship at the last harbor. No, the operator did not know why. No, a couple in the next port was taking over the cabin, so her parents definitely wouldn't be returning.

She'd barely snapped her phone shut when she heard a car door slam and voices carrying through the open windows. A peek through the paneled doorway glass gave a distorted view of two people. Verity and Matthew. Crap. She darted out of sight, pressing against the wall. She wasn't sure if she was ready to face them after last night's debacle. How could she face them with the knowledge that they might have drugged her? Heck, how could she look Matthew in the eyes after imagining him naked and feeling so sexually aroused toward him?

She didn't have time to decide what to do because they were on her front step and knocking on the door. Her heart pounded and adrenaline raced a path through her veins. She could ignore them and they'd go away. But eventually, they'd come back. Eventually, she had to face them. And if they'd been the ones to drug her, of which she had no proof, then this might be an opportunity to find out more about their motives. With a deep breath, she pasted a smile on her face and opened the door.

"Skye, darling. We were so worried about you, what with that beast dragging you out and all, so we came over to make sure you were none the worse for wear."

"Well, no, I..."

With Matthew on her heels, Verity stepped into the hallway, her perfume overwhelming with its heavy, musky scent. "You know, dear, Jerome Phips is, shall we say, of questionable beginnings. I'm sure you feel as if you're doing the right thing by being friendly with your neighbor, but I'd be remiss in my duties as a concerned friend if I didn't warn you about him. I'm sure you understand." Verity spared her a glance, but returned her gaze to an intent, organized sweep of the house.

Matthew only shrugged and gave Skye a sympathetic look.

Verity seemed satisfied with her search and returned her attention to Skye. "How are you feeling, dear? You did look rather peaked last night."

Rather peaked? Someone had drugged her; she'd vomited, fainted, been carried away, and all Verity could say was that she looked rather peaked. She smiled. "I'm fine, thanks for asking." Resigned to the unwanted intrusion, she offered tea to her unexpected guests.

"I'd love some tea. Do you have any white tea? Preferably darjeeling or silver needle."

"No. I'm afraid I've only got peppermint, chamomile, or regular black tea."

"Oh." Verity sounded disappointed, but not overly surprised. "I suppose I can settle for some black tea and Matthew will have peppermint. You won't mind if I browse while you prepare the tea?"

"I'm not sure..." Skye's words fell on empty air as Verity had already wandered into the library.

"Sorry. Mother can be somewhat abrupt when she has her mind set on something."

For the first time since her guests had arrived, Skye looked directly at Matthew, afraid that he'd see the truth of her sexual imaginings and doubts about him. But his eyes reflected innocence and his mouth turned up in a warm smile. She waited for the reaction she'd felt last night, but relief swept through her when all she felt was frustration at the interruption and not being able to pursue her search for her parents.

She grinned. "What exactly does she have her mind set on?"

"Seeing where the skeleton was discovered, of course. Come on, I'll help you make tea."

The next hour proved to be a mixture of light local gossip and discreet yet probing questions into Skye's background. She kept meaning to turn the conversation to last night's ritual, but embarrassment and a sense of self-preservation kept her quiet. Besides, talking about her strange sexual vision was the last thing she wanted to do, and if they had drugged her, she didn't want to warn them she was suspicious. She'd do some probing of her own. She just wasn't sure how. The two of them presented an intimidating, united front, and Skye doubted she'd get anything past Verity, who exuded self-confidence and a smattering of arrogance.

Okay, tons of arrogance. Skye knew she was no match for Verity.

Matthew solved her dilemma by offering to act as a tour guide and show her around town the next day. Her initial response was to decline politely, but she realized it was an opportunity to question him without Verity's stifling presence. She jumped at the offer and wasn't sure if a glint of self-satisfaction flickered in his eyes or if it was her imagination.

After sipping the last of her tea, Verity set the cup down impatiently, as if it was no good to her now it was empty.

"Tell me, dear, have you had any intruders or strange visitors?"

"You mean other than the skeleton?" she quipped, only to receive a pointed glare from Verity. "No. Why do you ask?" Verity uncrossed her legs and shifted in her chair, her gaze never quite settling on any one thing. Searching, sweeping the room like radar. "Curiosity seekers worry me. You live in a house with a history, you know."

"Well, yes, but it's been empty for years, so I think curiosity would have been satisfied by now."

"Trust me, darling, this house is always more interesting when it's occupied."

Reaching over, Verity patted Skye's shoulder. "Don't worry. We in Salem keep an eye on our own and filter out those who don't belong. Our forebears believed in binding together as a society and the rights of a single person were negated by the duty of the whole, so we stick together to ensure that the cycle of history does not find repetition in today's society. Thus, the purity of our beliefs is ensured."

"I see." She saw all right. Verity was an elitist snob. And what purity of beliefs was she referring to? Wiccan? Puritan? Christian? The woman's view was somewhat skewed, yet the intensity of the woman's speech assured Skye she meant exactly what she said.

"I'm not sure you do." Verity glanced toward Matthew and the tension sizzled. "A young woman went missing last night, and we want to make sure that you're safe. Living here on your own, no less."

"Missing? From where? How?"

"A horrible thing." Verity leaned close and lowered her voice to a whisper as if the house itself had ears." She left her job around midnight as usual, but when her mom went to wake her up for breakfast, she found that Chastity's bed hadn't been slept in, so she called the police."

Skye choked on her tea. "Chastity?"

"Yes. Did you know her?"

"I met her on my first day in town. At your store, actually."

Verity's narrowed gaze fixed on her son and she spoke. "Three other girls have been murdered over the last year or two."

"Murdered. You think Chastity's been murdered?"

Matthew and Verity shared a glance and spoke in unison. "Probably."

Her stomach twisted with guilt. A vision, rampant with blood and terror filled her mind, and she felt sick with the thought that she could have saved Chastity's life. She'd meant to call her, but with the distraction of the diaries, she'd put off calling the girl she'd met so briefly. She thought there'd be time later. But maybe she was still alive; no one had found her body yet.

Skye clenched her hands together until all feeling left them. Chastity had been so full of life and plans for the future. She'd also feared her own powers, afraid that using them would be dangerous. Did her disappearance have anything to do with her powers? Had Chastity's words been a portent of her destiny?

"Skye. Are you okay?" Matthew patted her hand, concern wrinkling his brow.

"I'm fine. I just can't believe it. I hope she's okay. She's so young...I just..."

"Maybe we're wrong. She'll probably show up after a weekend shopping spree in Boston and be all apologetic for worrying everyone." Matthew's eyes glazed over, and his hands twisted on his teacup.

"Maybe. Do the police have any idea who's behind the other murders?"

"Humph! Their incompetence precludes them learning anything. I wouldn't count on them." Verity rose and ran her hands down her silk pants. "We must be going. There's work to do. Come along, Matthew, darling." With a wriggle of her fingers, Verity glided from the room.

Matthew grimaced as he watched her leave. "Mother's always one for dramatic exits. Entrances, too. Don't let anything she said bother you. I'm sure you'll be quite safe here. See you tomorrow at ten." He flashed a white-toothed smile and followed his mother out of the kitchen.

Once alone, feelings of guilt bore in on Skye, along with the bitter regret of not telling Chastity about her vision. If she had, then maybe Chastity would have taken the necessary precautions. She slammed her palm against the nearest wall, and the swelling in her chest gave way to a wave of tears.

Enough. She'd seen Chastity's danger and done nothing. She'd done her best to keep her promise to her mom, but with the cold certainty that a malevolent force had taken root in the hospitable town of Salem, Skye vowed to understand her powers and use them in any way necessary to find the killer and bring justice. For the murdered girls she'd never met, but especially for Chastity.

Her presence in Salem had a purpose.

CHAPTER ELEVEN

Skye tossed well into the night, unable to still her mind or relax her body. Too many unanswered questions and a sense of impending danger clawed at her so that when she finally slept, restless dreams whispered through her sub-conscious.

Sensations of drifting or floating often interrupted her sleep, but that night she experienced the tug of a specific destination directing her journey. Her otherworldly self traveled a path of intent to a dungeon of clutching hands and dark corners shadowed with fetid smells. Hovering in the dark, her mind's eye detected a woman sobbing mournfully in the farthest corner.

There was something unusual about the woman's clothing, and Skye drifted in for a closer look. A dirty linen cloth hung awkwardly off to one side of her lank hair and a long gray skirt and waistcoat appeared even grayer and dismal in the dark cell. She recognized the clothing as resembling what she'd seen in some magazines. Exactly what a Puritan woman would have worn.

Movement flashed in the corner of her vision, and Skye came to the horrid realization that the dank cell held a young girl—bound and chained.

Shivering with cold, fear, or maybe both, the child stared wide-eyed at the sobbing woman. Something about the girl struck a familiar chord, and she drifted down for a clearer view. Suddenly, a vacuum of air grasped her within sucking fingers and dragged her into a downward spiral. Closer, she whirled toward the young girl until a slap of energy melded their beings together as one. With the sudden awareness of the person she'd become, Skye knew the girl to be Dorcas Good. Skye's own identity retracted into a barely there spark residing in Dorcas's body, so that what Dorcas saw, Skye saw. Worse, what Dorcas felt, Skye felt. Terror, hunger, and choking guilt lay heavy on the child.

No longer safely reading words in a diary centuries after the fact, she was now part of history and the aching wrench of first-hand experience would have brought her to her knees had she been in physical form. Instead, amazement and admiration rose for the young child who bore the agony of such abuse.

She tried to move, but found herself—Dorcas—chained to the wall. Who chains a child in a dungeon? Revulsion rose briefly, but the sobbing woman spoke, and her words quelled Skye into sobering understanding. The woman was Sarah Good. Mother and daughter. Of course, who else would Dorcas be imprisoned with?

Whispered words spoken with all the aching of a mother saying a final goodbye to her child. "My sweet child, I fear this to be the last of our time together. Oh, these accusers are cruel to taunt us with each other's presence, yet keep us restrained from touching." Sarah lifted her manacled hands in a helpless, frustrated gesture. "Dorcas, as scared as I know you to be, you must listen while I speak."

Dorcas whimpered like a whipped dog and cowered deeper into her corner. Skye did her best to lend strength to her. After all, their very souls were one. A stab of strength wended through Dorcas, who moved closer to her mother.

"Good, child. How fares your health?" Sarah peered into the inky gloom in an attempt to see her daughter. "I fear my words are harsh, but no harsher than the savage treatment we both bear. Dorcas, today these holier than thou doer's of God's will are going to drag me to Gallows Hill, where they will hang me until I'm dead."

Dorcas nodded, a tear slipping down her cheek.

Skye tried to close her mind to the vision of Dorcas's mother hanging from the gallows and, certain that Sarah was about to share important information, used all her ability to keep the young girl listening to her mother.

The sound of rustling cloth and something scraping on dirt shot through the darkness. "Here. Take these." With a determined thrust, Sarah shoved something across the dirt floor.

Tentative, fearful, Dorcas reached out a trembling hand. Dim light reflected off broken, dirty nails and Skye felt the urge to curl them under out of sight until she remembered that the hands weren't hers. Disgusted with her vain thought, she gave herself a mental scolding to reinforce the severity of the circumstances and the fact that dirty nails didn't even factor in as a concern. Not when lives balanced in the scales.

As Dorcas grasped the bulky object and ran her fingers over the surface of rough canvas, Skye felt the solid outline of a book, as well as the outline of a knife lying sideways atop the book. Sarah's diary and the infamous knife that was supposed to hold such power? But if Sarah had passed possession of both objects to Dorcas, why had Skye only found the diary? And how had Sarah smuggled them into her jail cell? Wouldn't the guards have searched her?

"Dorcas, look at me." Sarah's voice prodded persistently in the darkened cell. "Please, child, the task I set before you is more important than either of our lives."

Dorcas wavered, and then looked at her mother. Sarah's eyes shone with the light of a mother's love. But the love light dulled to the bitter pain of knowing that her horrible, unjust death would leave her young daughter to deal with circumstances beyond her understanding. Circumstances that would place her child in danger. Skye's soul screamed at the injustice. But, not knowing if her thoughts and feelings would pass on to Dorcas, she tried to control herself. "Remember the story I told you about a young girl who found a magic knife that all the evil witches had spent a very long time searching for?" Dorcas nodded. "Remember how I said the young girl had to learn how to protect the knife from the evil witches, because if they found it, they would do terrible things to many people?"

Entranced by the story, Dorcas tried to shift closer to her mother, but the chains kept her firmly in place. She whimpered.

"Oh, child, I'm so sorry that I couldn't protect you from this, but what you need to understand is that I was that little girl. And I didn't find the knife. My grandmother gave it to me and made me swear a blood oath. Because of that oath, I've spent most of my life making sure that the power of the knife was used only for good, never for evil. It is our family's birth-task to protect this knife from those who would use it for wrong purposes. You'll find the full history of the knife and its uses in my diary. Guard them both with your very life if need be. My jailers have allowed me my diary, my one luxury, but the knife has been spell bound and only visible to a Good, only visible to others if held bare in the hands of a Good. Keep it wrapped, and it remains invisible."

Sarah stuttered the last few words as if they'd been torn from her unwillingly. A quiet sob wrenched through the cell and then silence. A pulse beat passed, then Sarah's raspy voice broke the quiet. "Promise me, Dorcas. Promise me that you'll fulfill your birth-task at risk of your own life."

Skye felt the battle rage within Dorcas. A child's mind struggling to understand an enormous task passed through generations with the ultimate threat of death for failure. A quivering started deep in Dorcas's stomach and wound its way through her chest and up her throat until it broke from her lips. "I swear, Mommy."

Clutching the wrapped objects close to her chest, Dorcas scrambled back into her corner and rocked quietly as tears slid down her face. Trying to understand what she'd committed herself to overwhelmed her adolescent mind, but Skye sensed the dawning awareness of responsibility reinforced by the death-like seriousness of her surroundings.

Moments later, the cell echoed with the sound of someone approaching, their feet clattering on the uneven stone slabs in the hallway. Fear whipped through Dorcas as two men flung the door open and stepped into the cell. Squinting, they surveyed the dark room, one of them spitting on the floor in a gesture of disgust.

"There she be." He gestured at Sarah. "Come on, witch, it be your turn to die."

His guffaw ended abruptly when he clutched his stomach and doubled over in pain.

"Hey, Jonas, you al'right?" The other man stepped back as if afraid it was contagious.

The pain ended and as Jonas straightened, fear lit his eyes as he looked at Sarah. "Yep. Musta been something I ate."

He wiped his sleeve across his mouth and waved a hand toward Sarah. "Maybe you better grab the witch. We wouldn't want her to get away if I cramp up again now, would we?"

He laughed, but it was an uneasy laugh and he made sure to keep his distance from Sarah as his cohort unlocked her chains from the wall and dragged her out of the door. Just before he left, Jonas looked back at Dorcas. "Won't be long now b'fore yer goin' home. Of course, your mom won't be waitin' for you, now, will she?" Laughing at his own attempt at humor, he slammed the door shut. A moment later, his laugh turned to a gasp of pain and then a roar of anger. "Get that damn witch to the gallows b'fore she kills me."

"You're going to die soon anyway, bad man." Dorcas's whisper sat heavy in the small cell and her gaze blazed into the man's retreating back. Rank with the inevitability of death, the room lent an aura of belief to the words, and it was then that Skye realized the truth. Sarah had not been responsible for the guard's crippling cramps. Dorcas had sent out the energy that doubled him over. Now she threatened him with death. If she had the power to do something like that at her young age, with no training,

what would she be capable of when she came into full use and understanding of her powers?

Skye had no time to wonder, because she suddenly found herself wrenched from Dorcas's body. Very different from the relaxed feeling of floating she'd experienced when she came to this place. The jerking motion grabbed and thrust into her own body so forcefully that she ended up tumbling from her bed onto the floor.

"Ow." She rubbed her butt as she sat up gingerly and looked around. Relief flowed through her when she recognized the warm, rich wood of her four-poster bed, the beautifully carved dresser with a matching armoire, and a pile of clothing strewn across the chest at the end of her bed. Her relief was short-lived once she stood and realized that what she'd just experienced had been no dream. Her heart pumped a vicious tune in her chest when she looked down at herself and saw the reality of the grimy cell streaked across her long T-shirt in shades of black and gray dirt. A couple of her fingernails had also chipped or broken where she — Dorcas — had clasped the canvas-covered book and knife so tightly.

Breathless and terrified of the possibilities her brief journey signified, she plopped down on her bed and played the scene over in her mind. Stifling visions of death brought an ache to Skye, and she pitied the young girl exposed to the horror of a jail cell and seeing her mother dragged off to hang. Her stomach clenched into knots at the memory of Dorcas's last words, repeated over and again, "I swear, Mommy. I swear, Mommy. I swear."

Skye shivered and tears flowed freely with sympathy for the mother and daughter exposed to such unreasoning hate and death. Her ancestors. She tamped down the desire to hug her own mother and returned to bed, not sure if she could sleep. She made a vow to track her parents down first thing in the morning, no matter what. She needed her mother desperately. She also needed answers.

CHAPTER TWELVE

S kye had spent the night reliving her vision of Chastity's glowing face slashed by a knife and the streams of blood in darkness turning blond hair to red. Then lifeless blue eyes, once alive with hopes and dreams. Each time she woke in a sweat and returned to sleep, so returned the dream. Guilt tore into the dreams and a voice taunted her with the knowledge that it was too late. She'd let the girl die.

When she'd finally fallen into a dreamless sleep, she'd slept in and didn't get a chance to call her parents before Matthew showed up, ready for the tour he'd promised her. Surprisingly, he turned out to be a great guide. His casual, easy-going attitude relaxed Skye enough that she easily doubted his role in drugging her the other night. And although she kept meaning to broach the subject with him, in an offhand manner so as not to sound accusatory or obvious in case he was innocent, Matthew kept her so busy going from one attraction to another that she never found the chance.

Eventually, she gave in and just enjoyed the day. She decided that she deserved the time of relaxation, having had nothing but upheaval since she'd moved into town. The sun shone brightly, and she was with a handsome man who quite obviously found her attractive. What more could a woman ask for?

Even as that thought crossed her mind, so did Jerome's image. Unfortunately for Matthew, he chose that moment to flash a white-toothed smile at her, his eyes sparking with appreciation. Skye barely noticed him. She was lost in the memory of the kiss she'd shared with Jerome and wondering about the intense feelings he provoked in her.

Matthew reached out, hooked a wisp of Skye's hair over his finger, and tucked it behind her ear. Skye jolted to awareness, unable to suppress the uncharitable thought that Matthew paled in comparison to Jerome.

"The sun brings out shades of dark auburn in your hair. It looks nice."

Kudos to him for noticing such a thing, but nice? As bland a word as any feelings she might have thought she had for Matthew. And what exactly was she doing even considering him as a romantic possibility when it's possible he'd drugged her? Skye gave herself a mental shake to refocus her mind on the seriousness of the situation. She'd found a skeleton in her closet belonging to a woman who had probably been murdered thirty years ago and some sicko was running around town murdering young girls. What right did she have to enjoy the day? She looked at Matthew and wondered if his flattering, easy-going facade hid a deeper, darker personality.

Was he capable of murder?

Realizing Matthew was staring at her, she responded to his remark before he saw the truth in her eyes. "Thanks. That's so nice of you to notice." She hadn't meant to sound sarcastic and hoped he hadn't noticed, but he was too busy explaining their next stop.

"Old Burying Point Cemetery. The second oldest cemetery in the US of A."

Matthew took her arm and steered her toward an alley behind the Peabody Essex Museum. Peab'dy, as the locals pronounced it. Across the narrow street, nestled between buildings, modern and old alike, and surrounded by an old stone fence, lay a small cemetery, obviously old with its crumbling headstones that tilted at odd angles. A few gigantic trees had rooted deep in the soil, their gnarled branches stretching high as if to escape the confines of the place of death. Skye's pulse thrummed with the sense—not only of history—but also of the ever changing, ever continuing cycle of life and death. Breathing deeply, she felt a sensation of bittersweet love mixed with regret and longing.

Ignoring Matthew's droning recital of the history of each headstone, she moved further down the row of stones, noting the pervasive heaviness that settled on her chest. Sure, any cemetery evoked a deeper understanding of one's own inevitable demise, but this cemetery created an aura of despair and unfinished business. Skye moved on, and somewhere in the midst of the cemetery, the sense of despair turned to stark terror that slammed her to a standstill. She looked down at the nearest headstone. Engraved with curly designs and rosettes, as well as a grinning skull at the top, the inscription read,

Here lyes interd
Ey body of Colo john
Hathorne esq'r
Aged 76 years
Who died May ey 10
1717

John Hathorne, witch judge and prosecutor during the infamous trials of Salem. And the only one not to repent for his part in the entire fiasco, stating that his actions were well rooted in justifiable fact. No wonder Skye's senses had spun into overdrive. She snorted and resisted the urge to kick dirt on his headstone.

"You found him." Matthew breathed close to Skye's ear and made her jump back and trip over a young girl who'd been standing behind her. Instinctively, she reached out to steady the young girl and offer an apology, but before she could utter a word, a middle-aged woman grabbed the girl by the arm and pulled her away from Skye.

"Don't touch her." The woman glared at Skye and Matthew with suspicion while she stepped back, keeping the girl clutched behind her.

"But I was only..."

"I don't care," the woman snapped. "Leave her alone."

Skye raised her hands, palms out. "Sorry."

The woman turned and set a hurried pace away from them. The poor girl could barely keep up, and she cried out for her mother to slow down. She didn't.

"What was that all about?"

Matthew raised an eyebrow. "You mean you haven't noticed."

"Noticed what?"

"The atmosphere of the town." He shrugged. "People act strangely when they're scared, and with these murders, they have something to be scared about."

Skye could have kicked herself for letting the sunny day deter her from noticing what had been going on during their entire town tour. How could she have missed the clerk at the Salem Wax Museum who'd clutched her cell phone in hand, not even letting go to ring up their tickets, or the woman at the Salem Witch Museum who jumped nervously in the darkened theater room and backed herself up against a wall whenever anyone moved to close to her. Even the officer in the police cruiser at the stoplights had eyed them suspiciously. The helpful, easy attitude of Salem's residents she'd experienced her first time here had turned to distrust and accusatory glares. Her stomach roiled, and she felt ill.

"I think I'd like to go home now, Matthew."

"Oh. Sure. Are you okay?"

"Yes, just tired." *And scared.*

The short drive to Winter Island Rd. led them past Ye Olde Pepper Companie, the oldest confectionery store in America. Skye made a mental note to check that store out later, but right now, she wanted to go home, pop some antacid, and try to find her parents.

There was an awkward moment when they arrived at her house, and Matthew leaned over as if expecting a kiss. She pretended not to notice and jumped out of the car with a cheery goodbye and a brief thanks, but not before noticing a hint of annoyance flash across his face. Hmm, not so innocent and easy going, after all. It had her wondering, again, what else he kept hidden beneath the surface?

She didn't care. As nice as he was and as much as she'd probably be attracted to him under different circumstance, she wasn't feeling anything for him now. Jerome on the other hand. Well, she needed to work out her feelings for him and find out why he disliked her so much.

The rest of the day passed either calling her mother's cell phone and getting no response, moving knick knacks around unnecessarily, or cleaning something that didn't need cleaning. Finally, mentally exhausted and still not in contact with her parents, she crawled into bed and fell asleep.

Skye woke to the sound of someone pounding on her front door. Her heart skipped a beat. Now what? Anyone waking her this early in the morning could only mean trouble. Rolling out of bed, she drew on a silk robe over her short cotton nightgown and tripped bleary-eyed down the stairs. She opened the front door and immediately wished that she hadn't. In fact, she wanted to crawl back in bed and start the day all over again—without having to confront a stone-faced Jerome. Their shared kiss followed by his insinuation about her possible involvement in Chastity's murder flashed through Skye's mind and she moved to slam the door in his face, but the way he shifted his weight uncomfortably from one foot to the other and twirled his hat about his finger stilled her hand.

"What's wrong?" She clutched her robe closer, as if to shield herself against the answer.

His gaze flicked from her legs to her face, then back again. He cleared his throat and took a breath. "You need to come with me. To the hospital."

That didn't make sense. She hardly knew anyone in town. Definitely not anyone she'd rush to the hospital to visit first thing in the morning. She frowned at Jerome, prompting him to explain.

"There's been an accident. At least I think it was an accident. Your parents are in the hospital."

Relief flooded through Skye. "There's some mistake. My parents are on a cruise."

"There's no mistake. Flora Temple and Walter Adams." Even as Jerome spoke, she remembered yesterday's phone call where she'd discovered her parents' abrupt departure from the cruise ship. Relief turned to fear, and her legs turned to mush. Jerome reached out a hand to steady her and heat blasted through her body from the touch of his fingers brushing across her arm.

"Hey, are you okay?"

"I'm fine. I need to get dressed." She ran for the stairs, and then whipped about, dark hair flicking across her face. "Did you talk with them? Are they all right?"

His gaze fell to her legs again, and the memory of their kiss hung heavy between them. Despite the circumstances, passion flamed through Skye, and she ached to feel the touch of his lips again. The warmth of his hand as it grazed over her bare skin.

"Skye?"

His voice poured over her like warm honey, and she shivered. Damn him. Why did he affect her that way? And how could she stop reacting to him so fiercely? She cleared her throat.

"My parents...I just..."

"They're alive." He spoke reassuringly. "But the doctor can tell you more than I can. Look, the sooner you get dressed, the sooner I can get you to the hospital."

"Right."

She flew. It took about two minutes to throw on jeans and a T-shirt and grab her purse. Neither of them spoke on the way to the hospital, each for their own reasons. Skye shifted restlessly in her seat, quelling the urge to ask more about her parents. Jerome had already said to wait and ask the doctor. If something was seriously wrong, he'd have told her. Wouldn't he? What were they doing here, anyway? They were supposed to be on a cruise. Crap. It was her fault. She should never have told her father about moving to Salem. If she'd waited until they arrived home, she could have talked to them in person and prevented them from rushing here in such a hurry that they had an accident. But why had they felt it necessary to leave their cruise before it was complete and come hurrying to Salem?

Skye blew a breath out of her mouth and crossed her arms across her chest. No sense in wondering. She'd get the answers soon enough. She snuck a peek at Jerome and noted his rigid posture and compressed lips. The lips that had passionately kissed her the day before. She didn't understand how he could have kissed her the way he did and then cast doubt on her innocence in Chastity's disappearance.

Jerome wheeled the police car smoothly into a spot in front of the hospital, and Skye jumped out with a nod of thanks. Then she slammed the door with all the fear and frustration she could muster. It felt good.

Upon entering the hospital, a barrage of noise and confusion assaulted her. A single nurse was busy dealing with a crying baby, answering the ringing phone, and motioning to a persistent man intent on pushing to the front of a line of people all waiting to fill out a form before taking a seat in the emergency room. Skye cursed under her breath and looked about for someone she could ask about where to find her parents, but there was a decided lack of staff available.

Just then, someone grasped her arm and dragged her across the lobby. "Rather than stomp off in a huff, you could have waited for me to take you to them."

Reason fought with anger, and she fought the urge to wrench her arm from Jerome's hand. But the need to see her parents was stronger, so she let him drag her onto the elevator, where he finally let go of her. The doors slid shut, and the ensuing muffled silence grated on Skye's nerves. A glance at Jerome revealed a set jaw and eyes that stayed firmly focused on the elevator doors. "Have you found...is Chastity dead?"

"We haven't found her yet. But we will." He glared at her, his gaze burning and calculating.

Rebellion at the silent accusation sparked Skye's anger. "I didn't have anything to do with it, you know."

"Whatever."

His tone bristled Skye into an outburst. "You know nothing about me. How can you even make such an accusation in the first place."

"I'm only conducting an investigation based on the evidence."

"Evidence? What possible evidence can you have against me? I've only been in town for two days, for God's sake."

"You're part of this, whether or not you realize it. The only question remaining is whether you're an innocent participant or a master manipulator intent on gaining the power that your ancestors tried to protect."

CHAPTER
THIRTEEN

B efore Skye could answer, the elevator door opened with a whoosh. "Your parents are up the hall in room 314." He pushed the button to close the doors, forcing her to jump from the elevator. Just before the door slid shut, Jerome turned the corner of his mouth up in a half-sneer. "Tell your mom that Amanda's son says hi."

A mixture of confusion, anger, and something unidentifiable passed through her, but before she could sort it out, a familiar silver-gray braid drew her attention. Her mother's caftan did little to hide the slump of her usually proud shoulders, while the hallway lighting accentuated hollowed cheeks and the wrinkle of a frown that creased her forehead.

Skye's heart wrenched. She'd never seen her mother so defeated. Beautiful, even at her age, Flora usually exuded the kind of dignity that came with being secure in oneself. Gray hair didn't age her. Instead, the color provided a sharp contrast to her blue-gray eyes and highlighted her tanned skin. Her mother turned, and that's when Skye saw the bandage on her forehead.

A sob caught in her throat, and she moved forward. Her eyes filled with tears and relief as Flora saw her daughter and opened her arms in greeting. The silken folds of the caftan settled into place like a protective shield, and Skye felt more secure than she had since being a child. She inhaled the aroma of lilac that her mother favored above all others and then pulled away. She touched the bandage.

"Are you all right?"

"That? That's nothing more than a scratch."

"Thank goodness." She heaved a sigh of relief. "I had to call the ship so many times before I finally found out that you'd left in the middle of the cruise. I couldn't believe it when the police came to my house to tell me you were here, in Salem, and in the hospital, no less. Where is Dad?"

Her mom's gaze darted from the floor to the window of a nearby room.

"Mom?" Skye stepped forward, and dizziness overcame her at the sight of her father lying in bed with tubes protruding from his mouth and arms. "Dad."

Skye choked back tears and grabbed her mom's arm. "Oh my God. What happened? Is he going to be all right?"

"Honestly. No one knows. He's in a coma, but they can't figure out why. All his tests show normal brain activity and no major damage. He hit his head on the dashboard when our car ran off the road, you see. "Her voice shook and Skye felt shivers beneath the hand that rested on her mother's arm. "The police say it was an accident, but it wasn't. Something jerked the steering wheel out of my hands."

Skye's mind raced even as her stomach gurgled with fear. Her father was in a coma. How could that be? The last time she'd seen him, he'd been waving to her from the deck of the cruise ship, as healthy and robust as any man of his age. Now he lay in a hospital bed in a coma; the result of an accident that her mother said wasn't an accident. Guilt rippled through her. Her parents had been on their way here and look where they ended up.

"Is he allowed visitors?"

"Yes."

Skye squeezed her mom's hand. "Are you sure you're okay?"

Her mother smiled reassuringly, but the tautness of her features and the whiteness of the bandage against her tanned skin only accentuated the unspoken, and Skye shivered with dread.

The occasional squeak of a cart wheeling past, or the soft soled shuffle of a nurse entering a room to administer medication, check pulse and BP reading, or take a temperature reading, broke the silence. Skye paced while her mom sat close to the bed and stared into an unseeing face. Conversation during the day was polite and stilted. They talked about inconsequential things or nothing at all, each one afraid to begin a journey down a road that would offer no return.

The doctor's appearance shortly after dinner brought a welcome break to the heavy atmosphere of the room. Obviously tired himself, with dark circles under his eyes and disheveled clothing with stains attesting to a long day, Dr. Barker had nothing to add to what they already knew.

"I'm afraid it's a waiting game now. All I can say is that he's strong and healthy, with no reason to remain in a coma. There's a good chance he'll regain consciousness and recover fully." He shrugged. "That's all we know right now. As for the two of you, you both need some sleep, especially you, Mrs. Adams."

"It's Temple."

The doctor looked at his chart, obviously confused.

"We're not married. His name is Adams, mine is Temple."

"Mom, it doesn't matter." Skye grew frustrated at the age-old argument. Her father had insisted that Flora take his last name if married and she'd refused. As a result, they'd never married. Realization struck Skye. Her mother knew something, or she wouldn't have insisted on keeping her own name. Dorcas's false name meant to keep the Good descendants safe. She glared at her mother and was about to pelt her with questions, but the doctor spoke first.

"Look, you need to stay strong for when he wakes up, and right now you're hovering on the edge of exhaustion. Go home. Get some sleep. We'll call as soon as there's any change in your husband."

"He's right, Mom." Skye brushed her hand across her mother's cheek and realized that now was not the time for a confrontation. "You look tired."

"Fine. I suppose it's time for me to see your new house, since it's what started this whole thing."

Spoken with a bare hint of resentment and anger, the words thrust into Skye like a knife and her stomach wrenched with guilt. Even her mother blamed her. And she should, because it was her fault. If she hadn't moved to Salem, her parents wouldn't have been coming to visit her and they wouldn't have been in the accident. Tears filled her eyes and rolled unchecked down her cheeks.

The ride home in the taxi was a silent one, and it wasn't until they turned into the driveway that her mother said, "This is the house you bought?" Her face paled, and she gripped her purse with white-knuckled fingers. "Dear fates, it really has come full circle."

The taxi rolled to a halt, and Skye said nothing more while she paid the driver. She and her mom watched the red taillights cut through the gray of mist that heralded dusk and threatened a rainy evening. The hoot of an owl echoed from the nearby woods, a tribute to the start of his hunting period.

"Mom, it makes no sense to me, but you obviously know more about everything that's been going on around here than I do. Care to enlighten me?"

Flora grabbed her daughter's arm. "What do you mean? What else has been happening here? You need to tell me and don't leave out a single detail. Our lives could depend on it. Your father's life already rests on precarious ground."

"Dad? But that makes no sense." Skye shook her head in denial. "It was an accident." She put her key in the lock and opened the door. "You can't tell me that had anything to do with me buying this house." She stepped into the hall and turned on some lights, the dimness of the disappearing day not providing enough to light the house. "It was just an accident. That's what the police said."

She turned pleading eyes to her mother, seeking reassurance even as part of her screamed the truth. Flora was too busy surveying the hall and running her hands across the wooden banister leading upstairs. Face ablaze with memories and pain, her mom walked directly to the library door and slowly, carefully, swung it open. She gasped.

"The wall." A haunted expression crossed her face. "Of course. It makes sense." Her eyes glazed over, and she mumbled to herself as she disappeared into the library, leaving Skye to follow.

Shadows danced on the walls. Hovering between night and day, the light played games, dark one minute, flashing with the promise of light the next. Skye watched in awe as tiny pinpricks of translucent figures flitted from the shadows and wound around her mother. More entered through the doors leading to the deck. Familiar figures from her own occasional sojourn into the realm of the nature creatures. But they weren't there for her. They floated to her mother and surrounded her with a profusion of color; green and white hues of healing energy. Her mother reached up and pulled the bandage off. She watched in amazement as stitches disappeared, bruises faded, and swelling receded, leaving the skin unmarked by any wound. With giggles of delight and welcome, faeries and nymphs alike darted about the room in a dizzying display and then, in a single flash of light, disappeared as if never having existed.

Skye was stunned. Not because she'd just seen faeries in her library, but because they'd appeared so easily without anyone beckoning them. She'd been able to communicate with them since being a child, but never without consciously making the effort to connect and always she had to be in their domain of forest, field, or water.

Her mother sighed. "Dear Skye, you have a lot of explaining to do."

"Me? You're the one who just summoned faeries without so much as an incantation. You're the one who hid my bloodlines from me."

The ensuing gasp gave her a nudge of satisfaction, but she squelched it because she knew anything her mother had done would have been to protect the daughter she loved so much. There was also the possibility that her mother didn't know about their illustrious ancestors.

"How do you know? Who could have told you?"

She had known. Resentment flared hot in Skye's throat, and she had trouble speaking. "I found out. And it wasn't from you." She lashed out, wanting to make her mother feel as guilty as she was feeling. Not fair. But, heck, who said life was fair?

"Oh, sweetheart." Flora reached out and brushed a tear from Skye's cheek. "I think that we both have a lot of explaining to do."

The strain showed on her features, and Skye's heart tugged with sympathy for what her mother was going through. Not wanting to add to the burden of a situation she felt responsible for, and realizing her mother was wavering with exhaustion, Skye suggested they get a go to bed and talk in the morning.

"I suppose that would be best. I must admit that I am rather tired. Where should I sleep?"

"There's a spare room upstairs with a bed. I'll just grab some sheets."

With a weary nod, her mom headed toward the stairs as easily as if she lived here herself. Just as easily as she'd made a beeline to the library without hesitation. Skye chalked that up to one more mystery that needed solving.

CHAPTER FOURTEEN

They still lived. The black-cloaked figure hurled a candle across the room and cursed the warped humor of the dark arts. The incantation should have assured their deaths, yet they both lived. What good was it to command powers and mold people's lives if you couldn't shape their death as well? Pacing turned to focused contemplation of the young girl on the altar. Once blonde hair now spread in tangles of caked blood while ribbons of red streaked her naked body in a vivid display of the horror she'd lived through. Did she still live? It didn't matter. Her blood had served its purpose. A failed purpose.

Years of study and intensive cultivation of inner powers had wrought nothing more than the occasional fulfillment brought from torturing and killing small animals along with the occasional person. This time was supposed to be different. This sacrifice should have produced two deaths to keep the way clear to the real prize. Skye. When Sarah and Dorcas Good's descendant had shown up in Salem, the future had brightened. The thrill of Skye's closeness and the possibility of controlling her powers became an obsession.

But wait.

Flutters of morbid excitement raced through boiling blood and the body on the altar was forgotten. No more than a grim reminder of a life unfulfilled.

The mother. Could it be done? Would it need a special ritual? Oh, the ecstasy and attainment of power the transfer of power from both witches could achieve. The possibilities of such a triumph forced the figure to pace the packed dirt floor. Yes. It could be done, but not without the knife. Already a probable requirement for transferring power of one witch, it would be a definite necessity if someone were to drain and kill both mother and daughter. Hopefully, the array of forces that drove such a quest would oblige by providing what was needed, when it was needed.

Renewed with purpose, the figure knelt to the altar and extended a hand over the brass bowl. The girl's blood may yet serve a purpose. One slice of the knife across a palm and fresh blood dripped into the bowl to mix with the congealed stain of the girl's dark blood.

Time ceased to matter. Hours of chanting turned to pain from kneeling too long on a dirt floor. Aching shoulders stiffened and eyes burned with the smoke of candle flames sputtering to nothingness. The lure of the ancient power of the two witches lent urgency to the ritual, and the dark forces responded with lustful, selfish need. By the time dim light faded to smudges of shadow, forces had assured the figure that they would provide the knife. Buried within such assurance hovered the understanding that they would not tolerate failure. Promises given to the forces that ruled the darker side of magic demanded fulfilling. At any cost.

Jerome ran as if the demons of hell were on his heels. His feet smacked on warm sand and joined the rhythm of the churning ocean waves as he tried to escape old memories dredged up from recent events. Seared with cold in the early morning mist, the wind whipped about his face as his bare legs pumped in a fury of frustration.

His mother's face swam in the mists of memory as that night forced itself into the present. Reflections of her velvety brown eyes—soft brown, the color of dark honey—as she implored him to behave himself. Memories of how she'd hugged him close and explained that they were attending a simple solstice celebration. He wouldn't be participating, but he could sit in the corner and observe.

"You're only six, but within your heart," she touched a finger to his chest, "you have the soul of someone much older. You hold significant power, and must learn the responsibility and respect that goes along with it. Tonight, you take your first step toward understanding your own history and abilities."

A simple solstice celebration. Jerome attacked the rocky incline with a vengeance, not even caring about how the sharp rocks cut into his bare feet or scraped his hands and knees when he slid backward. Nothing about that night had been simple. The worst part was that he couldn't remember what had happened. His mother had died. No, someone had murdered her that night, and he hadn't seen a damn thing. He'd run like a coward and left his own mother to her death.

A sob escaped his throat as he broke the cliff's edge and stood high above the beach and shore. The waves crashed in mindless abandon, and a pattern emerged. He was good at watching, analyzing, and making sense out of things that made no sense at all. That's why he was such a great cop. And that's why he'd find out what had happened to his mother that night.

A force beyond sight or understanding had drawn all the players to town. Eldon had never left. Verity had returned a few years ago after her failed marriage. He himself had returned five years ago against his better judgment, and now Flora was here. Inextricably drawn together, with that blasted house at the beginning and center of it all.

Jerome set a more sedate pace back to his house, fighting the ever-present urge that had started when he'd returned to Salem. When no one had found his mother that night, he'd been sure she'd find her way back to him somehow. After all, she was his mother. Mothers weren't supposed to desert their children. He'd prayed to the spirits and attempted a ritual or two that should have returned a loved one, but it all met with failure. Blaming his mother and denying his own ability, he'd sworn a blood oath never to practice his powers. Until he'd returned here, he'd easily denied his birthright and stamped out any urges, but now his blood sang with need and it was harder each day to deny himself. Chance's familiar bark greeted him as he arrived home, and he smiled at the warmth and love he felt for his canine companion. One of his only friends. Samson was another, and as he rounded the corner of his house, Jerome noticed Samson's squad car sitting in the driveway while he sat on the front porch throwing a ball for Chance to fetch.

"Hey, what brings you out here?" Jerome was worried, because if Samson was here while still on duty, it had to be important.

"Hi, Jerome." Samson did a quick study of Jerome's bare feet, scrapes, cuts, and disheveled appearance. He raised an eyebrow. "Have I come at a bad time?" He sounded worried.

"No. I just fell on the cliff path, but I'm all right." "Come on, man. This is me you're talking to."

"I'm fine." He reached over to pet Chance, who was winding himself in and out of Jerome's legs and sucking up for attention.

Samson sighed. "Jerome."

The steel-edge tone of warning said that he wouldn't put up with any crap. Jerome recognized it well. He straightened and looked into Samson's blueberry-hued eyes. Filled with compassion, Samson's gaze bore into him in a way that only someone who knew his deepest soul could.

Jerome broke the stare first and strode into the house, where he used a wet paper towel to wipe the blood off his hands, feet, and knees.

"Real sanitary. Don't you have any antiseptic?" Samson opened the fridge and grabbed a couple of bottles of beer. "This'll do."

Slapping a bottle onto the counter beside Jerome, Samson sat on the bar stool and stared.

"Stop staring."

"Nope." Samson took a swig of beer. "What do you want?"

"To make sure you're all right."

"Are you asking as a friend or my boss?"

"Both."

"Great." Jerome sat on a stool and propped his elbows on the counter, chin in hands, where he gazed at his beer bottle.

"For God's sake, you've experienced something that would have turned most people into a quivering mass of emotion, yet here you sit as cool as the ocean breeze. Most people would think that you don't care, you're a distant person, you're disassociating, or something crazy like that. I happen to know better. I have to make sure that you can still do your job reliably so as not to put others in danger. That's my job. I also care about you as a friend—my oldest friend—so I want to make sure you're okay." Samson gave a tight smile. "Help me out here."

Chance whined and pawed at Jerome's leg. His canine senses warned him that something wasn't right with his master. Jerome scratched his ears absent-mindedly. "I don't know if I'm okay. What I do know is that forces are building. I feel a clinging sense of wrongness and the fact that all the people involved thirty years ago are back in town for the first time worries me."

"Are you being more sensitive because of finding your mother after all this time?"

"No. I think that's part of whatever is happening. I..." He flushed.

Samson laid a hand on Jerome's shoulder. "Listen, pal, I want the whole story. However strange it might sound."

"Even if it involves magic and witches and stuff?"

Samson laughed. A belly deep laugh of tension relieving proportions. "Hell, we live in the witch capital of the world. Nothing would surprise me." He looked at Jerome and stopped laughing. "Would it help matters any if I told you I'm a witch?"

Hope flared and then settled. "Come on, be serious. You're not a witch."

Samson stood to his full six-foot six-inch height, squared his shoulders, and declared, "I am. Do you want to make something of it?"

"But how can that be? You never...I didn't..."

"I told you, we live in the witch capital of the world. If you live here and you're not a witch, there's something wrong."

"Oh, hell, I'm so confused. I feel things that I don't understand and I'm not talking about feelings and emotions. There's some kind of tangible energy within me that keeps trying to take over."

"It's your power. And it's not trying to take over." He walked to the patio doors and motioned for Jerome. "Come on, let's go outside for a minute."

The distant sound of the ocean and ever-present gulls greeted them, as well as the tangy scent of lush gardens filled with tulips, alyssum, clematis, and the spicy aroma of surrounding trees. Samson waved a hand, encompassing the panorama. "Tell me, what do you see?"

"The ocean, trees, flowers." Jerome looked at his friend questioningly.

"No. Close your eyes and tell me what you see."

He shifted his feet. "Look, Samson, if this is some kind of joke."

"This is no joke. Close your eyes, breathe deep, and see."

One look at Samson's piercing eyes and Jerome closed his own. He'd known his friend long enough to know when he was serious, and when Samson was serious, no one fooled around with him.

"Breathe, Jerome. Relax. Clear your mind."

Samson's voice was soft, and each word spoken, softer still—becoming one with the singing birds and then washed away by the ocean. With each breath Jerome inhaled, he felt a sense of floating. His heartbeat pounded through his body and pulsed in his mind as he concentrated on the whispering sounds that he'd been unaware of before, yet now reverberated all around him. The flutter of wings, like a bird's wing, except more gentle and rippling. A whisper of breath on his cheek and a giggle surprised him, but not so much as the strange sensation of his body as it shifted somehow. Caught in a vacuum, he drifted. Then, with a jolt of understanding, he created a connection with the vastness of a previously unknown world.

Even with closed eyes, he saw the world. Whirling colors of vivid hues graced the landscape. Untouched and natural, grassy meadows lent way to ancient forests. Faeries and pixies cavorted with woodland creatures and the sky stretched into the distance until it reached the ocean in a fusion of sapphire blue and sea-foam green. Vivid. Extreme. Alive. Jerome saw the world as he'd never seen it because he was seeing the underlining of his own world. Another dimension that existed, yet until now, had always been invisible to him.

With this new sight and sense, Jerome tapped deeper into the part of himself that he hadn't touched since his mother's murder. His physical body was such a small part of who he was as a whole being and there would be no returning to a one-dimensional existence. With a start, he opened his eyes and looked about himself with a new wonder. Here and there, he glimpsed a flicker of wings, the twinkle of a faerie, the unnatural color of a world beyond. His own body buzzed with undenied energy, and with one wave of his hand, he created breeze enough to send a ripple of movement through the flowers in his garden. With a single breath, he lit a candle wick to flaming.

"Samson, tell me I'm not dreaming."

"You're not dreaming. You've always had these abilities, but you've denied them until now. Until circumstances developed to such an extent that you lost the tight control that you've kept on yourself all these years. Remember, you told me about that night, and what your mother said to you before going to the solstice celebration. She took you there as an initiation. She wanted you to find your own powers."

"Yeah. Instead, someone murdered her."

"That's no reason to deny your true self. She wouldn't have wanted you to hide away from what you really are."

"It didn't do her much good, did it?" Jerome spoke bitterly.

"I just wish I could remember more about that night. I get flashes, but never enough to know exactly what happened."

"Do you think events are setting themselves in place for a re-enactment of that night?"

"Maybe. Or possibly a conclusion to what began on that night."

"Are you okay with that?" Samson inquired lightly, though he locked his gaze on Jerome as if judging his reply.

Clenching his hands, Jerome raised them up and unclenched them. Turning toward them, he looked at them as if seeing them for the first time. "I'll be ready for whatever I need to be ready for. I promise."

A silent moment followed, then Samson spoke. "Good." One simple word filled with a lifetime of friendship, unspoken bonds, and unbroken promises. "So, the reason I'm here..."

"I thought it was to check up on me."

"Oh, sure, if you want to believe that." Samson chuckled, and then his face clouded with anger. "Seriously, though, we found the girl, and it's not nice."

"Damn." Jerome pounded his fist on the balcony railing and set off a roiling vibration that knocked three flowerpots off the deck to the ground.

"Watch it. Now that you've accessed your innate powers, you'll have to be careful to control your emotions, because you have the ability to do a lot of damage. The first rule of witchcraft is to harm none."

"Oh." Jerome looked at the shards of pottery and broken stems of the red roses he'd cultivated so carefully and felt a twinge of remorse for the once beautiful blossoms that lay crushed under dirt. He took a shuddering breath, drawing the crispness of the ocean air into his lungs, and quieted his mind. "I'll remember to be more careful. Where was she found?"

"Close to the North River, to the side of the railroad tracks. She was tortured like the others."

"A ritual killing," Jerome stated.

"I'm afraid so."

"And the witch's creed is to harm none?"

"This is not the work of a witch. This is some sick son of a bitch twisting the rituals of a benign belief into something dark and evil. Just the same as a killer who hears God talking to him and then kills in his name. You can't blame the belief. You have to blame the sick person doing the killing."

"Let's get whoever's doing this and let's do it before he or she, kills again."

"I'm with you." Samson clapped him on the shoulder. "One more thing."

Jerome moaned. "With you, there's always one more thing."

"This is simple." Samson couldn't look him in the eye, so Jerome knew it wouldn't be something too simple. "I have the belongings of Flora Temple and her husband."

"They aren't married."

"Whatever. Her other half. I retrieved them from the car wreck and went to the hospital to return them, but found out that Flora had gone back to Skye's house. I have the stuff in my car. Could you take it over to her?"

The last place he wanted to be was the house where his mother's skeleton had spent the last thirty years. And the last person he wanted to see was Flora Temple, because as far as he knew, she was as responsible for his mother's death as Verity. "Come on, Samson. Ask me to do something else."

"Nope. Listen, you want to solve the mystery of your mother's death, and the best place to do that is to return to where it happened. Besides, I'm working."

"Oh, sure, what happened to *I'm working* when you were sitting in my kitchen with a beer?"

Samson shrugged. "Perks of being the boss. I'll leave the stuff out front. Talk to you later."

"Right," Jerome grumbled even as he stared intently at his garden. The world looked so different now, and he wanted to experience it to its fullest.

CHAPTER FIFTEEN

Upon the awakening of powers long latent, a bond shall form that holds the key to destroying the darkness before it destroys again. Love, pure and strong, needs the richness of fertile ground to grow and only through cultivating the love-energy inherent in all, will the two who have bonded succeed in their specific tasks.
Excerpt from *Faerie Enchantments and Sorcerer Magick*

"And then he had the nerve to warn me I'd be sorry if he found out I had anything to do with Chastity's disappearance. Of course, at that time, I didn't know what he was accusing me of. I found that out later. Can you believe it? How could he even think I'd have anything to do with something so horrible?"

A breeze trickled in through the open kitchen window and rustled across the table. In just over an hour, Skye had recounted everything that had happened, right from how her first sight of the house set her senses to shivering, to the body in the library, being drugged at the ritual at *Witches Haven*, her failed attempt at crossing to the dimension of dead souls, and the strange figure who had prevented her from being drawn into the dark hole, quite likely saving her life.

She held nothing back and through it all, her mother had remained stoic, a sure sign that she was upset. Unknown forces seemed intent on coming together to create a situation beyond her control, and her mother was the one person Skye trusted to put things right. Skye had to put things right, because she was definitely in a situation that far outweighed her knowledge and abilities.

She reached for another shortbread cookie from the tin and jammed it into her mouth, while her mother sat in heavy silence. Finally, Flora cleared her throat and leaned forward.

"You've been very busy, haven't you? I'm sorry you didn't feel that you could come to me before making the decision to buy this house." Though softly spoken, the words held a smidge of anger mixed with the disappointment.

"You would have stopped me."

"You don't know that." Flora shifted the sleeve of her caftan and took a sip of tea. "But I probably would have tried."

"Why? What do you know? Why did you leave in the middle of your cruise to fly here as soon as you found out I'd bought a house in Salem? And what do you know about this house? I saw you head straight to the library and show no surprise when you saw the open bookcase and hidden cubbyhole. I also noticed how you walked right to the kitchen with no direction from me. Mom, it's time for you to tell your side of the story. I told you mine."

"Yes, you have. And thank the fates that your father and I flew here immediately. Well, as soon as he mustered enough nerve to tell me what you'd done."

A cloud crossed over her silvery blue eyes, which bothered Skye because she'd never seen her mother worry about anything. Flora was usually the cool head in any given situation, or the one who could bring logic and calm when most needed. Of course, having one's husband in an unexplained coma because of a stubborn daughter whose actions had precipitated the situation would stress anyone out.

Flora mumbled, as if talking to herself. "So much to think about. So much to do." She reached out and clasped Skye's hand so hard that Skye yelped, but Flora didn't ease the pressure. "Stay away from Verity and her son, they're very dangerous. I can't believe that bitch had the nerve to drug you."

Skye yanked her hand back and rubbed it to restore circulation. "You know Verity and Matthew?"

Her mom continued talking as if Skye hadn't spoken a word.

"We need to find that knife. I thought Verity possessed it, but if that were the case, she would have used it on you at the summer solstice ritual. And if she wasn't using the authentic knife thirty years ago, that would explain her failure."

Skye's heart sank, and she suddenly felt nauseous. Thirty years ago. The same time that someone murdered Jerome's mom. "Mom, you're scaring me, and nothing you're saying is making any sense. Talk to me."

"Oh, sweetheart, I don't know where to begin."

Her mother twisted her braid around a finger. Such a simple gesture, yet it mirrored inner turmoil and Skye worried that events of the last few days had roots in a distant, murky past. Her mother had always been able to handle things. But now, with her forehead creased in a frown and whirling emotions muddling her silver-blue eyes, she didn't look capable of dealing with anything. Skye would have to be the one to calm this time, even though she felt anything but.

She reached out, took her mother's fidgeting hand in her own, and smiled a smile she was far from feeling. "How about starting with what happened thirty years ago. That seems to be the beginning."

"Yes, I suppose, although some would say it started long before then." She dropped her braid and took another sip of tea before placing her pale pink china cup gently on the saucer. "You're right about me being in this house before. Although it wasn't in nearly as good condition as it is now, someone must have done some work on it over the last thirty years."

"The real estate agent who sold me the house said someone bought it and spent some major money on renovations, but eventually moved out because they thought it was haunted. It sat empty for years until I bought it."

"When I lived in Salem, this house stood empty. Had been empty for years, as far as I know."

"You lived in Salem?" Skye searched her mind for a memory of her mother ever telling her this before, but there was nothing. "Why wouldn't you tell me that?"

"I'm telling you now, so please don't interrupt, or I'll never finish the story."

Skye made a gesture of zipping her lips and motioned her mother to continue.

"I'm sure you've learned by now that practicing witchcraft in Salem is as normal as joining a gym or reading a book. Everyone does it. Of course, as with anything, there are those who take things seriously and work at their craft, and those who play. Some have taken a commercial approach and turned Salem's history into a tourist trade that attracts people from all over the world. The more serious practitioners have had innate magic passed down from their ancestors, dating back to the witch trials or before. Even some accusers and judges possessed powers they weren't aware of at the time, but as practicing magic became more accepted, their descendants developed these powers. I was one who approached my training and studies very seriously. So were Verity, Eldon, and Amanda."

"Eldon Lambert?"

"Yes. Do you know him?"

"He's the real estate agent who sold me this house."

"Hmm, how strange."

"Who was Amanda?"

Flora put a hand over Skye's and squeezed gently. "She was Jerome's mother. The skeleton found in your library."

That explained Jerome's comment at the hospital about Amanda's son saying hi. Skye had no idea he'd been talking about himself, but if she'd remembered to relay the message to her mom, she might have found out sooner. And if her mom had been present the night Amanda disappeared... "You knew her. My God, Mom, do you know something about her death? Is that why you rushed back here when you heard I'd bought a house in Salem?"

Her mother's simple nod set a whole new set of thoughts spinning in Skye's mind. "Please don't tell me you had anything to do with her death."

"Not directly, no. Although I was there the night she disappeared. The group of us had come to this house to do a ritual."

"Shit. Shit. Shit." Skye stood and started clearing the kitchen table. When that was done, she wiped the countertop, which wasn't dirty, and then pulled a half-full garbage bag from the container under the sink. Anything to keep busy. Anything to keep at bay the situation rapidly developing.

"Skye."

She whirled around to confront her mother. "Does Jerome know you were part of the group that night?"

"Umm, he was there as well."

"What?" Skye's racing mind tried to place the pieces of the puzzle into some kind of order that made sense. "But, he had to have been a child. What was he doing there? Crap, no wonder he hates me. As well as thinking I might be some insane murderer, he probably holds you partly responsible for his mother's death."

"Oh, I've no doubt that he does."

She stared at her mother, trying to understand the situation and having trouble dealing with the speed at which events seemed to be unfolding.

"Skye, close your mouth, sit down, and listen to the rest of my story."

"I don't think I want to. In fact, I'm calling Eldon right now and putting the house on the market. We can go back to the way things were and forget any of this happened."

"That won't work. Events are in motion. You can no sooner deny your newly found knowledge and abilities than you could stop breathing. Not only that, but you are no longer a non-entity. The one reason I made you promise never to practice alone was so that I could keep you from accessing that part within you that would elevate you to more than what you were. I could protect you. As long as you flew under the radar, so to speak, you were safe from detection."

"What you mean is that my whole life has been a lie. Everything you told me about my powers, the promise not to practice alone, your past, my childhood—all lies. Mom, I don't want to hear any more."

If she forgot everything she'd just learned, then maybe she could go back to living in blissful ignorance. She'd been happy that way. Or had she? Her restlessness had led her all over the country searching for the unknown. Her dissatisfaction with life had led her to Salem, where she'd found a part of herself that had been so long hidden, yet prodded her daily for acknowledgment. Could she forget what she'd learned and experienced since being here? Could she deny that part of herself newly awakened?

With a deep, shuddering breath, Skye plopped onto the chair and faced her mom. "I guess I don't have a choice."

"You always have choices, dear. The thing to remember is that it's you who has to live with the consequences of your choices so it's a good idea to make the right ones."

Skye flicked a crumb off the table and watched it ricochet against the cupboard door and shatter into an array of tinier crumbs that fell to the floor. "Great. So how do I know I'm better off staying instead of selling it all and running?"

Her mom patted her hand and smiled. "Trust me on this one, staying is the right thing to do."

She considered her mom, noting the lines etched into a worn face and eyes filled with a depth of knowledge. Pleading eyes. Eyes of a woman that Skye had loved and trusted her entire lifetime. Why stop now? She sat up straight and pulled her shoulders back. "Okay, I'll stay. So explain this flying under the radar thing to me."

Flora's smile lit her face with an inner glow, and her shoulders visibly relaxed at Skye's decision. "There are those who are always searching for someone who possesses pure bloodlines. As long as a witch practices minor spells or participates in simple ritual, there's not a problem, but as soon as one takes on the manipulation of energy or crossing over to another dimension, they cast an energy trail that leaves them vulnerable. Sure, the trail will eventually fade, but because there are so few with pure bloodlines, it's like flashing a neon sign to anyone who has feelers out for just such a thing."

"It sounds like something out of The Twilight Zone." Skye's attempt at humor didn't lighten the mood at all. "Okay, as I understand it, you're saying that I have pure bloodlines and that's why you didn't want me practicing alone. You wanted to keep an eye on me and make sure I didn't call attention to myself."

"Yes. There are ways to sap a witch's powers, an act that leaves that person not only powerless, but mindless as well. I would have done anything to keep that from happening to you."

Skye reached over and hugged her mother. "I'm sorry for all the trouble I've caused you over the years. I had no idea."

"I did. I knew, because it's that very act of soul-sucking that Verity tried and failed at thirty years ago."

"The knife." She recalled the words in Dorcas's diary. "It's the birth-task of the Goods to protect the knife from those who would use it for evil." The pulse in Skye's throat beat fiercely as dizziness overcame her. "Are you telling me that the ritual you were part of thirty years ago was an attempt to use the knife to sap another person's powers? Amanda. That's why she's dead, isn't it? Mom..."

Frantically, she searched her mother's face, afraid of seeing an unwanted truth.

"Don't look at me like that. I had no way of knowing what Verity was up to. Remember, it was thirty years ago, and I was young, naive, and headstrong. Much like you are now. As far as I knew, it was a simple summer solstice celebration. That night taught me a lot about what was possible if a person's heart was filled with greed and hungry for power."

Skye couldn't fault her mother because she'd been just as easily led with the story of a simple summer solstice and ended up drugged. She shivered at her own narrow escape from whatever had been in store for her that night. Her life had depended on Verity's whims just as her mothers had thirty years earlier. "Sorry, Mom." She laid her hand over her mother's. "Tell me the rest of it."

A demanding knock at the front door caused renewed fear to shoot through both women. "Don't worry, Mom, if there was any news, the hospital would call. They wouldn't send someone to the house."

"Of course. You're right."

Skye opened the front door, anxious to get rid of whoever was interrupting their enlightening—and long past due—talk. When she saw the visitor, her heart flipped an extra beat or two. "What are you doing here?"

Jerome had come intending to be polite. After all, he had no proof that Skye was involved with anything, even if he had doubts about her mother. But her belligerent tone and flashing blue eyes bit into his newly heightened senses and caused him to respond in kind. Hefting the suitcases off the porch, he thrust them toward her.

"I'm dropping off your parent's things." Skye kept glancing toward the kitchen, as if she had something to hide. It bothered him she couldn't look at him while he stood right in front of her. He wanted her full attention, and that fact bothered him. Why should he care? And what was she hiding? Curiosity piqued, he decided to stick around and find the answers. "I also have a couple of questions to ask you."

A frown wrinkled her brow, and her tongue darted in and out, wetting her lips. A sure sign of nervousness. Jerome's gaze fell to her mouth and couldn't help but notice how the upper lip was not quite as full as the lower one. The slight upward arch of her lips, even when frowning, drew his attention, and he fantasized about their shared kiss. Her teeth tugged at her lower lip, and his groin tightened with wanton need. Heaving a breath, he shoved past her and dropped the suitcases in the hallway.

"Wait a minute. Now is not a good time."

"I don't know. It seems like a great time to me."

"You insensitive son of a bitch...I..."

"Skye, dear, who is this? Oh, you've brought our suitcases. What a wonderful gesture."

Skye tried to shove Jerome out of the door, but he stood as solid as a tree trunk that had been rooted for a century. Now he understood Skye's anxiety. Her mother was here. But it begged an answer as to why she was nervous about the two of them meeting, unless she knew more about what happened thirty years ago than she'd let on. His gaze swept over the older woman, and he noticed the resemblance to her daughter. They had the same slashing high cheekbones and full lips, although Flora's eyes were a softer hue than Skye's intensely blue ones that were currently burning a hole into his back.

"Skye, do stop pushing the young man and introduce us."

"I don't think..."

Ignoring Skye, he stepped forward until no more than a foot separated him from Flora. "I'm Jerome."

Those simple words wrought such a fierce reaction in Flora that Jerome would have been worried, except he was too busy feeling satisfaction. Fear streaked across her face. Her chest drew in a quivering intake of breath, and her eyes filled with enough guilt that he knew this woman held answers. Bile rose in his throat and he fought the urge to curl his fingers into a fist and show her some of the pain he'd lived with over the years. But even that wouldn't be enough because physical pain healed, whereas emotional pain continued to live on with each thought, each breath, and each sentiment that found itself warped with doubt and distrust.

Then he saw the trail of tears that wound a path down Flora's cheeks and the genuine sympathy replacing the look of guilt in her eyes. She fixed her gaze on him, and the connection between them jolted him from the ground up. Flora reached out and brushed a hand across his arm, as gentle as a touch of whispering wind. Calmness filled him, and the knots of pain he'd lived with for so long eased ever so slightly.

"Nothing will heal the pain of what you've lived through, but I am sorry for your loss and all that has risen from that night thirty years ago. I vow my powers, my very life, to finding out the truth and enabling you to step from the shadows of the past."

Even though the distant sounds of a clock ticking and the laugh-like chee-chee-chee of seagulls continued, time in the hallway ceased to move. Jerome's emotions rolled like the undulating waves of the ocean in a storm as he tried to reason through what this woman he'd hated for thirty years said to him. She was willing to give up her life to help find out the truth. For him? But if she'd been there that night, didn't she already know the truth? She was probably lying to him to throw him off the trail, but her voice shook with genuine sincerity.

A pinprick of a breath and a whisper tickled in his ear. "Open your senses. Use your abilities." A giggle and faerie-like chatter followed the words.

Jeesh. He wasn't used to hearing voices in his head or having faeries dance around him. Silently he cursed Samson for kick-starting his senses, but took it back when he realized it had been inevitable. Eventually he'd have discovered that inner part of himself and he'd much rather the awakening be instigated by someone he trusted.

He looked from Skye to Flora, both of them staring at him as if he'd grown two heads. Too many thoughts and senses reeled within and without. It was too much. He wanted to scream. He wanted to stay and find out the truth, but his unstable powers overwhelmed him and the two women just kept staring at him. Their faces shifted into soft focus and disappeared from sight altogether.

Visions of the past wound with the present as the light receded and the hallway became the dark tunnel that he remembered from thirty years ago. More voices whispered, but this time they were voices of the past, laughing as they set up an altar and planned their evening. Candlelight reflected the warmth of his mother's smile when she looked at him, her dark eyes gleaming with pride. Events moved in fast forward, through the aborted ceremony. The argument between his mom and Verity, right up to the moment that he had fled from the room, intent on escaping the heated anger and the feeling of sticky fingers clawing at him.

He re-lived the fright that had spurred him to run from the room as anger pulsed and tempers flared. His side stabbed with pain as he ran until he could run no more. When he realized his mother wasn't coming for him, he'd cried himself into a state of exhaustion and curled into a tight ball against the coldness of the night. His mother never came.

The touch of a hand on his arm pulled him from the past. He jerked to awareness and stared into Skye's blue eyes, filled with an eerie understanding of what he'd just been through, almost as if she'd shared the experience. It wasn't until he looked at Flora that he realized a remnant of the past had followed them to the present. His mother's face wavered fog-like in place of Flora's, her soft brown eyes pleading silently, and her lips moving soundlessly as if begging him for something. Warmth rushed through him, lending strength to his limbs. That's when he turned and fled.

CHAPTER SIXTEEN

"**M**om?" Skye whispered, afraid to attract attention or bring back the mist of magic that had formed in her hallway. It hadn't been the whirling mist or the colorful pixies and faeries darting around Jerome that set her heart to beating. No, something else had caused her wavering legs and sweaty palms, and judging by the icy chill radiating from her mother's trembling body, she'd seen the same thing.

"Come on." Skye pulled her mother away from the still open front door she seemed to be fixated on and into the living room. She flicked on the gas fireplace and silently thanked whoever had the foresight to update the old house. As warmth seeped into the room, she ran into the kitchen and poured some lukewarm tea into her mother's cup.

She sat on the sofa beside her mom and offered the cup of tea. "Are you okay?"

"I'm not sure." She sipped her drink, her gaze drifting to the hall, and then flicking to the library. "But I hope that young man is all right. He ran out of here like the hounds of hell snapped at his heels."

Skye stifled a laugh at the thought of Jerome being afraid of anything, then remembered his white-faced shock and the flash of denial that crossed his face just before he ran. The urge to go after him rose, but she realized he wouldn't accept any act of help or reassurance from her. He believed her mother had murdered his mother.

"Don't worry, Skye, he'll be fine. He just needs time to adjust himself. I'm sure he has friends to help him understand and direct his abilities."

"Sure, yeah, okay," Skye muttered, still thinking about the scene that had engulfed the three of them without so much as a by your leave. "Did we see what I think we saw?"

"We just saw a young man of extraordinary abilities coming into his own. The surrounding air rippled so erratically that he obviously hasn't learned how to curb and conserve his forces." She smiled. A soft one of reminiscing. "He possesses Amanda's powers, and they're far more than she imagined them to be when he was younger."

"Yeah, but what about the rest of it? We were standing in the hallway, but it was different. And there were other people there as well. I recognized Eldon and Verity, although they were both younger. A couple of children stood in the shadows." Skye pointed a shaking finger to the hallway. "I saw an argument and then Jerome running and hiding. My God, the pain that poor boy suffered." Her throat tightened with tears as she recalled the memories of every thought and emotion she'd lived through, just as if she'd been there. "He was terrified and wanted his mom so badly. She never showed up. It had to be devastating for him." Her voice fell to a whisper. "No wonder he hates us."

"Yes. No wonder. But we'll make it right. I have no doubt that's what we've been brought here to do." Her mother's eyes darkened and she slapped the sleeve of her caftan against the arm of the couch in a restless movement. "Damn, the cycle continues no matter what we do to avoid the eventuality."

"Cycle? Mom, if there's more, you need to tell me. Now."

She wasn't used to demanding anything from her mother because their relationship had always been one of distant affection. They loved each other, but had left so much unsaid as they glossed over important issues, avoided meaningful conversations, dealt with day-to-day circumstances without ever reaching into their souls to explore a deeper relationship. Afraid of her own feelings overwhelming her, Skye had agreed long ago with her mom never to practice her craft alone; it had relieved her of the responsibility of her own powers.

It was strange to know that her mother's carefree ways had masked the intensity of deeper pain. Always laughing, looking for the next social event, traveling to far-off places, acting the part of a blithe gadabout, her eyes now reflected a deeper knowledge. Guilt shot through Skye for bringing them to this place; a place that heralded the reshaping of relationships and personalities. The lightness of living carefree was no longer possible.

"I'm afraid you're right, dear." Skye had never been able to hide her thoughts from her mother. "But it doesn't mean the end of. Rather, it's the beginning of a new understanding of ourselves as well as each other, and that can be a wondrous thing."

"Maybe." She shifted on the sofa to face her mom. "Talk to me."

"You need to know your history. It began long ago. Long before the witch trials of Salem. Though it's that era that has lived on the most in people's memory. Interestingly enough, it was shortly after Christianity was cemented as the officially sanctioned religion of the Roman Catholic Church that people started being executed for witchcraft. Until then, the populace had respected witches for their craft and sought them out to alleviate sickness. Never harming, never judging, humble and benign in their belief of nature and her ways, those who practiced the craft were harmless yet powerful. They used the natural bounty of the earth to heal and gave respect to nature's cycles. The Church felt threatened by the belief that someone besides God could heal, never once thinking that maybe God was working through these people."

She paused, as if trying to remember a forgotten thought. "We would gladly burn a hundred, if just one of them was guilty." Her voice rustled through the air, much like dry leaves scratching along the ground in the last days of fall.

"That's horrible. Who said such a thing?"

"Conrad of Marburg, first Inquisitor of Germany. Anyone who denied the tenets of the Church, or opposed their teaching in any way, lay themselves open to persecution and execution by the Church. This common method of getting rid of the opposition by accusing them of witchcraft gained popularity and quickly became the perfect excuse for execution. But we can't blame only the Church because many adopted this convenient belief over the centuries. Yes, this attitude branched out to governments looking to exert their power, as well as local merchants looking to pad their coffers with confiscated property and money. Talk about a cycle of needing to destroy what one cannot possess."

A heavy silence settled in the now warm living room. A silence of respect for the sacrifices of the dead. Skye had known the lives of witches in the past hadn't been pleasant, and various periods in history had warranted a time of death for some of them, but she never really considered it. Never given it more than a passing sigh or consideration. Confronted with the brutal truths of persecution, torture, and even murder on nothing more than the whim of a church member or greedy merchant, caused a tide of heat to flush through Skye. Breathing deep, she let the fullness of emotion previously unknown vibrate her senses and resonate within until she thought she'd explode with the extreme pain of knowing. Of being.

Her shoulders shook with the resulting sob and when a gentle hand touched her arm, she buried her face in her mother's shoulder and cried for the dead. The innocent.

"That's when the knife took on new meaning. Legend tells that the Priestesses of Avalon had forged and blessed the knife. Originally meant as a tool to pass knowledge and wisdom from a ruling priestess to her successor, its purpose had become warped and misused through history until it became a danger. Since it is indestructible, our ancestors inherited the birth task of guarding the knife and ensuring that those not so pure of intent would never use it for evil. Times in Salem were dangerous, and the thought of losing the knowledge of slaughtered witches was unacceptable. The idea was to focus the power of the Goods into the knife and enable the abilities and knowledge to be preserved and passed through the generations despite the fervent attempts to wipe out all witches. It was no longer safe to practice the craft and there was no time to develop one's powers over a lifetime, as had been done in the past. No, if one of our own was threatened, they could instill all their knowledge onto another in a single ritual with the knife."

Her mother heaved a sigh. "It became a receptacle of sorts. Unfortunately, there are always those who are corrupt and searching for ways to twist the goodness inherent within the craft. It was for that reason that a second knife was fashioned; a replica of the original. The one difference being, that the replica holds none of the power of the first. It's merely a red-herring."

Her voice ran smooth, like honey on a humid August afternoon, and she brushed a stray bit of hair from Skye's cheek. "I've been wrong to keep you from your powers. I should have known better because your grandmother did the same thing with me. She tried to protect me from the truth, so that when events of thirty years ago confronted me, I had no idea what was happening until it was too late. Amanda stood up to Verity when I should have. Her death should have been mine. Now we need to make up for the past by building your powers and then protecting you. We also need to find the knife before it can be used for harm."

Skye straightened, wiped her hands down both sides of her face, and sniffled. "Okay, where do we begin?"

Jerome paced Eldon's office, his glowering face enough to drive away anyone who might have been foolish enough to come in to inquire about real estate. Eldon sat with his elbows propped on his desk and his fingers peaked steeple-like under his chin. He watched. He listened.

"It's Samson's fault. He sparked all this stuff inside me and now I can't control a single thought or emotion." He slammed one fist into another. "She was standing right in front of me, and all I could do was turn tail and run like a whipped puppy."

"Give yourself credit, Jerome. From everything you just told me, you experienced a major shift in your consciousness, which left you open to an onslaught of overwhelming forces. Not only that, but you somehow transported your mind into the past to relive the most horrible night of your life. I'm surprised you're here and not home in bed in the middle of some sort of meltdown instead."

Jerome waved a hand dismissively. "No time to sleep. Don't you feel it in the air?" He moved to the front window and scanned up and down the street. "It's heavy. It wants, no, it demands fulfillment, and the cost will be a human life...more human lives. I feel a connection with whatever—whoever is doing these murders. Even more so, now that Samson has helped me do whatever it is I've done." He held his hands in front of his face, turned them about, and snorted. "It's amazing how much more sensitive all my senses are now. I feel as if I've been living in a fog."

A look of longing crossed Eldon's face. "Your mom would have been so proud," he whispered.

Restless, Jerome moved from the window, locked gazes with Eldon, and asked the question he'd been too afraid to ask Flora earlier. "I want you to tell me about that night. I have to put a stop to whatever's happening any way that I can, and the more knowledge I have about the past the better equipped I'll be."

Eldon bolted upright in his chair and raised an eyebrow. He ground his teeth, the movement of his jaw serving to wriggle his beard around as if it possessed a life of its own. "Well. Thirty years it took you to ask me that."

"Then it's about time. Especially since everyone involved has returned to town. Almost as if an unknown hand is gathering us all here for a re-enactment of that night."

"Don't sound so morbid. It wasn't that big a deal." The words barely left Eldon's mouth, and his face paled. "Christ, I didn't mean it like that. I only meant that nothing out of the ordinary happened that night to make me think that there was some force at work. No clue indicating that remnants of history had reared up to engulf us in some kind of dark performance." He quieted his voice and almost whispered, "Your mother's death was either an accident or the result of a human hand, not some dark force of evil."

Jerome didn't believe him. Not because he thought Eldon was lying...at least he didn't think so. He needed to believe that his friend was too loyal and steadfastly moral to lie, but with events, both past and present, he wasn't sure he could trust anyone. Jerome believed that even if his mother's death had been by human hand, a hand other than human had directed the events.

"Tell me."

"It was a summer solstice celebration, nothing else. Verity led the ceremony. Even though your mother possessed stronger powers, Verity was the ambitious one and was older by a few years, so she felt it was her place. Flora and I had only begun tapping into our innate abilities and never would have presumed to push our way to the forefront."

"The rain was torrential that night, so we held the ritual inside. We lit some candles, cast a circle, and gave a blessing for growth and rebirth."

Frustrated, Jerome rubbed a hand back and forth across his head, the short hair prickling his palm. "So what went wrong?"

"I don't know. Near the end of what would be a typical blessing verse, Verity drew out a knife, laid it on the altar, and chanted a strange verse. Your mom gasped and jumped back to the edge of the center circle. She demanded that Verity stop immediately, and when she didn't, Amanda started to recite something that made Verity blanch. They shouted at each other for a couple of minutes—something about upholding the ways of our ancestors and not dabbling in things we don't understand."

Eldon paused for breath and shot a look at Jerome. "That was when you ran from the room."

"I remember. The air sparked with anger and stifling heat until I felt suffocated. The dark scared me and I'd never seen Mom so angry. I thought I'd done something wrong, so I ran. I was shaking by the time I stopped and I'd gone so far into the woods that I had no idea how to get back. That's where the police found me the next day. Shivering under a pine tree." The memory wrenched Jerome because he'd always blamed himself for his mother's disappearance. If he'd stayed in the house, everything would have been different.

Eldon reassured. "Don't blame yourself. If you'd stayed, you might not be alive today. Besides, you were only six years old. I don't know what you were even doing there."

"Mom said I needed to understand my power so I could control it and not let it control me. She was trying to help me because I'd been having horrible nightmares and I think she believed it was a result of not understanding my power."

Eldon shrugged. "It's a moot point now, I suppose. After you left, Verity and Amanda argued for a couple more minutes while Flora and I watched, totally confused. Your mom finally said she could have no part in such a vile act, and she'd do whatever she could to stop Verity from completing whatever she'd started that night. She warned Flora and me to leave if we knew what was good for us, then she left to find you."

"That's it?"

"Flora and I left right away. We assumed Amanda had found you and taken you home. I never saw her again." He cleared his throat and wiped a tear. "I should have looked for both of you. I'll never forgive myself for going home that night."

"It's okay. I'm sure you couldn't have known."

"I should have. I should have known something was wrong." His voice trailed off, and he sighed. "The entire event scared me enough to forget about practicing any kind of craft ever again."

"What was so special about the knife?"

"I didn't know at that time, but afterward I did some research. All I could find was some brief reference to a knife passed through the generations of Goods and that it needed to be protected from, *Doers of evil.*"

"How do you know it's the same knife?"

"I don't for sure. I'm only going by the description and even that was sketchy. But, as far as I could tell, it described the knife I saw that night." He frowned and his eyes glazed over as he recited a poem from memory.

She wields the black-handled knife
As an extension of her thoughts and intuition
The knife's edge gleams and dances in moonlight
As she spirals her energy
Ever focused on her prey
Twisting round the handle, clawing its way upward
Twines a dragon with a single ruby eye that glimmers
When the creature's gaze fixes on you
Your power is lost, your life is forfeit."

"Jesus, Eldon, that's morbid. Where did you hear something like that?"

"In an old diary at the Peabody Essex Museum. Believe it or not, one of Sarah Good's ancestors wrote it. The man thought it his duty to warn his descendants of the knife's power or something. I can't really remember, but I do know the knife I saw that night was black-handled with a dragon winding up the handle and a ruby for an eye."

"So you think this knife has some kind of special ability and Verity was trying to use it that night to steal someone's powers."

Eldon threw his hands up in denial. "I don't think anything. I'm only telling you what I read and that was thirty years ago, so I'm not sure I even have that right."

"You sounded sure enough when you recited the verse. But it's still not enough. We need to read that diary and find out what happened to the knife."

"It won't do you any good. Someone broke into the museum and stole the diary shortly after I read it."

Jerome smacked his palm on Eldon's desk. "That proves it. The knife holds powers that someone, probably Verity, doesn't want us to know about. She killed my mom and now she's on a murdering rampage and killing off young girls."

"Slow down, son. We don't know for sure that she killed your mom and there's no reason for her to kill those girls. Remember, the knife is supposed to drain a witch's powers, so she has no reason to kill the girls."

"Unless they happened to be witches."

"That's a stretch and you know it."

"A stretch? We are talking about Salem here, Eldon. What I know for sure is that we need to find that knife and put a stop to the killings."

"Jerome, whether or not Verity has the knife, she's a dangerous woman and a powerful witch. You can't go accusing her of crimes of this magnitude without evidence and even then, I'd worry about your safety. Your power is too young and untried to stand against her."

"Then help me."

Eldon shook his head and shuffled the papers on his desk. "No. I haven't practiced the craft in a long time. I'd be no help to you."

"Come on, I need your help. I know your magic is strong. Mom always said so."

"She did?" Eldon's eyes brightened and his face lit with pleasure.

That single moment slammed Jerome for being a blind fool. All these years, and he'd never seen the truth. "You loved her."

"What?"

"Mom. You loved her."

"No. We were just friends."

He laid a hand on Eldon's shoulder and felt a tremor. He realized that Eldon was on the verge of crying. "After all this time, don't you think I deserve the truth? Don't you think Mom's memory deserves the truth?"

Eldon breathed out as if the air had been let out of him. Unabashed tears streamed down his cheeks as he looked at Jerome across the desk. "You always had a way of getting the truth out of people, you know. Samson says that's why he lets you interrogate so many prisoners."

"Why have you never said anything?"

Eldon blew his nose and shrugged. "What good would it have done except to open wounds better left healed? You and I have remained friends through the years. That's all that matters."

A knot of emotion wound up Jerome's chest, and he realized how much this man meant to him. Eldon had always been there for him with an encouraging word, a handout when needed with no payback expected, a place to crash when Jerome returned to town and had nowhere to stay.

He'd been the father Jerome never had. Eldon had loved Amanda, no way would he have killed her. Any doubt that he might bear some responsibility for his mother's death left Jerome at that moment.

"Okay." Jerome stood and took a deep breath. "I guess I can count on you to help me out now."

"I guess so."

The two men smiled at each other with a new understanding of their relationship.

CHAPTER SEVENTEEN

With the bonds of blood and camaraderie coming full circle, the force that darkens the day shall be forced to hide in the night. When souls touch and love blooms, the bonds shall strengthen more until the darkness is banished into a realm beyond the reach of man. Safety is imminent, but only as long as each follows their heart and remains pure to the past.

Excerpt from *Faerie Enchantments and Sorcerer Magick*

Morning dawned, imbuing the day with light and fresh hope. Skye and her mom decided to visit the hospital after breakfast, and then her mom wanted to stop at one of the local stores to pick up supplies. The accident had damaged most of hers, and according to her, 'There are some things no self-respecting witch is ever without.'

The sun had barely crested the distant line of the ocean, traffic was light and the hospital parking lot near empty. After a sleepless night, Skye didn't feel like talking, and her mother's usual chatter was noticeably absent. They moved carefully through the hospital, taking care not to interrupt the early morning schedule of the nurses attending waking patients. With a one-finger dictate from the nurse, Flora motioned Skye into the room for the first visit.

The door closed soundly, leaving her with stifling heat and the constant beep, beep of machines. She felt nauseous. Her father looked gaunt, so unlike his usual tanned, muscular, energetic self. She moved to touch his cheek and hesitated when she saw a flicker of movement from his eyelids, but she remembered a nurse saying that might happen and that it was nothing more than a reflex. Sighing, she cupped his cheek with her palm and shivered. He was so cold. But that wasn't all. There was more. A hint of malignancy washed over her so quickly she could almost convince herself she'd imagined the sensation. She needed to probe with her own senses, which could be somewhat dangerous considering her father's condition.

But she had to try. This was her father, for goodness sake. The man who raised her with love and an unwavering ability to step between her and her mother whenever circumstances called for an intermediary. Relaxing her mind, she probed deep inside her body for the flow of her own lifeblood. It was a vital connection to make if she wanted to explore her father's aura or inner being. Without full control of her own energy flow and blood path, she couldn't hope to read another's. Relax. Breathe. Spinning and whooshing through her veins, carrying the oxygen and nutrients to sustain life. There. She'd made a connection. She was one with herself.

Now she reached out. Bursting from within, she let her senses probe and fuse with her father's aura. Oh, so wavering thin. So weak. She felt herself weaken. Couldn't go too deep or she might not be able to return. She recognized his essence. Warmth engulfed her in a comforting embrace and then nudged her forward, almost as if he were trying to show her something. Yes. That's what she was here for. Giving herself fully to her father's essence, she was shocked when she suddenly smashed into a hard wall of resistance.

Her father screamed a warning. Fear. Anger. He fought whatever force threatened her, and she felt him weaken. She had to get away, or he'd use all his life force to save her. With a wrenching grasp of her senses, she yanked away and found herself promptly falling butt first onto the cold, hard hospital floor.

Her mother tore into the room, cursing like Skye had never heard her do before. She knelt down and placed a hand on Skye's forehead, tugged her eyelids up, and looked into her eyes. Satisfied with what she saw, she swore again. "For Heaven's sake, Skye, what do you think you were doing?" She yanked her daughter's arm and pulled her to her feet.

"Mom, he's not in a coma. Something else has a hold of him and it tried to get to me, but Dad saved me."

"Yes. I know it's not a normal coma. And because of your thoughtlessness, you almost cost him his life." Her eyes swelled with tears. "Maybe yours as well."

"I'm sorry, I just...I thought..."

"Don't think or you'll get us all killed."

Skye flushed. The beep, beep of monitors filled the hurtful silence.

"Oh, my dear, I'm the one who's sorry now. I didn't mean it. It's just that I already knew the coma wasn't a normal one, and because you bull-headed your way into a dangerous situation, you almost destroyed the two people I love most in the world. You need to trust me."

"Then stop trying to protect me. If I'd known that you already knew about Dad's coma, I wouldn't have tried what I did. You need to trust me as well."

Surprise and then respect lit her mother's eyes. "Okay. I guess my own daughter has just set me in my place. I better watch out or you'll surpass me in both power and wisdom." Her smile and watery eyes softened the mood.

Skye put an arm around her mom's shoulders and hugged her close. "I doubt I'll ever know everything you do." She sniffled and wiped the back of her hand across her eyes. "So what now?"

"Plans have changed. I was going to induce a trance myself and try to weave the path to whoever is holding your father in this coma, but not anymore." Her gaze settled full force on Skye. "I tried to connect with him yesterday to no avail, but you connected with ease, so I guess you'll be the one going into the trance."

"But you just said that it was a dangerous thing to do. Besides, I almost didn't make it back this time, so how can trying again help?"

"Next time you'll be better prepared to enter the ethereal plane, and you'll have me guarding you on the physical plane. It's the only way to get a clue to whoever is doing this and help your father. We need to act soon. For each hour he's in this state, he loses a part of himself. Before long, he'll have no memory of us or himself." She gestured toward her husband, lying prone, and her voice cracked. "We need to find the knife for the sake of the innocent, but we have to save him for my sake. I can't live without him."

Understanding of her parent's love welled within Skye and she hoped one day to be as blessed to find the kind of love that transcends time and boundaries.

"Give me something. Anything," Jerome mumbled as he thumbed through his rarely used by-law manual, while Eldon poured them both another mug of the police station's strong, black coffee.

"Jerome, we can spend more time over at the Peabody. We only covered a small area of archives yesterday."

"That's the point; we only covered a small area. We need to find that knife before another girl is murdered and it could take weeks of digging through boring old diaries and documents before we turn up a single clue."

Eldon placed the mug of coffee none too gently onto Jerome's desk. "And you think that finding a reason to search Verity's store is going to get you further ahead?"

Jerome gulped his coffee and grimaced at the bitterness. "Yes. If she has the knife, she'll have it close. I know it. We just need a by-law infringement, some excuse for reasonable justification to have a look around."

"Thin. Very thin." Eldon shrugged and sat. "How'd you sleep last night?" He slurped a mouthful of coffee, his gaze fixed on Jerome over the edge of the mug.

"Fine," Jerome replied absent-mindedly.

"You're sure?"

"Of course I'm sure. I had a couple of dreams, that's all." He looked up from the manual and fixed a narrowed gaze on Eldon. "Why?"

"I had dreams too, but they weren't nice ones. I kept reliving that night, but each time it was someone else who died at the end. In the last dream, everyone died." Pained, he looked to Jerome as if waiting for him to deny such a thing was possible.

"That will not happen, Eldon. It's just your mind's way of reacting to the dredging up of events from that night. Nothing more, nothing less."

"If you say so." Eldon slugged down the rest of his coffee and rose to pour himself another.

Jerome's coffee sat on his desk, barely touched, and it remained that way as he turned his attention back to the manual. He wouldn't admit it to Eldon, who worried too much, but violent, twisting visions of blood, gore, and death had haunted his own dreams the night before. He'd also dreamed about the death of a group of faceless people involved in a horrid ritual. That was why he was so intent on ending this entire situation before anyone else was murdered. He knew the killer hovered on the edge of killing again, and he couldn't let that happen.

"Why don't you just say that you found something on one of the bodies that leads back to Verity's store? That should give you reason enough to ask questions and maybe do a search."

"To quote someone I respect, 'Thin. Very thin.'" He grinned at Eldon. "But if we say it was clutched in her hand as if trying to give us a clue, we might have something."

"Can you do that, though? I mean, if you're trying to get a search warrant, doesn't it have to be based on fact?" "If I were trying to get a search warrant, sure. But chances are that Verity wouldn't want word spreading around town that we're searching her store regarding a murder, and she's arrogant enough to believe that she's smarter than us. She'll co-operate."

"What if she does and then finds out that you lied to her? You could lose your job, or worse."

"I'll deal with that if it happens. Let's go." With a face of granite and eyes burning with a purpose honed over years, Jerome strode from the room without waiting to see if Eldon would follow.

***

The store was smaller than *Witches Haven*, but seemed better stocked for craftwork. While Verity's store catered to touristy, wanna-be witches, The Magic Corner was packed from floor to ceiling with jars of dried herbs, vials of essential oils, crystals, candles, amulets, brooms, cord, and divination tools such as tarot cards and runes. The back wall boasted a glass showcase of knives—athames for ritual and bollines for cutting and carving—as well as a bookshelf stocked with some very impressive books.

Stepping into the store was like entering the past. A world of enchantment, solid earth-magic, time-honored natural remedies, and a perception of one's own eternal cycle of life.

A woman approached them. Dressed casually in jeans and a lavender blouse ruffled at the V-neck and wrists, she exuded warmth and calm. She glanced knowingly at Skye and Flora while her mouth curved into a smile of welcome and a nod of acknowledgment. Without a word spoken, the woman recognized them as fellow practitioners of the art of magic.

"Good morning, sisters. I'm Nora. And I know you two are Flora and Skye."

Flora chuckled. "I guess Salem is still a small town at heart, isn't it?"

"Yep. Not much goes on around here that doesn't get talked about. Especially when one of our own returns to town."

Flora's eyes brightened with unshed tears. "What a nice thing to say. Thank you." Her gaze landed on the glass case of a leather-bound book. Resting on a raised podium, open to reveal yellowed parchment under the glass, and protected with an elaborate lock and alarm system, the book was obviously old and revered. With a gasp, she moved forward and ran her hands lovingly over the case in a gesture of reverence. "No. This can't be what I think it is. I always thought it was mere legend and myth."

"It's real." Pride filled the woman's voice. "I was fortunate enough to find it in a box of books I purchased at an auction about ten years ago. As soon as I held it in my hands, I knew what I'd found."

Skye looked at the book, but saw nothing special other than it was obviously old. Yet when she laid her hand on the glass, a jolt of heat shot up her arm and set her heart to fluttering. "Wow." She withdrew her hand.

Her mom and the store owner laughed at her reaction. "Yes, the book has a tendency to make itself known to those of the craft. The true craft, not the pretenders."

"But what is it?" Skye questioned.

"It's called, *Faerie Enchantments and Sorcerer Magick* and it's estimated to be over two thousand years old."

"But that's not possible. No book could survive that long. Did they even make books with parchment and leather that long ago?"

"Ahh, legends tell that the book transmutes into whatever form is appropriate for the time. It also holds tales of magic and ritual from its inception to the present."

"But who would dare write in such an ancient text?" Skye knelt for a better look and saw no difference in color from one page to the next. "And how could they even begin to match pages and color?" She peered closer at the book, but there was nothing that marked any recent additions.

"The book writes its own stories as needed. Kind of a guide to future generations who will need the knowledge." Nora spoke softly. Reverently.

Skye laughed, but realized no one else was. "You're serious. How can that be?"

"The book is imbued with pure, ancient magic. The kind that existed when intent was without ulterior motives, and people's beliefs were respected rather than condemned."

"Oh." Skye pondered the information as she stared at the book. The knowledge, experience, and history that must lie within those pages was unfathomable. "No wonder you have it under lock and key." She still couldn't believe that the book wrote its own stories, but she supposed it made a fascinating tale for tourists.

As if reading her thoughts, Nora smiled and said, "So what can I help you with today, ladies?"

"I need some of your parchment, ink, a brass table cauldron for burning, orange candles, dragon's blood oil, some cord, some mugwort, and I think some violet as well."

Knowing warmth filled Nora's soft gold eyes, and she placed her hand gently over Flora's. "You're going to attempt reviving your husband, aren't you?"

Skye was about to deny the claim, not wanting anyone to know what they were up to, but her mother spoke first. "Yes, we are."

"How could you possibly know that?" asked Skye.

"I've been in this business for years, so I recognize the ingredients." She smiled at Flora. "It's also that small town thing again. I know about your husband. Besides, I know everything that has anything to do with that woman."

"That woman?" Skye and her mother echoed simultaneously.

"Verity Parker." The store owner practically spit the words.

The color drained from her mother's face, and Skye squeezed her arm reassuringly. "Why do you think she has anything to do with my father's coma?"

Seemingly perplexed, the woman looked from mother to daughter. "I just figured, you know, with the history between you and the fact that you've all returned to town." She shrugged. "Stands to reason she's involved somehow. She's involved in every other horrid event that goes on around here."

"Oh. Like what?" Skye asked.

Deftly packing the supplies into a bag, the woman continued talking. "Missing pets, lost jobs, robberies, you name it." Skye didn't like gossiping, and felt the need to defend a woman who wasn't here to defend herself. "Pets go missing all the time. They run away."

"And show up gutted and hanging from someone's front porch?"

Skye gulped. "People lose jobs every day and robberies happen everywhere."

"Jobs are lost by people who have ticked Verity off for one reason or another, and the robberies, these same people have their houses broken into and personal items like hairbrushes stolen. Usually right before they lose their job. Verity takes money to put spells on people."

Skye didn't know what to say. Nora might be paranoid, but she appeared to be mature, intelligent, and successful. On the surface, she was far from some loony spouting conspiracy theories on the street corner.

"She taught her son the ways of the Black Art as well."

"What?" Skye hadn't been paying attention.

"Her son. He's just as bad as she is. Or worse."

"Matthew. Come on...Matthew?"

"Don't let him fool you. I've seen him grow up, and he's polished that act of innocence over the years. Ask your mother. Even at eight years old, he was worse than a mouthful of wormwood. Excuse me." Nora moved to help another customer inquiring about a book at the back of the store.

Skye pondered Nora's assessment of Matthew's personality and found that she couldn't reconcile the slightly gawky, outgoing man she'd met with the dark personality Nora portrayed. Not knowing the history between Nora and Matthew, or Nora and Verity for that matter, she didn't want to take the shop owner's words verbatim. People tended to color their opinions and beliefs based on their own life circumstances and events. Nora might very well believe what she said about Verity and Matthew, but that didn't mean it was true. She had learned that beliefs and opinions were usually multi-layered with many truths. She'd reserve judgment.

Skye looked around for her mom and saw her staring at a shelf of crystals. "Mom, are you all right? You haven't said a word since Verity's name was mentioned."

"I've been thinking. It makes sense. Verity's involvement in the accident, as well as Walter's coma. I sense the closing of a circle and since Verity was the one who started this whole thing, it stands to reason she'd be the one to bring it to a close."

"What about Matthew? Is it true what she said about him?"

"I'm sorry. I wasn't listening to what she said about him. I do remember him as being quite a handful, especially when Verity wouldn't allow him to take part in the ritual thirty years ago. He threw a major temper tantrum."

Skye shivered. Cold fingers crawled up her spine and shimmied up her neck. "Come on, let's get out of here and go save Dad."

They moved to the door, but a shout from the back of the store stopped them. "Wait." Nora strode toward them, her eyes blazing. "Wait. I have to give you something." Withdrawing a chain with key attached, she unlocked the showcase and lifted *Faerie Enchantments and Sorcerer Magick* carefully from its resting place. Hesitantly, she handed it to Skye. "You'll need this."

"What. No." Shocked at the offer, she drew her hands behind her back. "I can't take that. It's far too valuable. Besides, I wouldn't know what to do with it."

"You'll know when the time comes. Trust me. This is what needs to happen. Don't ask how I know, I just do."

Flora placed her hand on Skye's arm. "Take the book, and trust that Nora's being led to do what she must."

Skye swallowed and accepted the gift. The same jolt of heat shot through her, but this time it settled into a soft warmth that went bone deep and swelled within her. Her mother and Nora shared a knowing look.

"I think the book has decided it's time to change ownership. It now belongs to you, Skye." Nora's tone held a hint of regret, but she shrugged and smiled. "All things come to an end. I wish you the best and please keep in mind that the day will come when you must pass the book on to someone for the greater good as well."

"I'll remember," Skye murmured, still stunned at coming into possession of such a treasure. Such a responsibility.

CHAPTER EIGHTEEN

Jerome stepped into the sunshine and cursed. There was a certain wrongness about spending such a beautiful day on a needle-in-a-haystack search for a centuries old knife that might have been the weapon of death for several young women. Anger and a fierce sense of reckoning drove him ever closer to *Witches Haven* and the woman he was convinced was responsible for his mother's death.

Eldon fell into step beside him. "Look, I know Verity. She'll have her craft tools well organized, close to her altar, and in a chest of sorts. It won't be a cheap or tacky one either. Oh, no. She'll have the best, most elaborate one she could find. If you locate that chest, you'll more than likely find the knife." He shot a glance at Jerome. "That is, if she's got it."

"She's got something. Whether it's the one we're looking for is the question."

"So, what if we find it, but it's not the same one?" Eldon weaved off the sidewalk to avoid a woman and her young son, who seemed to have taken it in his mind to have a tantrum in the middle of downtown.

"The same what?" Jerome pinned his gaze on *Witches Haven* and never flinched, even as they crossed the road and a speeding vehicle almost ran them down.

"Knife, of course." Eldon panted, out of breath from jogging to keep up.

"That's what I have you here for. Identification."

Eldon slid to a halt and grabbed Jerome's arm. "Hey, I can tell you with some certainty if it looks like the knife I saw thirty years ago, but no way in a month of Sundays can I tell you if it's the knife. Heck, the story is not a secret, but I'm sure there's more than one knife with that description. Unless..."

He shook off Eldon's hand and strode across the cobblestones to the front of *Witches Haven*. Before entering the store, he turned and gave Eldon his full attention. His friend did have a point. If myths and legends held true and there was a knife of unimaginable power, they needed to find it and keep it from the hands of anyone who would use it irresponsibly. If the knife used by Verity thirty years ago was a different one, it was still the one most likely used to murder his mother. They needed both.

"Unless what?"

"Unless we get a Good to tell us. If you can believe gossip and legends, they're the only ones who would know for sure."

"How? Until a couple of days ago, Skye supposedly didn't even know she was descended from the Goods."

"It doesn't matter. It's in their blood."

"Maybe." Jerome's attention turned to the heavy wooden door guarding the entrance to the store. With his mother's face flickering on the edge of his mind, he yanked it and stepped inside. It took a moment to adjust to the dim light, and he took that time to focus his mind and open his senses. Since discovering the part of himself he'd been unaware of, he has found that he needs to concentrate and categorize, or go crazy. Battered with a myriad of sounds near and far, it took time to distinguish each one and filter out the unimportant. As for scents, he could smell the cinnamon buns being baked at the Black Cat Bakery three blocks away, the salty tang of the ocean, the exhaust from numerous cars, a hint of lavender from Maeve's Flower Shoppe, the musky aroma of someone's sweat... the list went on.

He needed to learn to ignore the distant and unnecessary and focus on the nearby and important. Samson had given him a few tips and Jerome heeded his friend's advice now with a deep breath, a visual scan of his surroundings to qualify what was there and how that related to the sounds and smells he was experiencing. Everything else, he filtered into the back of his mind.

"Why, Jerome, twice in the same week. What are you here to accuse me of this time?"

Verity glided across the highly polished wooden floor, her high-heeled shoes clicking a sharp staccato. Elegantly dressed in a black pantsuit with white accents edging the sleeves and pant legs, she certainly didn't look like a murderer. Unless you looked into her eyes. Jerome could have sworn he saw a dark shadow pass across her blue eyes when she fixed him with her gaze. An unfamiliar touch brushed through his mind as if searching, and he repelled it with an instinctive thought of protection. Surprise glimmered in Verity's eyes before she could settle her features into a blank facade of greeting.

"I'm not here to accuse you of anything. Why? Are you feeling guilty about something?"

Verity's red, lipstick coated mouth turned upward in an attempt to emulate a smile. "A lady's allowed some secrets, isn't she?"

"Sure. As long as it doesn't involve murder."

Nostrils flared, and the coldness crept back into Verity's eyes. "I don't have time for games. What do you want?"

"I'd like to search your store."

"No."

"Yes."

Their gazes locked, neither one wanting to waver first. "We found something clutched in the hands of the last murdered girl that leads here. I can get a search warrant based on that evidence, but I thought you'd rather keep things quiet." Jerome's gaze never left her and he was rewarded when all color drained from her face and her lips pursed.

Verity snapped her head away from Jerome. "This is preposterous." She acknowledged Eldon's presence for the first time.

"How much of this is your doing? You've hated me for years, but I wouldn't have guessed you'd go to this extreme to bring me down."

"I don't hate you, Verity, I feel sorry for you."

If there hadn't been customers in the store, Jerome was sure Verity would have shrieked out loud. Hate she could handle. To her way of thinking, it went hand in hand with jealousy, and if someone were jealous of her it meant she had something worthy of jealousy. But pity was unacceptable. She would hate being pitied. Jerome watched her struggle to rein in her emotions and regain her favored demeanor of self-control.

"Fine," she said. "At least let me clear out the store and put up the closed sign. The last thing I need is for gossip to fly around town. I have a reputation to uphold, you know."

He bowed his head in acquiescence and stepped into the shadows to allow her to usher her customers out of the store. It gave him a chance to watch her closely. She might be good at maintaining her composure, but reading people was the part of his job he excelled at. Her movements were efficient, and it took only a minute to herd the few customers from the store, but during that time, her gaze shifted a few times to the curtains that led to the back of the store. That's where he'd start his search.

Motioning to Eldon, he crossed the floor and entered the back room. It was a typical storage area, although better organized than most, with boxes piled neatly on one side of the small room and unpacked stock resting on a trolley, ready for moving out onto the floor. Empty boxes had already been broken down and tied together for garbage pickup, and the packing material was bagged and resting at the back door.

"What did I tell you?" Eldon whispered. "She's a neat freak."

Jerome's mind worked at full speed—cataloging, analyzing, configuring. They wouldn't find what they were looking for here. But where? Eldon answered his unspoken question quickly enough.

"She usually does rituals out in the back garden, so I assume she'll have her altar and tools out there."

"Good plan." The afternoon sun shone brightly and Jerome shielded his eyes until they adjusted. The garden was just as he remembered from the night he saved Skye from an uncertain fate, except the raised altar no longer held center focus in the garden. How could that be? He knew he'd seen a stone platform that night, but now there was only a flat patio stone lending a sitting area to a couple of chairs and a table. Inspiration struck.

"Help me get these things out of the way." He moved the table off of the stone, while Eldon moved the two chairs. Kneeling on the stone, Jerome ran his hands around the edge of the slab, curling his fingers under the stone's edge as much as possible. Sure that he'd felt some movement of the stone, he continued working his way methodically around its circumference. Then it happened. He felt himself rising from the ground. He'd activated a mechanism that raised the flagstone from the ground until it was waist height. With a wide grin, he sat back on his butt and looked at Eldon, who stood open-mouthed.

"Voila. I'm magic."

"Amazing. Now we need to..."

"How dare you?" Verity ran through the back door, unceremoniously tripping on an ornamental figurine and barely righting herself before continuing her forward forge. "You have no right." Panic raised the pitch of her voice an octave or two, and Jerome knew they were on the right track.

"Sorry, but you gave me the right by allowing me to search."

Obviously not satisfied with his explanation, Verity grabbed his arm with a surprisingly forceful grip and tried dragging him off the altar. Usually perfectly coiffed, her hair had worked loose from its hair-sprayed helmet and hung in disarray to her shoulders. Her eyes were the wild blue of the ocean in a storm and Jerome worried for her sanity, so he complied with her attempt to pull him off the altar. She seemed to settle down.

"Thank you." Verity straightened her shoulders and nervously worked her hair into a semblance of order. "Now, if you'll see yourselves out, I have a store to run."

"I'm not finished looking yet."

"But you have to be." She looked over her shoulder as if afraid of being discovered, and whispered, "You have to go."

"Not until I'm done." Jerome knelt to look under and around the moveable altar and saw nothing more than smooth stone, but Verity's rapid breathing let him know he was on the right track. If there'd been one device to hide the altar, there could be another one to hide her chest. He probed the underside of the altar stone with his fingertips, ignoring Verity's strident declaration that she was going to call the police. Her unusually harried state must be affecting her mind. He was the police. As his exploration brought him around the backside of the stone, her verbal demands to stop turned into physical ones when she grabbed his arm and tried dragging him away again.

"Damn it, Eldon, keep her off me, would you."

None too gently, Eldon clutched Verity's arms and wrung them around behind her back just as Jerome triggered a switch. With a smooth movement and almost silent rasp of stone on stone, a drawer slid from the base of the altar. Verity's struggles increased as he shot a triumphant glance at Eldon.

"Well, well, well. It looks as if we've struck gold." He glared at Verity, who stopped her struggles when confronted with the full bore of his accusing eyes. He pulled a finely etched mahogany chest from its hiding place. "You had better hope the weapon used to murder my mother isn't in here."

In a decisive movement, Verity ceased her movement, squared her shoulders, and stared over Jerome's head into the distance. Eldon let go of her arms, and they dropped to hang by her side.

About twice the size of a breadbox, the rectangular chest was inlaid with mother-of-pearl. With a fiercely beating heart and a deep breath, Jerome touched the hinged lid and lifted, suddenly unsure whether he was ready to find what he was looking for. Resting on one side of the chest were a couple of tarot card decks with various colors of blue, lavender, and gold, the primary colors in the top card of each deck. A red leather-bound book, probably a Book of Shadows, took a prominent position in the center of the chest, while candles, incense, and oils lined the other side. No knife. But the depth of the chest attested to the fact that there was probably another shelf.

Jerome's gaze scoured the interior until coming to rest on a small tab of red velvet. Pulling the tab released the shelf, which lifted up and back on hinges.

Bingo.

Obviously the place for Verity's most revered treasures. The lower shelf held exotic crystals whose essence sparkled in the sudden light, timeworn books with titles such as, *Beyond the Realms of Reality* and *Rituals of Ancient Magicians*. But the best part was the dark wooden box inlaid with black symbols that nestled innocently upon a raised platform. Heart pounding, Jerome lifted the lid and stared at the contents. He swallowed and calmed his breathing before acting. With shaking hands, he raised the box to Eldon. Sunlight pierced through the trees and lent an unearthly glow to the red velvet lining of the box, but mainly, the light ignited the red jewel that was the dragon's eye.

He recited Eldon's earlier words. "Twisting round the handle, as if clawing its way upward, twined a dragon with a single ruby eye that glimmered intermittently. When the creature's gaze fixes on you, your power is lost, your life is forfeit."

Eldon blanched and nodded. "That looks like the knife I saw that night."

Sudden pounding ignited a headache in Jerome's skull and he fought the urge to strangle the woman who stood as if entranced by some unseen specter. Closing the lid and tucking the box under his arm, he stood and faced Verity. A flicker of hate flashed in her otherwise strangely flat eyes and he ground his teeth to keep from screaming that she was a murderer. As much as he'd love to choke the life from her, he'd let the courts handle her. No way did he want her getting off on a technicality. He'd rather see her suffer all the indignities a woman like her would have to bear in jail.

"If this knife matches the stab wounds in my mother..." He choked as his mother's face swam through his vision like a shaft of sunlight pierced the forest. "Do not leave town, or I'll find you and drag you back for the punishment you deserve." He spun about and strode through the back gate before he lost the last thread of sanity remaining and made that woman pay for killing his mother. He was sure she was guilty. It made sense. She'd been the ringleader at the ritual thirty years ago; she still had the knife used for the foul deed of murder. Okay, the alleged knife. But a deep sense of knowing told him that the knife he carried under his arm most definitely was the knife that had struck his mother down at the very pinnacle of her youth and beauty.

Eldon finally caught up to his long stride. Out of breath and jogging, he grabbed Jerome's arm in an attempt to slow him down. As a concession to his friend, Jerome slowed his pace. With a sigh of relief, Eldon asked, "Are you just going to let her remain free? What if she leaves town?"

"She won't. She's too arrogant to think that we'll pin a thirty-year-old murder on her. Even with the murder weapon."

"But she'd be wrong. Right?"

Jerome clenched his jaw. "I hope so, or it'll fall to my shoulders to mete out justice."

Fear crossed Eldon's face and his beard rode up and down as he chewed his lip. "Your mother would not want you to destroy your life, avenging her death."

Jerome stared at his friend and wondered how different things might have been if his mother had lived. This man probably would have ended up being his stepfather. But did that really matter? He'd been like a father to him all these years, anyway. Eldon's statement made him wonder about himself and how far he would go to avenge his mother's death. He didn't know the answer and hoped it wouldn't come down to that.

He pulled the keys to his police cruiser from his pocket and said, "We have one stop to make with this knife before I hand it over for testing. Are you coming?"

"Just try to stop me." Eldon grinned and slapped Jerome's back in a gesture of camaraderie.

CHAPTER NINETEEN

"**A**re you sure you've remembered the poem exactly the way I taught you?"

Skye watched her mother twist her hands fretfully and wished she could reassure her, but the closer they came to inducing a trance, the more of her own energy it took to remain calm. She had nothing left for her mother. "I remember, Mom. I promise."

"It has to work, Skye. It's our only chance to save him and I can't imagine life without him. He's my rock, you know. He always encourages despite what he calls my strange ways, and he never judges or demands. I can be somewhat overwhelming to some people, but your father has never been intimidated by my exuberance." Uncertainty shadowed her mother's gray-blue eyes, darkening them to the sheen of a storm-ravaged sea. She looked old and frail, attributes Skye would never have associated with her mother, who usually sparkled with youthful health.

"It will be fine. I'm sure he recognized me when I connected with him at the hospital, and now I'll have the poem he dedicated to you on your anniversary to remind him of who he is and give him a link back to consciousness. Come on, the sooner we get started, the sooner he's back with us." Brave words, but her heart pumped with fear. How would she ever face her mother? How would she live with herself knowing that the responsibility had been hers and she'd failed? How would she live without her father?

Before letting the doubt and tears overwhelm her, she stepped into the circle of candles and sat on the cushion she'd taken from the couch. Smoky drifts of incense filled the air, she'd rubbed dragon's blood oil on her wrists and forehead, orange candles flickered all around the room, and she'd written the poem she needed to recite on parchment and then burned it in the cauldron. Her mother sat crossed legged outside the circle they'd cast, as she'd be Skye's guide and anchor. They'd make a connection before casting the circle so that Skye had a physical tie to return to in case something went wrong.

Her mother started to chant in a low, pleasing tone. Skye inhaled the soft scent of lavender and focused on the flickering candle flames. Chanting drifted through the flames and wafted with the smoke, entering Skye's subconscious and stimulating her senses. Becoming less aware of her surroundings and physical body, she became aware of wisps of light darting about and patterns of color emerging through a mist. A quick tug and she was free of her body, able to float at will.

At first, she felt fear until she heard the faraway chant of her mother's voice reassuring her, urging her forward. But where to go? She'd been able to reach her father when she was touching him physically, but how to find him now? As far as her gaze reached, she could see misty expanses of swirling colors, arcing lights, and illusive shadows enchanting her, urging her forward. A giggle, a shushing sound, and then a gentle tug on the hem of her jeans. Faces appeared through the mist, undulating and shaping into solid form and then, just as quickly, melting away and leaving Skye alone. But she wasn't alone. The presence of many haunted her steps and tugged at her with an urgency that fogged her intent. Overpowered by the hunger of wandering souls and the questing needs of the damned and lost alike, she became confused.

What was her purpose again? Where was she?

She fought to remember repeating the poem over and over again until the miasma that clutched at her mind fogged out the purpose of the beautiful words. Why fight to remember a poem she had no need for? Why fight the pleasant feeling of floating at all? All these souls surrounding her wanted her to be one with them. Why not? They looked friendly enough. Numbness of emotion claimed her and it felt good to have no cares, no worries. She smiled and drifted towards the grinning faces.

The chatter of insane twittering shattered the peace. Chittering like little chipmunks, the darts of light she'd seen earlier surrounded her and tugged her away from her waiting friends. She fought, but was no match for the hundred tiny hands that directed her forward. The further they got from the mist, the more her awareness returned. Skye cringed at being so easily, almost fatally, influenced. Her mother had warned her about the mists of the damned, yet she'd almost walked right into the midst of them and would have been condemned to walk with them for eternity. An eternity with souls who had sinned so horribly in life that they were fated to wander the mists of a place that was no place at all. A world between what was and what lay beyond.

She looked at the tiny creatures who still led her forward and realized they were pixies and will-o'-the-wisps. Their bright faces shone like beacons of love and innocence, and Skye was surprised to see them so deep in the chamber of the souls of the dead. Usually, they stayed in their own world that hovered on the outskirts of this place. One of them smiled sweetly at her and touched a minute finger to her cheek. A tiny spear of warmth tingled Skye's face, and she smiled at the brave pixie. Before she could ask why they'd wandered so far astray, they disappeared in a whiff of air that blew through the mists and cleared an area around her. As the air receded, it sucked away all sound and light, leaving her in a vacuum of nightmarish silence.

Before panic rose, sound came crashing back in a painful roar and light returned in a bright, piercing glaze that forced Skye to shield her eyes. As everything settled, her breathing returned to normal, and it was then she realized she was no longer alone.

"Daddy." Standing in the vastness that stretched forever, even her father appeared diminutive. Skye tried to run to him, but found that her movements resembled a turtle slugging through the mud. Frustration tore at her, and she tried to reach out to him. Get his attention. Anything.

"Daddy." The screech tore from her lips, but obviously didn't reach his ears because he continued to stare into the distance, his hair lifting and sweeping across his forehead by an unseen breeze. His mumbling intertwined with the drifting breeze and carried to Skye, who struggled to get closer to him. She must have made a sound that drew his attention, because suddenly he looked directly at her. His usually blue eyes darkened to black and he raised his hand, palm forward as if to caution her to stop.

"Dad, it's me—Skye." Her voice sounded high pitched and not at all like her. She cleared her throat and tried again. "Dad. I've come to help you get back to us. Me and Mom."

He shook his head and turned away. "I don't know you." Raising both arms up to encompass the vast emptiness of mist, he proclaimed, "This is where I belong. Go away and leave me alone. This is my place."

Fear clenched at her. What if his memory had deteriorated too much? "You belong with us, not this godforsaken place." Wind whistled through the nothingness and mists swirled fiercely about her feet.

With a dismissive wave of his hand, her father started to walk away. Dark fingers of fog swirled around his ankles and crept up his legs, claiming him for its own. Panic flared, and Skye couldn't remember the poem. Disjointed words tumbled through her mind, but none of them were the right ones. Suddenly, her mother's face floated in the mist, her eyes pleading that she bring her husband back.

With clarity brought on by love for her parents, Skye remembered the poem and shouted it with all the passion she could wrench from the deepest part of her.

I love thee, as I love the calm
Of sweet, star-lighted hours!

I love thee, as I love the balm
Of early jes'mine flow'rs.
I love thee, as I love the last
Rich smile of fading day,
Which lingereth, like the look we cast,
On rapture pass'd away.
I love thee as I love the tone
Of some soft-breathing flute
Whose soul is wak'd for me alone,
When all beside is mute.
I love thee as I love the first
Young violet of the spring;
Or the pale lily, April-nurs'd,
To scented blossoming.
I love thee, as I love the full,
Clear gushings of the song,
Which lonely--sad--and beautiful
At night-fall floats along,
Pour'd by the bul-bul forth to greet
The hours of rest and dew;
When melody and moonlight meet
To blend their charm, and hue.
I love thee, as the glad bird loves
The freedom of its wing,
On which delightedly it moves
In wildest wandering.

Time stopped, if such a thing could happen in this Nether-land of Nowhere, and her father heaved his shoulders in a deep breath. "Skye?" The whisper was quiet enough to become lost on the muffled density of mist, yet to Skye, it rang clear and true. Her heart jumped.

"Dad." She moved toward him, only to watch in horror as he dispersed into particles of reflecting light and then—nothing.

Sobs wrenched from the pit of her stomach, climbed her throat, and broke free from her lips only to become a lost wail in the thickening fog. Barely discernable words mixed with her cries and gave her leave to hope.

"I remember, Skye. I remember everything."

Could it be? If he remembered, why had the mists claimed him? Dear goodness, she prayed that he knew the path back to his body, and he was making his way there. But she had no way of knowing and couldn't do anything about it. It was time to return to her own body. With a perfect sense of timing, her mother's voice beckoned her. Warm and whispering, it gave her direction, and she didn't hesitate to follow.

Picking up speed and enjoying the sense of floating, Skye suddenly slammed into an obstacle. Shaking her ethereal head, she realized that her surroundings had taken on the look of a stone and dirt structure. What the heck? She was supposed to be in the ethereal world, not the primal world, and as far as she knew, the ethereal didn't cater to stone and dirt buildings. Before her stood a two story, roughly hewn, gray stone building, similar in architecture to some of the older places still standing here and there in Salem. Hesitantly, she peered around the corner and saw the front door, carved from oak, swing open to reveal the dark shadows of the building's interior. Someone, or something, wanted her to enter. No way.

Nervous now, she listened for her mother's voice, but heard nothing. A hand beckoned to her from the doorway. Cripes. Mom, what do I do? Nothing. No voice, no guidance. A man stepped from the doorway and frowned at her. He reminded her of a grizzly bear, except he wasn't as hairy, just huge, muscular, and looked about ready to eat her for lunch. Wait a minute. A welcoming smile replaced the frown, and he didn't look so fierce. In fact, with his square-cut jaw, full lips, and blueberry colored eyes, he was kind of handsome. Where had she seen eyes like his before?

She stepped closer, not afraid of him at all. Soft feelings of acceptance warmed her, and she knew he meant no harm. He had something important to tell her. He stretched out his hand to welcome her and she reached out in acceptance. But before they could touch, the landscape heaved violently.

Skye lost her balance and began to fall until the building and the man became nothing more than a pinprick on the horizon. And then they disappeared altogether. The light faded and gave way to the thick fog of earlier, and her senses flared into full alert. This was not right. Fog crept over her body and tightened until she found it hard to breathe. Mom. Mom. She screamed inside her head until it felt ready to explode. Weakness overcame her, and the fog reformed itself into a sneering face, black eyes glittering triumphantly.

Wavering at first, her mother's voice broke through the murk of evil that almost claimed her. "Skye, breathe. Don't give in."

She struggled against the chains of dark fog that bound her. Breathing deeply, she concentrated on her mother's voice and the hope that her father would soon return to his body. She sensed pulsing anger with each chain she broke, and that gave her the strength to keep fighting until she floated free. Pulling the last of her strength from deep inside, she imagined being inside her body and shot forward until one jarring motion set her back where she belonged.

The strangeness of physical form brought with it the fact that she had to force herself to breathe again. Her mother pounded on her back and yelled at her to breathe. She pulled one gasping, gut-wrenching breath of oxygen into her lungs until she choked. Tears wound a path down her cheeks as she attuned herself and gave thanks to whatever powers that be that she was back home safely.

Her mother's anxious face obscured her vision. "Skye, are you all right? What happened? You were coming back fine and then

I lost my contact with you—twice. Did you...your father...the poem...tell me."

Skye leaned back on the couch and took a cleansing breath. "I found him, Mom. I found him and recited the poem."

The light of relief brightened her mother's eyes. "Then he's all right. Everything's fine."

"I'm not sure. He disappeared right after the poem, but he remembered us. He said he remembered."

Her mother twisted a strand of hair around nervous fingers. "Well, if he remembered, it should be all right. I never thought about what would happen after you said the poem. What if he remembers and still can't make it back to his body? Dear heavens, he'd be better off existing in that place if he has no memory. Maybe we made it worse for him."

"Mom. It'll be fine. You told me that all he needed to return to his body was the memory of who he was. That's all. We'll get a phone call from the hospital anytime saying that he's regained consciousness. Just wait and see."

Insistent pounding on the front door put an end to any further conversation.

"You stay here and get your strength back. I'll go see who it is."

Skye nodded, crawled up onto the couch, and sank into its welcoming embrace.

Chapter Twenty

S he'd almost succumbed. But some force had intervened again, and the dark fates didn't deal well with almost. Time was running out. Deliver the knife or become one of the hapless souls wandering endless eternity. Bah! A well-placed kick sent altar, candles, and incense scattering in all directions. Nothing mattered anymore. No more rituals, no more killings. Nothing without the knife. What insanity had possessed agreement to living a life in this weak physical body in exchange for finding the knife? Oh, yes, the endless eternity thing. Too much time spent mindlessly, hopelessly lost. Too many screeching souls vying for favor from the dark fates.

The pact allowed the figure to feel the earth beneath feet and wind upon face again. Though the body change had been an adjustment, it was worth it for the chance to revel in power and manipulate the naive and trusting imbeciles who believed such insipid sentiments as love and peace. Oh, yes, the temptation had outweighed the consequences of failure.

Born again to live in Salem, but a far different Salem than remembered from centuries before. No longer tolerated were blatant tortures and judgments against the innocent. No, present-day laws had forced the necessity of a modest face in public with the practices of the dark arts for private rituals and only the occasional torture and murder of some unsuspecting fool. Escaping the stifling, infinite arena of Hell and having the chance to re-explore forgotten spells and expand on latent powers had been worth everything.

Until now.

Now, everything would be lost if the knife was not delivered. And there was another consideration. Damn Jerome Phips to the fires of eternity. The shift in his powers had sent ripples of energy into the atmosphere. How the blazes could anyone accomplish anything with descendants of the Goods and the Phips family combining their full power? The evidence of their unity was obvious. Palpable even, with the taste of purity and elemental energy that grew stronger with each generation. That sickening connection to nature that was inherent in both their lines would prove to be a deterrent to plans of revenge.

Amidst the shaft of fading afternoon light shooting through the basement window, the figure gave pause and considered. To be outmaneuvered again by the descendants of those who had been responsible for past life disappointments would not be tolerated. No cost was too great, no sacrifice too extreme, and no action unwarranted. Which brought to mind the question of the knife. If the knife was so powerful that the darker fates desired it desperately, what powers could whoever held it in their grasp access? The intoxication of sheer domination flooded the figure's brain like a drug.

But no. Thoughts like that would only bring hideous retribution. Better to follow the pact and complete the assigned task, so life could return to normal.

Dissatisfaction welled. Normal was no longer satisfactory. Seeing the descendants of such putrid enemies, watching them blatantly flaunt themselves in public, wreaked havoc with long-buried emotions of hate. That bitch-child, Dorcas, had escaped centuries ago and perpetuate the bloodline, but now there was a chance to eliminate the family who'd been an ever-constant thorn. And Jerome Phips's do-gooder ancestor, William Phips, who had started the trials with such vigor, had eventually been responsible for questioning the proceedings.

His distaste of the path of questioning and presentation of evidence had sent him to Boston to consult the ministers, who decreed he pursue the guilty as vigorously as ever, but enabled him to throw out anything based on ghosts, specters, or unseen evidence. The embarrassment at having her, or rather, Ann Putnam's, testimony repealed had been mortifying. Ann's eventual apology had cost dearly and the bitter betrayal had never left. Over the years, then and now, it had festered and grown until revenge colored every thought, every emotion.

The knife was the instrument of retribution and ultimate power. Visions of such power lent substance to the figure's desires, raising a flush and the thrill of domination to know that before the night was over, someone else would die. The last stopgap on the way to sweet revenge.

The door swung open to reveal a white-faced Flora. Jerome felt a moment of regret for intruding on her while her husband lay in a coma. But circumstances didn't allow for niceties, so he squared his shoulders, pushed the door open, and stepped into the hallway. With an apologetic shrug, Eldon moved into the hallway beside him.

Regret turned to suspicion when his senses buzzed with the unmistakable ring of a recent ritual. Flora's white-faced appearance took on an entirely new meaning and a growl of anger rolled about in Jerome's throat as he tested the barely there threads of forces that permeated the house. At the best of times, he had trouble entering this house without reliving the past, but now, with whatever had occurred, he had to force his sweaty hands into fists to keep control over his own thoughts and emotions.

Weakness poured through his legs, rendering them almost useless, and his vision wavered, creating a panorama of shifting im-

ages of dark and light, sharp and soft. Sneering faces mingled with faces etched with confusion. The vortex of swirling
faces and encompassing mist led him on a journey of intense
fulfillment and ragged fear as he struggled to remember his
own identity. Haunting words of a love poem touched his soul
and filled his heart with such emotions he would never have
thought to experience. It took him a moment to recognize the
voice of the person reciting the poem, but he realized it was
Skye's voice soothing him, leading him through the mists.

He watched her plead with her father and almost crumble
when he turned away and disappeared. She moved forward
as if led by a purpose, and then she disappeared. He tried to
follow her, but sticky hands of otherworldly entities clung to
him. With a curse, he slapped at the intangible souls.

Before he could break away and follow Skye, the pressure of
a hand on his shoulder yanked him from the souls clutching at
him. He jerked to dizzy awareness, shook his head, and looked
around for a place to sit. With Flora and Eldon expressing their
concerns and asking if he was all right, he stumbled into the
living room and dropped into the nearest chair.

That's when he saw Skye stretched out on the couch, eyes
closed, face blanched and worn as if aching from exhaustion.
And no wonder. Even if she'd experienced only a fraction of
what he'd felt in that nether world. She stirred and mumbled,
a movement that sent her hair tumbling like dark glory across
her shoulder and over the edge of the couch. Heat shivered
through Jerome as his gaze rested on the luscious curve of her
hips and how her deep blue T-shirt stretched tightly across her
breasts.

As if sensing his scrutiny, a frown creased Skye's forehead, and
her eyelids flew open. Her incandescent blue eyes shot a thrill
through Jerome, and he cursed the fact that this woman could
affect him so much. Her mother was a suspect in his own mother's
murder, so Jerome hardened his thoughts against Skye's trembling

lips and the visible shake in her hands as she pushed herself into a sitting position.

"Are you here to stay this time, or are you going to turn tail and run again?"

He flushed at her sarcasm, but respected her for standing up to him despite his veiled accusation about her innocence. There was a possibility that her mother was a murderer, but frustration had sparked his snarled warning to Skye when he'd dropped her off the other day. It wasn't feasible that she held any responsibility for Salem's recent murders. She had no motive, and based on his investigation, she'd never even been to Salem until last month while the murders of young women had started approximately five years ago.

Of course, there was always the possibility that she might be protecting her mother. His steely gaze clashed with her defensive one, and invisible sparks flew. Jerome stared at her, through her, until a worried Eldon stepped between them and peered into his face.

"Jerome, are you okay? What's happening?"

Jerome nodded. His thoughts returned to the strangeness of his journey. It hovered on the edge of his mind, teasing and tantalizing—like a dream not quite remembered. Analyzing reality and suddenly realizing the extent of the ritual Skye and Flora had performed. He shoved Eldon aside, strode to the couch and wrapped his hands around Skye's arms until she flinched.

"I just re-lived your entire ritual. Every sight, every sound. What the hell do you think you were doing?"

With a wrench, she freed her arms and stared at him belligerently. "What do you mean, you saw everything?"

"I mean exactly what I said. It was the same as yesterday when I was here. You lived what I was feeling as if through my own eyes, just as I did with you a minute ago."

Skye looked like she wanted to argue, but the truth lay undeniably between them. An unwelcome bond existed between them that allowed the sharing of experiences and visions. Jerome had never heard of such a thing and wasn't sure he liked being bonded with such a stubborn, independent woman. He also wondered what reason lay at the root of their connection.

Skye watched him closely, her features mirroring his thoughts. She shrugged. "If you saw everything, then you already know what I was doing."

Her off-hand acceptance and resulting sarcasm flared the anger and frustration that Jerome seemed to experience whenever he was in the same room with her. Flora placed a hand on his shoulder and the connection sent warming waves of calm through him. He inhaled deeply, and was able to center and focus. He noticed the bright red bands of fingerprints on Skye's arms and realized how hard he must have gripped her. Regret and shame forced an apology.

"I'm sorry." He raked his fingers over his bristly hair and down the back of his neck. "But you shouldn't be playing with forces beyond this world."

"I wasn't playing. I was trying to save my father." She regarded him with eyes as blue as a summer ocean. Defiance and independence set her face into a mask of restrained beauty.

"Christ, you were doing a retrieval spell." Eldon glanced around the room. "Yes, it makes sense, but I can't believe you would defy nature like that. The last person I know who tried that kind of retrieval spell lost her mind and ended up in a sanitarium."

Skye's gaze flickered to her mother, and Jerome realized she might not have known the risks of what she'd attempted. Flora shook her head imperceptibly and sat in the armchair he'd recently occupied. "Skye is powerful enough to achieve that, and more. She just hasn't done anything of this magnitude until today."

Eldon moved to the window and stared out at the ocean, while each person sat lost in their own considerations. Skye looked intrigued, but not surprised, while resignation lent a shadow of worry to Flora's features. It was Eldon who broke the silence as he turned from the window to face Flora.

"It seems you and Amanda both bred children of immense powers. The power of your ancestors."

"Yes." Flora smiled. "Remember how, when we were young, we used to pretend we were the ones who had inherited the absolute power our ancestors could wield?"

Eldon nodded in agreement. "Our rituals now seem so foolish and naïve compared to what these two can accomplish."

Jerome was confused. He'd only just acknowledged his abilities. Why were the two of them talking as if he was a witch of extraordinary power? And he'd sensed no aura of potent magic on Skye when he'd first met her. Although, her presence now filled the room with rich, vital power that set his pulse to racing. The thick, sweet scent of maple and the more tangy scent of fall leaves wafted around both he and Skye and Jerome could only figure it had to do with the recent crossing over they'd both just experienced.

"It was more than just a retrieval spell. Wasn't it, Skye?"

"What do you mean? We quite definitely prepared for a retrieval spell, nothing more." Flora was quick to protest.

"It was more, Mom. So much more."

Skye's voice changed. The light innocence was gone, and in its place had slipped a husky timbre. Her eyes were different as well; where once they shone with guilelessness, they now showed depths and shadows of age-old wisdom. It was as if by crossing over into another dimension, she'd crossed over a threshold within herself and emerged as a woman more aware...more powerful. A woman with a deeper understanding. Great. She'd been stubborn before. Now what?

Jerome was even more attracted to her than ever. An attraction that went deeper than the physical, more of a melding of souls. He sighed. He didn't have time for complications because he needed to focus on finding his mother's murderer and preventing any more deaths. Personal relationships would only complicate matters.

"Tell us what happened, Skye." Flora moved from the armchair to sit beside Skye. She took her hand and comforted her with a look. "And don't leave anything out. It could be more important than it seems."

Skye told her story and every inflection of her voice, every twitch of lips, lift of an eyebrow, or shift of weight had merit. Her words strung together to create a tale that would have had most people shaking their heads and whispering behind their hands. But Jerome had been there and seen what she'd seen, so he had no doubt. He re-lived the vivid colors, encroaching mists, and souls stranded in a place he wouldn't have wished on his worst enemy. Skye's voice hypnotized him with her tale of the pixies and his heart melted when she recounted the poem she'd recited to her father. The words of love that had floated around Jerome. Now he understood their meaning. Romantic. The kind of love that literally transcended worlds.

He suddenly realized that Skye's story had veered off from his own journey. She was talking about a stone building and a man with blue eyes beckoning to her, trying to tell her something. Then the seeping evil that had wrenched her away from the man before he could communicate with her. He bolted upright.

"Wait a minute. I didn't see any of that."

Skye stiffened in defiance. "That doesn't mean it didn't happen."

"I don't doubt that it happened, but explain it to me again. Maybe I can help figure out what it means."

As he listened to the description of a stone building and the man beckoning her forward, something niggled at the back of his mind. He knew the place, and he knew the man, but identifying either of them eluded him. Skye's voice drifted into the background while he tried to pin down what she'd said that kept prodding him. Then it came to him.

CHAPTER
TWENTY-ONE

"The eyes. Tell me again about the eyes."

Surprise lit Skye's own eyes, and she recoiled at the snapping urgency in Jerome's voice, so he took a calming breath and repeated his request.

"His eyes were blue," she offered.

"No. Describe them the way you did the first time." With a heave of her shoulders and a sigh that made it quite clear she wasn't happy about repeating herself, she did what he asked. "His eyes were dark blue, but not a shadowed dark. They bordered on a shimmering purple that, when mixed with the blue, created kind of a..."

"Blueberry color," Jerome whispered.

"Yes. Exactly. How did you know?" She gasped. "Oh, I re-member. Your friend Samson had the same eyes. When I met him, I thought about how unusual his eyes were. But he wasn't the man I saw."

"No, he would have been one of Samson's ancestors. Most likely the one who held the thankless job of head jailer at the Salem jail during the witch trials."

"Jailer? That means that the building he was so adamant I follow him into was probably the Salem jail."

"From your description, yes. What do you think, Eldon?"

"Now that you mention it, it fits. But why would Samson's ancestor want Skye in the jailhouse?"

"He's probably the dark force that assaulted Skye the other day when she entered the dimension of dead souls." Flora turned to her daughter. "You said you saw the same dark force today, right? So it makes sense. It's a good thing you didn't follow him into the building." She put an arm around Skye's shoulder and hugged her tightly. "I can't stand the thought of losing you, too."

"You're not going to lose me, and Dad will be fine, I'm sure of it. But the guy with blueberry-colored eyes wasn't the source of darkness, neither the other day nor today."

"Not if he was a relative of Samson's, he wasn't." Eldon spoke. "Samson is as straight and honest as they come, and anyone related to him would be the same. I can't see it any other way."

"Eldon, he was the jailer, for goodness' sake. How can you be so sure he wasn't evil?" Flora stood, hands on hips, to face down her old friend.

"Doesn't matter. People had to make money somehow in those days. Besides, how do you know the plight of the prisoners wouldn't have been worse under someone else's rule?

"Okay, guys, let's get back on track here." Jerome stood and placed himself between Flora and Eldon. He tended to agree with Eldon, as his own ancestor's role in the past wavered on the shady side at times, but now was not the time for useless arguments. They had a murderer to find.

"Eldon's right, Mom. Sarah's diary mentioned someone tending to the sick prisoners, and someone who didn't care wouldn't have allowed that. Besides, there's more at stake here than someone's reputation. We have an extremely powerful and dangerous knife to find before it falls into the wrong hands," Skye cautioned.

"And who's to say who the wrong hands are?" Bitterness colored each word that left Jerome's mouth and his glare shot flames at Flora.

"Whoa. Now who's getting off track? We're all friends here, so let's try to work together and help each other." Eldon laid his hand on Jerome's arm to calm him down, but Jerome shook it off as if it was a pesky mosquito.

"No, it's right on track. My first order of business is to find whoever is killing young girls, second order of business is to find my mother's murderer, and then maybe I'll have time to make friends." He jutted his chin out defiantly and stood with his arms crossed, while three pairs of eyes rested on him thoughtfully. Skye broke the tension when she stood, folded her own arms across her chest, and faced Jerome.

"Fine, since you're so full of things to do, maybe you should just be on your way and do them. In the meantime, stop accusing my mother of murder, or I'll have you charged with slander."

She was magnificent. Her anger sparked green to mix with blue in her eyes and the resulting sea foam color cut short his breath. He wondered if she was as wild as the raging ocean her eyes emulated and, after staring at the determined set of her lips and remembering how she'd bravely crossed over to another dimension to save her father, decided she probably was. But it was a storm that he had no time for now.

"I'll stop accusing your mother when I find out who killed mine."

Skye waved a hand at Eldon. "Why not accuse him? He was there that night?"

"Eldon didn't kill Amanda." Flora's soft voice stilled the arguments. "He was too in love with her to harm her. And, contrary to what you might believe, I didn't kill her either, Jerome. That leaves only three people."

"Three?" Eldon, Jerome, and Skye questioned.

"Yes. Verity, Matthew, and you." Flora stared him down with all the fierceness of someone defending her own honor. Rage shot through Jerome. He clenched his fists and the pulsing of his blood reached a fever pitch before he was able to speak. "How dare you accuse me of such a terrible thing?"

"Hmm, if memory serves correctly, you've accused me of that same murder on more than one occasion." Flora's eyes flashed with indignation, frustration, and a hint of pleading. Jerome remembered her earlier vow to find his mother's murderer at the expense of her own life. That could have been an act. He had been in no mood to listen to her then, but today was different. He heard the ache of sincerity in her voice as she pleaded for his understanding. As stubborn and single-minded as he'd been about his mother over the years, the realization washed over him that maybe Flora was innocent. Maybe he'd have to look elsewhere for his mother's murderer.

The weakness of emotional release turned his knees to jelly, and his jaw ached from tension until he remembered his reason for being there. He'd have to sort out his feelings later. Not speaking, he lifted his shirttail and drew the slender box from the waist of his jeans where he'd shoved it after retrieving it from Verity's.

With a heartfelt pause, he opened the lid and exposed the knife to Flora's questioning gaze. Darts of light shot from the ruby-red eye and the black handled dragon's grin shone with wicked intent. Flora gasped and her face paled.

"Can you tell me if this is the knife without touching it?"

Flora reached out and passed trembling fingers over the top of the silver blade and the knife handle. Fear and tension hung palpable in the room.

"Is it the knife?" Husky with emotion, Jerome's voice cut through the strained silence.

"That depends," Flora replied.

"Don't play games. I ran out of patience years ago."

"You're asking a question that has more than one answer. If you want to know if it's the knife that is meant to be guarded by the Goods, then no. If you're asking if it's the knife used on that night thirty years ago, probably. What do you think, Eldon?"

"I agree with you. We found it at Verity's, so I assume it's the knife she used."

Jerome hissed air between his teeth. "Too much information, Eldon."

"They're as much a part of this as anyone. They need to know everything. The time for secrets and individual action is past. We need to work together if we want to find the knife and find a murderer. Or two murderers, as the case may be." Eldon crossed his arms and thrust his chin out, his gray beard jutting awkwardly.

Jerome battled with his years of ingrained thoughts. To trust a woman who might be responsible for his mother's murder. No, wait, he had to stop thinking like that. He'd already decided she most likely wasn't responsible, but old habits were hard to break. He considered the woman before him and did something he'd never done before. He used his senses to creep into Flora's mind to determine her guilt or innocence. Maybe wasn't a satisfactory deduction, he had to know for sure.

At first, a barrier blocked his probe, soft and pliable, but definitely not allowing him through. About to retreat, he was surprised to feel the blockage disappear and his probe given free roam of her mind and emotions. Just for a second, and only to the part of her that held memories of thirty years ago, but it was enough to assure him of her innocence. Suddenly, the gut-wrenching belief of responsibility and a sharp ache of regret that had followed Flora all these years almost drove him to his knees. Tears filled his eyes, and he pulled his probe back.

Flora's gaze held his defiantly, until Jerome inclined his head ever so slightly in acknowledgment of her self-inflicted guilt, and the two formed an unspoken bond of understanding.

Clearing his throat, he asked, "Okay, where do we start?" A simple statement, yet it showed his acceptance of Flora's innocence and set a tone of camaraderie in the room.

"I have a question." Skye, who had been silent, spoke. "Mom, how do you know that's not the knife meant to be guarded by the Goods...us? I mean, you could be mistaken."

"I'm not mistaken. Here, take it in your hand." Flora lifted it from the box still held open by Jerome and placed it in Skye's outstretched hand. "What do you feel?"

"Well." She frowned. "It's warm and I feel threads of sticky energy emanating from it." She closed her eyes and concentrated. "There's a dark shadow resting over it, a shadow that makes me feel as if someone has used it for dark rituals."

"That's all?" Flora questioned.

"Isn't that enough?"

"No. If this was the knife we're looking for, you wouldn't be able to hold it without preparing yourself. Even with proper ritual, ancient, long forgotten powers would overwhelm you. Trust me, it's not what we're looking for. Although it is likely what Jerome is looking for." Flora scrutinized Skye, whose brow was wrinkled and lips pursed in concentration. "Is there something wrong, Skye?"

"No...not wrong, but there's more to the knife—something I feel I should know, but can't remember."

The sharp ringing of a phone interrupted them, and Eldon hastened to reach inside his jacket to answer his cell phone. While he took care of business, Skye closed the lid on the knife and offered the box back to Jerome. "I suppose you'll be taking it in for forensics testing."

"Yep. I'm not sure what we can find on it after all these years. It will depend on if anyone had used it since that night and how often. Hopefully, we'll find some small bit of my mother's DNA, which would prove that Verity is the murderer and I can finally have closure. Virtue of elimination tells us that."

Flora fixed him with a considering gaze. "Oh. How do you figure that?"

"Well, she's the only one left strong enough to move Mom's body." It hurt to say the words, and Jerome struggled to remain calm. After all these years, you think he'd have become used to the fact that his mother was dead. Maybe once they caught the killer, he'd be able to put it behind him, pain and all.

"Yes, it would take an adult to move her, but not necessarily to kill her." Flora's tone was respectful and calm, even if the subject was horrible and hurtful. "And, no, I'm not accusing you."

It took a second for Jerome to understand. "I don't believe it. Matthew would only have been about eight or nine. There's no way he could have killed her. What would his motive have been? How could he have had the strength? It makes no sense."

"It doesn't have to make sense, Jerome. Forget what's normal and acceptable, and realize that we're dealing with alternate realities and age-old magic steeped in rituals and mastery we can't even imagine. A nine-year-old boy would be more than capable of murder if an apparition or presence from another plane led his hand."

"Great news. I finally have a bite on a pink elephant of a house I've been trying to unload forever." Eldon stepped back into the room and stopped talking when he noticed the tension. "Oh, oh. What did I miss?"

"Flora seems to think that Matthew might be responsible for Mom's murder. Her theory is that an apparition might have given him the strength to commit murder despite his age and size." Jerome sounded unbelieving.

"I see." Eldon didn't seem to see at all and didn't know what to say.

"Remember how Verity opened the ritual in a different way than usual and we felt some kind of shift in the air, a heaviness that pervaded the room. I know you felt it as well because you shivered the same as I did." Flora reminded him.

Eldon frowned and chewed on his mustache. "Now that you mention it, yes. It felt as if the air had been sucked from the room and left something rancid in its place. You think that was some kind of presence that she brought into the ritual?"

Flora shrugged. "She was always searching. Always stretching her powers over the borderline of what was safe. I think she

188

opened a doorway to something more than what she'd expected and the result was Amanda's death."

"So, instead of stealing my mother's powers, Verity got her murdered. But how do you know Matthew killed her?"

"I don't, I'm only guessing. It was Verity, or Matthew with Verity as a co-conspirator after the fact."

"I've got to get this knife to forensics. Maybe we'll get answers then."

"Go ahead, but I have a feeling we'll know the answer before we ever see the results of the tests." Flora crossed her arms across her chest and trembled. "Darkness is creeping closer, and it has a hunger for fulfillment that it's waited a long time for. We need to find that knife before it does."

"There's not much we can do now." Jerome glanced at his watch. "Salem jail closes at three and it's shortly after already."

"Can't you get a warrant or get whoever runs the place to let us in?" Skye asked.

"A warrant to search for a magic knife that we need to find before some evil force from another plane of existence manages to? I don't think so. And the person who runs the jail museum visits his sick mother in the nursing home after work. I'm not interrupting him there. Besides, I have a feeling one night won't make a difference. If we can't get in, neither can anyone else."

"Anyone else might not have the same sense of morals as you and could try breaking in." Skye's voice held more than a little sarcasm.

"Fine, I'll get this knife booked into evidence and then set up a stakeout for the night if it'll make you feel better." He glared at her, challenging her to find a flaw in that logic. She seemed determined to keep the flame of dissent burning between them. Why couldn't she be pliable and agreeable like her mother? Christ, what was he saying? Up until a few minutes ago, he'd believed her mother capable of murder. He shrugged off all negative feelings he held toward Skye and focused on her positive traits: hair that shone like raven wings, eyes rippling with vivid colors of blue and the occasional shot of green, and lips made for kissing.

"Jerome. Hello." Eldon waved his hand in front of his face and broke the spell Jerome had been weaving. "I need to meet this client, so let's get moving."

"Sure." Terse and direct, just the way he needed to be to stay on track. "I'll see you two at the Salem jail museum at 9:00 a.m." Without a backward glance, he strode out the front door and waited impatiently in his car for Eldon to catch up. He tuned out his friend's comments about how being rude and impatient was not the way to win friends. As he'd said earlier, making friends was low on his list of priorities.

CHAPTER TWENTY-TWO

S kye and her mom approached the hospital room with trepidation. She reached for her mother's hand and clasped it. Seeking, as well as giving, comfort. Sounds and scents of the hospital ward drifted down the hallway—the usual beep, beep of monitors, the squealing wheels of the food cart, the chatter of nurses discussing patients, and the sharp scent of cleaning fluid. The gleaming shine of the floor attested to a recent cleaning, and Skye's running shoes made that horrendous, squelching squeak that sent shivers up her spine.

They stopped outside the door. Her mother's lips trembled, a motion that carried through her body and into Skye's. Knowing her mother would stand in the hallway all night, too afraid to open the door, Skye made the move. The sight that greeted them shocked her. Someone else occupied her father's bed.

Her mother moaned, and Skye gave her a reassuring pat on the arm. "It could mean that he's awake, and they moved him out of intensive care."

"Yes. That would make sense. We should ask the nurses." They didn't need to go far. One of the nurses must have seen them enter the room, and she scurried up the hallway. But Skye didn't like the array of emotions on the woman's face. Uncertainty, pity, and a hint of fear. She was obviously dreading being the one to impart bad news. A knot lodged itself in Skye's throat and tears threatened. But she had to stay strong for her mother. Even if Skye was losing a father, Flora was the one losing a soul mate.

"I'm so sorry. We tried to reach you at home, but..." Skye met her mother's worried expression with a look of compassion. The tired-looking nurse fixed her gaze on Skye. "I'm afraid we moved Mr. Adams to the long-term care unit. We needed the room and since there have been no signs of improvement. I...I'm sorry."

Silence. Coming here filled with such hope after actually having communicated with her father, Skye felt as if her own world had just crashed and burned. Flora looked ready to collapse, so Skye put an arm around her shoulders and guided her to a chair in the hall. The nurse helped by bringing over a glass of water and handing it to Flora.

"It doesn't mean anything more than we needed a room. There's still hope, honestly. Would you like to see him? He's just one floor up in room 420."

Skye didn't know how much more her mom could take. Especially after the shock of finding another person occupying the bed when they'd hoped for so much more.

"Yes. Yes, of course." Flora dabbed at her tears with her fingers, squared her shoulders, and stood. "I need to be with him. Whatever his condition."

They rode the elevator up a floor. This room was identical to the one her father had come from, except the view now looked out over the parking lot rather than a courtyard with trees and flowers. The reasoning must be that someone in a coma, and not likely to recover, didn't need the view. As illogical a feeling as it was, Skye felt slighted for her father. He deserved better. Hell, he deserved to wake up and live his life.

A lump rose in her throat and threatened to turn to tears. She stepped back from the bed so her mother wouldn't see her cry. The desperate hope that had filled them both on the way here now faded to desperate resignation. While her mom sat on a chair by the bed whispering to deaf ears, Skye's mind raced through childhood memories of her father. The pink bike she'd wanted for Christmas so badly, and how her father had helped her learn to ride. A serious talk about how it wasn't fair to send a legion of frogs chasing after another girl just because she'd teased her and stolen her lunch. Or how when a boy tried to kiss you, it meant he liked you and it wasn't a good idea to turn his lips fluorescent orange. Then came the promise to her mother not to practice magic alone. Skye didn't know how she grew up without getting herself into serious trouble. Her gaze fell to the still figure on the bed, and a sense of futileness settled into her. It didn't make sense. She'd communicated with him so effortlessly. He was alive and vital, so why was he just lying there?

She closed her eyes and focused on her center. The area just below her belly button and deep inside, where power churned and life-energy simmered. An imaginary flame heated her core, swelling like a bubble until ready to burst from her body. At that moment, Skye sent a blast toward her father, a streaking shaft of colors that wrapped around him and pulsed with green and pink. Colors of love and healing. She recalled the moment she'd found him on the other plane and relived every word spoken. Those she sent to him along the shaft of light.

At first, nothing happened. So she tried harder. A gasp of disbelief from her mother caused Skye to lose concentration, and her eyelids flew open. A white flutter of movement caught her eye. The blanket that shrouded her father shifted and something traced an uncertain pathway to the top of the blanket where her father's hand emerged. Pale and shaking, he reached out, as if grasping for a lifeline. He found Flora's hand and held it, even as his eyes connected with Skye in a silent bond of eternal gratitude and understanding.

It had been so simple. A single phone call with the right bait and Eldon bit the hook like an idiot. The first step toward destroying

Jerome was almost in place. The sun touched the distant horizon and shadows fell through the windows while the figure waited for Eldon to keep his appointment. An appointment that would end in his death. Anticipation needed to be subdued lest the careless emotion interfere with a well thought out plan. Passion and satisfaction at finally fulfilling an age-old hate could wait. Right now, the task required detachment and logic.

A mantel clock showed about ten minutes before Eldon should arrive. The stupid man was punctual, if nothing else. The figure shifted in anticipation and relished the thought of bringing to final justice those who had earned such hatred centuries ago. Ann Putnam's hate. Now reincarnated, but with full memories of that time long ago. That had been the deal. In order to fulfill the task of placing the knife in the hands of darker forces, Ann Putnam needed to remember the hate, the bitter rivalry, and the trials that had fueled her accusations back then and drove her present day incarnation.

Damnation to Jerome, a descendant of Governor Phips, who had fought the trials at all levels and had any evidence thrown out whose roots rested with specters, ghosts, or magic. An act that had forced Ann to apologize grudgingly for her part in the trials. Empty words forced from her lips, while her heart screamed out for revenge and death.

Eternal Hell to Skye, whose ancestor had refused Ann Putnam's command to enter their circle and learn the ways of their magic. Sarah and her daughter had paid for that slight.

Sarah died a horrible death, while townspeople ostracized Dorcas and forced her to flee her home to live a life of fear.

Eldon...well, he was no more than a means to an end. A piece of the puzzle that would garner both revenge and the knife that had started this entire sequence of events. Oh, yes, that night in the clearing when Ann and her friends had witnessed Sarah during her ritual, Ann had understood. The power that emanated from the knife, even when wielded by someone with only good intentions, had jaded Ann; beckoned her mind and soul until the need to possess the knife transcended all. Even after her apology, even after years of living a dull life as a God-fearing, true-believing person, the taint of the knife and the thrill of power seethed deep within her.

That's when the dreams had started. Voices that taunted and defiled her for failing to exact proper revenge. The knife was beyond her reach. The others had won, even if their lives had been forfeited or lived in fear. The voices continued for years. Sometimes, as a distant hum, other times as a full-blown scream that ravaged her senses until she couldn't think straight. They continued until she lay on her deathbed.

That's when the dark forces had offered her the deal. When the time was right, they'd bring her back to the earthly plane where she could exact her revenge. A long life with access to ancient magic and power would be hers if she delivered the knife to them.

The body chosen this time was much different than Ann's, but the choice was not one to regret. Along with more powerful magic, the figure possessed a stronger physical body. An interesting difference from the pampered softness of Ann Putnam.

A car door slammed, and the wait was over as all thoughts and senses sprang to the present. Once Eldon was a prisoner, there was one more stop to make before the phone call was placed. Centuries of hate wove through a darkened soul, and the time for retribution and fulfillment was at hand.

CHAPTER TWENTY-THREE

Jerome turned his car into a spot that would allow him a front view of the primitive stone jailhouse and the walkway that led around back so that anyone trying to gain entrance would have to pass him. For the sake of keeping a low profile, he'd decided to use his own car, a black Grand Am, rather than his police cruiser. With a sigh, he adjusted his seat back, stretched his legs, and reached for his coffee cup. Actually, it was a caramel cappuccino with chocolate sprinkled on top of the foam. He'd long ago given up regular coffee in favor of the fancier drink, but it had taken a long time for him to admit it to the guys at the station.

The routine was that whoever was on duty took turns making a daily coffee run to the local Starbucks, giving them a break from the station coffee, which was dark and bitter. Jerome always ordered regular coffee and chose to save his indulgence for after work, when no one could see him drinking his fancy cappuccino. One day he figured, screw it. When Jaks asked who wanted coffee, Jerome piped up with his order for a caramel cappuccino with chocolate on top. Silence had fallen in the room until someone snickered and made a comment about girly drinks. Laughter had erupted and Jerome took the good-natured ribbing with grace and regretted the decision that seemed to have provided fodder for jokes from then until perpetuity. The funny thing was that when the scent of caramel filled the station, some of the others had wandered over and sniffed his drink. Someone even gathered the nerve to ask for a taste. Within a week, most of the men had switched from coffee to something more elaborate, like soy milk latte, toffee nut latte, caramel macchiato, or some other form of fancy drink. Now, Jerome could drink without fear of his co-workers teasing him.

A movement from the corner of the building caught his attention, and he brought his night-vision binoculars to his eyes. It would be the shortest stakeout on record if he found someone trying to break in now. Heck, he'd only been there five minutes. He scanned the front lawn from one side to the other. A figure leaped from the shadows with a mewling screech and pranced off triumphantly with mouse in mouth. Damned cat out tomcattin' around.

Jerome settled back and slurped a mouthful of cappuccino. Damn, it tasted good. He had a feeling he was in for a long night. And it was all Skye's fault, since it was her idea that someone might try to break in overnight. Although, to be honest, he would admit that the possibility should have occurred to him. He was the cop, after all. He'd learned over the years that it was never a good idea to judge others by your own standards. Just because they were waiting until the jailhouse museum opened in the morning, didn't mean whoever else was after the knife would have the same ethics.

A pair of headlights arced through the dark night, and he sank down in his seat to avoid the glare trapping him. He tensed for a moment, but the vehicle passed without slowing down. Jerome's heartbeat returned to normal, and he straightened in his seat, almost hoping that someone would try to break into the museum; at least then his night wouldn't be a total waste.

He downed more cappuccino, regretting that his cup was almost empty, and let his mind wander. Unfortunately, the traitorous thing kept returning to visions of blue eyes and raven dark hair. He gave his head a shake and tried to focus on the case; the evidence, who might be guilty of his mother's murder, the current murders of young girls who invaded Skye's dreams...oh, there it went again. Soft waves of hair wafted like dark silk through his mind, while sapphire blue eyes invaded the corners he'd closed off long ago.

It baffled him he couldn't keep his mind off her. He'd never had trouble dating a woman as a pleasant distraction and then forgetting about her when she began expecting too much from him, or he just got bored. Cavalier, yes, but they'd always known the score before entering any kind of relationship with him. He supposed it was divine retribution. He knew his actions had unintentionally hurt more than one woman he'd dated, and here he was finding out what it was like to crave the touch of someone who didn't seem interested in him. Damn her.

To block her from his mind, Jerome focused on the search ahead. The immediate task was to find the knife which should, in all likelihood, draw out his mother's murderer. Verity had instigated the ritual thirty years ago to access the power of the famed knife. But she'd failed because she didn't have the real one. Had she known and tried to fool the fates? Had she been misled? If so, by whom? Had she murdered his mother? Was she slaughtering young girls in a perverse ritualistic fashion? If not her, then who? Were the killings merely for pleasure or part of a ritual offering to otherworldly forces to attain aid in finding the knife and using its power?

He shook his head and prayed that time would answer all his questions. The first step was to find the knife and draw out of hiding whoever else was looking for it, which led him to another consideration. Once he found his mother's murderer, what would he do with his life? He frowned and concentrated on the shadows dancing about the building. Where had that thought come from? Although, it was a valid question. Everything he'd done from that night thirty years ago until now was geared toward finding out who'd taken her away from him. Whose hand had wielded the knife that had so mercilessly ended the life of a young, vibrant woman and left a boy alone in a cold, harsh world? What purpose did his life have besides finding her killer? Once the killer was found, who was Jerome Phips?

A wavering movement drew his attention to the building, now bathed in moonlight and shadows that lent an otherworldly quality to the chipped and worn stone. His eyes roamed across the jailhouse and searched out the darkness of the surrounding bushes. Nothing. Then he saw a whisper of mist take shape—pale against the dark backdrop of the wooden door that led into the jail.

He shook his head. No way was he seeing what he thought. The mist had taken the shape of a man whose face looked spookily like the photo Jerome possessed of his ancestor, Governor William Phips. And the specter raised its arm to beckon him. No. Rather, the gesture seemed to be an attempt to gain entrance through the door. But it didn't work. The ghostly apparition paced back-and-forth mumbling words that Jerome was too far away to understand, but the wild gesturing and stamping of feet conveyed frustration.

Just then, the ghost stopped pacing and turned his glare toward Jerome. The scrutiny of gleaming ghostly eyes flashed across the distance and stabbed him with a force that left him gasping. As he struggled to gain his breath, a voice rasped across the distance.

"You are a Phips. Undo what I have done. Set free the innocent."

Then silence reigned in the dark night and left Jerome feeling numb and amazed that he'd encountered his ancestor—an ancestor in ghostly form, no less. And it seemed as if the governor felt remorse for his role in the trials and eventual deaths meted out to those deemed guilty. Wow. Even though Jerome had always defended his ancestor, a small bit of doubt had burrowed itself deep, like a pesky sliver that couldn't quite be dug out. But if William's ghost haunted the jail attempting to free the innocent, well, that was a good thing.

A weight of guilt he hadn't even been aware of lifted from him and he smiled. Realizing now was not the time to ponder the past. He brought his mind back to the present and swept his gaze across the surrounding area to make sure he hadn't missed anything. All was still and quiet. With a sigh, he gulped the last of his cappuccino and settled in for a long night. Unfortunately, his mind had a mind of its own and whispered to him the words of a familiar love poem that he remembered from his journey to the realm of lost souls. Strangely enough, the whispering voice resembled Skye's.

Skye and her mom spent the night in the hospital. Relief overpowered every thought, every emotion, and it was difficult to stay focused on the knowledge that someone had put him in the coma. Whatever she was feeling, Skye knew her mother was experiencing tenfold. Events of the day had left Skye too weak to do much besides sit and stare at her father, her eyes brimming with tears. And her mother...well, no way could anyone have dragged her from her husband's side. Not until she was ready to go.

Conversation was sparse because of his weakened state, but her father's stories about wandering in a place beyond his understanding was enough to have both women aching with compassion for his ordeal. Whoever had sent him into a coma had sent him somewhere that even Skye had never been. Tales of serpents, dark-hued specters shifting and darting about, as well as the endless pits of seething souls seeking to escape, raised goose bumps and shivers on their arms.

Just before falling into a restless sleep, her father whispered, "It was the poem that brought me back, Flora." He brushed a shaking finger across her cheek and smiled tremulously. "I've never forgotten the words of love we vowed so long ago, and I mean them as much today as I did then. More."

Tears flowed down Skye's face when her father's tear-filled eyes met hers. "And how much more fortunate am I to have a daughter who risked her life to save me? It was your voice that led me from that horrible place, Skye. Like a sweet song of life, it broke through the suffering and endless moaning to lead me to you. And then, just before I gained consciousness, I heard you again. This time, your energy shone like a beacon, and any doubt I had that I was heading the wrong direction was gone." His eyelids drooped and his words slurred with exhaustion. "I love you both."

Night passed into dawn and Skye contemplated the rising sun and shifted her aching butt in the chair quietly so as not to wake anyone. If only this were the end of it. But it wasn't.

Someone out there had tried to kill her father. Worse, they'd condemned him to an eternity of wandering in a hellish place of suffering. Skye gained a new understanding of what had driven Jerome all the years since his mother's murder. Someone was going to pay, and if the same person was responsible for both horrendous crimes, then she and Jerome would have to flip a coin to see who got the first stab at justice against the warped bastard, or bitch.

Her mother moaned and opened her eyes. When the realization of her surroundings dawned, her gaze flew to the bed where Walter rested easily. She heaved a sigh of relief when she saw the color had returned to his face and his chest rose and fell more deeply than when he'd been in a coma. Rubbing her neck and stretching, Flora turned to Skye with the understanding look that it was time to leave. A tear fell as she touched her husband's arm lightly, lovingly, and then strode from the room before she could change her mind.

Skye ached for her and wished there was a way her mother could stay at the hospital, but they needed as many eyes as possible to look for the knife. Hopefully, it wouldn't take long and they could return before her father woke up.

The best time to set a fire was the shift change at the fire station. There'd be enough confusion to delay the firefighters a couple of extra minutes. That was the plan anyway, as rags shoved into a gas can were ignited. Simple and effective. By the time the rags burned down to the gas, they'd be outside the house. Damn good thing the mangy mutt was knocked unconscious and in the back seat of the car. The unholy beast had put up a fight, and it had taken longer than considered to corner and render it unconscious. Stupid beast had even left a jagged bite mark on a now throbbing right leg, a leg that also seeped with blood. Shit.

Death would come extra slow and painful for the mutt, and Jerome would get to watch the death of his favored pet. The only question was, would Eldon die first, or the dog? Circumstances would dictate the answer to that question, and licks of anticipation flamed at the thought of what lay ahead.

Not only was Jerome in for a taste of hell, but the meddling, arrogant, holier than thou Goods were about to find out what it meant to cross the wrong person. So what if it was more than three centuries later? Revenge could be savored just as sweetly.

It was easy to hide in the woods until catching sight of the first flames. Glowing through the sliding glass doors to the back deck, the fire danced with orange hues that contrasted with the reflected blue of the ocean. Assured that the fire was spreading freely. It took only a minute to slink back to the waiting car. A glance into the back seat revealed both dog and man lying unconscious. Good. Not long now. A short drive and they'd be transferred to the basement where the altar waited.

A chuckle of delight escaped through lips drawn tight with anticipation. Not only would revenge prevail, but it would come full circle in the house built by that brat, Dorcas. Years ago, a child's exploration of the house known about town for being actually haunted—and not just staged to collect money from curious tourists—had led to the uncovering of a secret room in the basement. Layers of dust and cobwebs had been easily brushed aside and discarded boxes disposed of to reveal an altar carved of stone and markings on the wall that the child had no way of understanding. An interesting enough secret at the time, the room had been left alone and forgotten about — though not completely — until years of study of magic had helped to develop power and brought about a ripening of inherent abilities.

A childhood of hazy memories had led to confusing teenage years of demanding voices, strange dreams, and finally, a dawning realization as a child passed into adulthood with a full memory of past life resentments and a bargain with the dark forces. Realizing the importance of finding a place for secret rituals, the figure revisited the room, understanding that the dark forces had presented its existence for the sole purpose of revenge and fulfilling the bargain. In a day or two, its existence wouldn't be a secret anymore. It also wouldn't be needed once possession of the knife came to the one who deserved it the most.

CHAPTER TWENTY-FOUR

A nd as the time of conflict draws closer, and all forces align in a way to render the strongest advantage to the side of Light, the knife shall appear. Raging out of control with souls having lain stagnant and restricted for centuries, it will take the pure hand and true heart of a Good to spellbind the unruly, unjustly accused.

Excerpt from *Faerie Enchantments and Sorcerer Magick*

"Damn it, why isn't he opening?" Jerome checked the same watch he'd looked at less than a minute ago. "And where's Eldon? He knows how important this is."

Too busy fighting off the strange sensations that had flooded her since arriving five minutes ago, Skye ignored Jerome's restless ranting. She was also worried about her mother who had hardly spoken a word since leaving the hospital and, upon arriving at the jailhouse, had wandered over to the garden and now sat on a small stone bench to stare blankly across lush flowers and winding pathways. Skye wondered about the reason for her pensive silence.

"Finally," Jerome exclaimed as the door creaked open to reveal a short, gray-haired man dressed in jeans and a T-shirt that proclaimed, *Jailers Do It With Handcuffs.* "You're supposed to open at 9:00."

"Don't get your shorts in an uproar, young man. It's only 9:01."
The man extended a shaky, spider-veined hand toward Jerome.
"Nice to see ya, son."

Jerome shook the old man's hand and seemed to put his impatience in check long enough to inquire about the man's mother.

"Oh, she's doin' fine as can be expected for an old lady." He chuckled. "Don't you know, before too long, I'll be joinin' her in the home."

"I doubt that, Samuel." Jerome shifted his feet, his gaze searching the darkened shadows behind Samuel. "You're too cantankerous to let someone else take care of you. Besides, you'll probably outlive most everyone you know just to be stubborn."

Samuel snorted. "Stubborn. You should show respect to your elders."

"I show respect enough. Now, how about turning on the lights so we can look around."

"Oh? And what's the hurry? Official business?"

Samuel stared pointedly at Skye and her mother, then back at Jerome, an implicit request for an introduction. Expelling a breath of exasperation, Jerome stepped aside and introduced them.

"Samuel, this is Skye Temple and her mother Flora."

Everyone shook hands, but it wasn't until Samuel actually raised his chin to look Skye directly in the face that the blue of his eyes struck her. Dark blue mixed with purple. Blueberry-colored eyes. She gasped. The same color eyes as the man who'd beckoned her in the dimension of dead souls.

Jerome noticed her stare. "A Wilder has always run the jailhouse. The eyes are hereditary."

"Yep, these eyes are a curse. Can't get away with anything, too easy to be identified." Samuel chuckled, as if he thought it humorous that he'd be capable of committing any kind of crime. "So, Jerome. Give it to me straight. Yer too antsy for this to be a social visit."

205

"Come on, Samuel, if it's official, you know I can't tell you anything." Jerome glanced pointedly at the light switches and folded his arms across his chest.

"Okay, fine. Don't let an old man have any fun." Samuel flicked on the lights, which filled the hallway with a feeble glow.

"Thanks. You can go about your business now. We'll be fine."

Skye heard the respect and gentleness in Jerome's voice and was glad he'd dismissed the old man without being rude.

After all, the jailhouse was Samuel's place. It would be easy for him to take offense at someone ordering him about. Instead, he shrugged his thin shoulders and shuffled off down the hallway to disappear behind a door marked Office. Jerome waited for the slamming of the door before he turned the Open sign in the front door to Closed, something Skye was sure Samuel wouldn't have been too happy about.

"Okay, now what?" she whispered, almost afraid of disturbing what had been left undisturbed for so long. Like waking the dead, or something worse. She shivered.

Jerome considered Skye and Flora for a minute before answering. "I think we should split up and search. We can cover more ground that way."

Skye wasn't sure about leaving her mother alone in her pensive state, but Jerome was right. They needed to cover a lot of ground quickly. And Eldon's unexplained absence wasn't helping matters any.

"If we're this close to the knife, one of you must be able to feel something. Hone in on that and give us a direction."

Skye frowned. She didn't know about her mother, but her own senses seemed to batter her with unknown recognition. Drawing her forward. She felt led, as if she should know or understand the force leading her, but she didn't. Even as they spoke, disembodied voices rasped her nerve endings and sensations of drifting kept her struggling to remain centered. She felt fear in every fiber of her being and was terrified that if she felt like this now, just being close to the knife, what would she feel like when they actually found the knife?

"Jerome's right, you can lead us to the knife, but he's wrong about splitting up. We need to stay together for safety." Flora spoke for the first time since they'd arrived at the jailhouse, her voice soft, yet determined. Her eyes flashed with the usual spark of stubbornness that Skye hadn't seen since before the accident.

Clasping Skye's hands between her own, Flora squeezed tight. "I almost lost your father. I can't risk losing you as well. We could have avoided so much if I'd only trusted and been honest with you, Skye. I feel so horrible about that."

"Mom..." Skye began, but her mother silenced her with a shush.

"As it is, I consider myself wholly responsible for what happened, and I need to make things right. Whatever, or whoever, is after the knife will know that we're here, but that's not the only danger. The knife itself can be dangerous for someone not prepared for its influence. When we find it, the knife will affect you more than me. Your powers are stronger by far. You'll need me to act as your anchor just like when you crossed over to the dimension of dead souls, and we'll need Jerome to keep an eye out against any physical threats while we're bringing the spiritual aspects of the knife under control."

"Christ, this just keeps getting more complicated." Jerome brushed his hands over his short hair and down the back of his neck. "I thought we'd just find the knife and turn it over for testing."

"What?" Flora and Skye exclaimed.

"I said we'd turn it over for testing. What else did you think we'd do with it?" He frowned and looked from one to the other.

"Keeping the knife from falling into the wrong hands is the birth-task of the Goods. You're not equipped to deal with the forces that want to gain possession of such a dangerous weapon." Flora folded her arms across her chest and stared him down. "The knife stays with us to do with as we think necessary."

"The knife is possibly the one used to murder my mother. It goes in for testing." Jerome folded his arms and stared right back.

Skye shook her head and considered the two people now locked in a silent battle of wills. Her mother had the gall and tenacity to match even the most stubborn person, but Jerome had the fire of revenge burning deep inside him. They both possessed a desperate reason to claim the knife and do with it as they would. Not knowing who'd win this confrontation and afraid of the shards of intent she felt rising in both of them, she realized that she'd have to settle the argument. Protecting herself with a hastily thrown up shield of white energy, she stepped between them.

"Look, you two, we need to find the knife before the wrong person does, right?"

They looked at her, but remained firmly locked in a confrontational stance. They nodded warily.

"Great. I'm sure we can also agree that we need to find Amanda's killer and whoever has been killing young women." She glanced between them for confirmation. They nodded.

"There's also no doubt the knife we're looking for holds age-old powers that we can barely understand or control, so why don't we come to an agreement. If we discover the identity of whoever murdered your mother, then you won't need the knife and we keep it. You've already handed one knife over for testing, so why not wait for those results before we hand another one over." She hesitated. "Besides, I have a feeling that it'll be very obvious when we find this knife that it's been hidden for centuries, so all this arguing will be moot, anyway."

Jerome's face reflected his internal struggle. A battle between frustration and anger, and logic and sanity. His need to find a murderer and avenge his mother's death against his responsibilities as a police officer. With a shuddering breath, he nodded.

Only able to imagine what demons he must be fighting in his quest for the truth, Skye gently touched his arm. "Jerome, we will find out who killed your mother, but you won't find the answer with this knife. I have a feeling that the knife might have been the cause, but not the instrument used."

Her mother nodded in agreement, stepped back, and drew a calming breath. "I agree with Skye. Let's go find the knife." Jerome's muscles twitched under Skye's hand, and warmth spread a comforting touch between them. With one sharp inclination of his chin, he strode down the hallway and pulled open a door that led into a darkened maw of a stairway. As dim as the upstairs light, it appeared to be even worse downstairs in the dungeons.

Following Jerome's descent, Skye took a tentative step onto the first stair where the unholy stench of must mixed with aged dust and stale air to assault her nostrils. She sneezed and mumbled, "Great, I always enjoy spending a day in a dark dungeon inhaling mustiness and mold."

Her sarcasm earned a chuckle from below where Jerome waited, and her belly clenched at the rich warmth of his laughter. She found it hard to believe how attracted she was to him, despite how much he frustrated her. It had started before their kiss, no doubt. Probably the first time they'd met. Even though his animosity that night had been obvious—and understandable, now that she knew the circumstances—she seemed to remember a sharp tug of sexual longing. Although, that he could ever have thought her mother responsible for his mother's death made Skye feel sick, she supposed she understood his reasoning. After all, only a few people had attended the ritual that night, and her mother had been one of them. Of course, she'd be a suspect. But it was time to clear her family name and expose the killer.

It was also time to understand the powers that her mother had—with good intentions—withheld her from exploring.

Her newly unleashed senses gave way to an inherent recognition and control of her own abilities. As ancient as the earth's soil, her connection to all that existed, here and in other realms, seemed as natural as breathing, yet she had a hard time adjusting.

She felt as if she'd taken a step off a cliff's edge and dangled above a rocky shoreline and even though she had the capability of flight, wasn't sure if she could spread her wings and fly.

She shivered and sent a silent prayer to the powers that be that she wouldn't screw up. Until lately she'd never committed herself to anything; skipping from job to job, flitting from boyfriend to boyfriend, never committing to anything or anyone. But her responsibility here was too important. She had a generations old birth-task to ensure the safety of others and she meant finally to take responsibility for her actions. She needed to access that part of herself that now lay bare and pulsed with new awareness.

A light touch on her shoulder broke Skye's train of thought and she looked at her mother, who stood beside her. "You'll do fine. Without realizing it, you've been preparing for this your entire life. Every decision you've made, every action you've taken, has brought you to this point in your life. Trust me, circumstances have unfolded as they needed in order for you to be who you have become. You should regret nothing about your life; you are who you are because of it." She smiled lovingly, and moved past Skye to join Jerome, who waited impatiently at the bottom of the stairs.

Skye wiped the tears from her eyes and took the last few steps into the dungeon. It was time to find the knife and protect it from whoever was searching for it. It was her birth-task.

CHAPTER
TWENTY-FIVE

I t didn't take long. Each step into the dark, lower regions of the jail, and Skye felt the tingle of a thread of energy drawing her forward. Each tiny, depressing cell gave off waves of revulsion, pain, and emotional distress, but no sense of the knife. Skye remembered the room she'd been in when she had become one with Dorcas. But so far, none of the ones they'd looked into was that cell. She'd have no doubt when she found the right one.

One more tiny, oppressive cell and one more negative shake of her head made Jerome glare at her. "Are you sure? I mean, really, how do you know for sure?"

"I just know, okay. You're going to have to trust me."

"I don't trust easily. Not with something this important."

Jerome thrust his chin out, shoved his hands on his hips, and spread his feet shoulder width apart. The overall effect might have intimidated some people, as he was an impressive sight with his tanned, compact, muscular body, square jaw, and flashing green eyes. But Skye wasn't intimidated. She was aroused. And she understood his reason for being short-tempered and abrasive. For those reasons, she'd give him some leeway.

"Well, I guess you'll have to learn to trust me, won't you?" She knew that both of them understood the hidden meanings of her statement. There was no doubt of the attraction between them, not only physically, but on so many other levels that she didn't have time to figure it out now. His sharing of her trip through the mists of another dimension to save her father proved that connection. She knew they'd settle the issues between them once this was over, and she looked forward to the confrontation. With a smile filled with promise and primal temptation, she moved to the next cell. Jerome snorted and followed.

The very second her fingertips touched the scarred wooden door, Skye knew. This was the place. Her chest knotted with memories—Dorcas's memories—of imprisonment and horrified terror as the men dragged Sarah from the cell to her death. Tears fell unbidden as Skye swung open the door and faced the hellhole of despair and death. A sob caught in her throat and quivers washed through her body as all blood seemed to drain from her. Distant echoes of voices and screams whipped through her mind and beckoned her forward. She stepped into the darkened cell and her gaze razed the room in search of something, anything, that would indicate the knife's hiding place. A bright flash of light nearly blinded her, and she rushed to the far wall, barely aware of Jerome and her mother's exchange of worried frowns.

As if being directed in one of her wanderings to another realm, Skye dug furiously at the dirt-packed wall, her fingers burrowing and gouging. She pulled her lower lip between her teeth and bit down as she clawed frantically. With each chunk of dirt or stone she dislodged, her senses reeled until she was sure it would send her spinning out of control. The thrum of indistinct voices increased to a howling melee that caused Skye to wince and dig faster, hoping to put an end to the racket in her head.

It didn't.

As soon as she broke through to a hollowed recess in the wall, she motioned for Jerome. "I need the flashlight. Hurry." A sob caught her words in her throat and Jerome laid a comforting hand on her shoulder as he passed her the flashlight.

The swath of light cut a pathway into the hole and revealed a piece of cloth. Torn, dirty, gray canvas that someone had shoved out of sight and almost out of reach. Skye fumbled to get a hold of the fabric and was finally able to clutch a piece of cloth and pull it out of the hole. She raised her gaze to her mother and Jerome. Her hands shook as she lifted a fold of cloth back. The voices of lost souls reverberated through the tiny cell as they dived and leaped about chaotically. She folded another piece of cloth back and the din of voices increased so much that she wondered why Samuel hadn't come down to see what was wrong. Her mom and Jerome didn't seem bothered by the noise, only excited by the prospect of what she held in her hands.

"Doesn't that hurt your ears?"

"Doesn't what hurt my ears?" Jerome asked.

Skye's brow beaded with sweat and her heart raced at twice its normal speed. She turned a worried look to her mother. "Mom?"

"I don't hear them, but I know what you're hearing, and what you're feeling. It'll pass, dear."

She nodded and unwrapped the last piece of canvas until the dim, yellow light of the cell revealed the knife. Even the lack of light couldn't detract from its craftsmanship and beauty. Skye touched a fingertip to the cool blade. Suddenly, a spinning web of otherworldly energies grabbed her. Her breath pressed from her body as spidery fingers grasped her, seeking to draw her to them. It was as if she'd let loose the Hounds of Hell.

Shadows and light swelled from the knife and darted about in confusing patterns. Some shot here and there as if searching, while others merely drifted, all desire for redemption or release gone. Skye tried to ignore the masses of lost souls, even when they insisted upon moaning in her ears and touching her body with their cold essence. There was a sucking sensation when the frantic rush of souls caught Skye's ethereal self as they circled the knife. Terror gripped her as she lost all connection to her physical self. She hadn't been prepared before touching the knife. Fates forbid. She was lost.

Through a foggy gloom, she watched Jerome grab her body and shake. His mouth formed words but she couldn't hear him. She felt souls who had been loved, but the worst were the ones who'd given up. No hope lit their souls, and no life flared their thoughts.

No, as sorry as she felt for the wrongly executed, Skye needed to get out.

Quelling her fear, she concentrated on loosening tight muscles, even if they were only ethereal, and breathing deep into herself. She calmed her mind and blocked out everything except the beat of her heart and pulse of her blood, just as her mom had taught her. Slowly, she unwound her own soul from the twist of frantic souls seeking the knife. The more she relaxed, the lighter she became, and the higher she rose above the melee. With the same sucking sensation that had drawn her from her body, her ethereal self rushed back into her physical self. Gasping, she drew a breath and bolted upright, only to find that Jerome held her in his lap.

It took all her effort to speak the words that hovered on the edge of her sanity. "They're here. They're all here. In the knife." A choking sob cut through her, and she tucked her face into Jerome's chest. His strength seeped into her, warming, comforting, lending support until she could wipe her face of tears and pull away. Her mom helped her stand and enveloped Skye in a tight hug.

"For a minute...I thought...Oh, Skye, thank the Fates you're all right."

"Thanks to you." She hugged her mom back and whispered, "You've prepared me all these years, haven't you?"

"Of course." Flora pulled away and straightened the voluminous sleeve of her caftan. "You don't think I had you learn meditation for the good of your health, do you?"

They looked at the knife, partially covered with canvas and lying innocuously on the ground. "Are you sure you're okay?"

"Yes, I'm fine now."

"What happened, anyway?"

"The knife is so much more than we realized. It's not only able to transfer power and knowledge from one person to another, but it steals souls." She shivered. "Can we go outside and I'll explain what I saw. I really need to get out of here."

With the souls now quiet and the knife re-wrapped and in Skye's possession, the trio made their way to a wooden bench in the garden, a haven of heavenly aromas and a riot of nature's colors. Once settled, she turned her face to the sun and reveled in the heat beating down. Warmth flowed through her limbs and dispelled any residue of the cold that had crept into her in the dungeon. After experiencing the discordant emotions of the trapped souls, she appreciated life more than ever and gave a silent prayer of thanks for her own life.

Jerome paced the stone pathway and shot the occasional look of impatience at her. Finally, he stopped in front of her, arms crossed over his chest, his gaze piercing. "Okay, tell us what happened."

Skye observed the view in front of her for a moment, then let her gaze wander up past a trim waist, toned abs nicely outlined through his T-shirt, a chest that begged for someone to run their hands over it, and to his face, which had paled a shade once Jerome realized the suggestive stance he'd assumed. With an effort, he relaxed and sat on a bench on the opposite side of the narrow pathway and Skye almost laughed at how incongruous he looked next to the delicate structure of the wooden bench so elegantly carved in a Chantilly pattern.

"It's kind of hazy, but when I touched the knife, I must have disrupted what had lain dormant for centuries. All these souls leaped from the knife and raced around the room in a frenzy, as if seeking an escape, but the knife held them fast. When it drew them back in, I became entangled in their mass. Any sense of self disappeared within the memories of so many lives that I couldn't even distinguish one from the other. Their anguish, love, hate, terror."

She shivered and Jerome was quick to move, to wrap an arm around her shoulders and pull her close. Skye breathed deeply of the scent of him; a masculine, earthy scent that immediately calmed her.

Her mother frowned. "It wouldn't have surprised me to find one or two lost souls absorbed into the knife, since it's been around for centuries, but nowhere near the numbers that you're talking about. Were you able to tell who all those poor souls belonged to?"

Skye sniffled and scrubbed the back of her hand over her cheek. "I know who they are. I saw what happened." With a smile of thanks to Jerome, she sat up and straightened her shirt. "It started in the grove that night when Ann Putnam interrupted Sarah Good during a ritual with the knife. You remember, Mom, I told you about Sarah's diary entry."

"Yes, I remember. Ann Putnam was upset because Sarah refused to share any knowledge with her, especially about the knife."

"Well, when Ann interrupted the ritual, she prevented Sarah from completing the spell that would bind the powers of the knife, but Sarah didn't realize it. Before her execution, we know she passed the knife to Dorcas, who eventually hid it where we found it. All those years hidden in the Salem jail, the knife has sucked in any unhappy, unfulfilled, or restless soul that passed through these walls. The souls of all the executed witches are here." She lifted the canvas wrapped knife. "They've been trapped for centuries."

"Great Mother Earth." Her mother's face paled and her eyes rounded with fear. "Skye, be careful. The one who controls the knife, controls the souls housed within. Except, I'm afraid you don't have the strength to control them. They'll be in rare form and ready to cause trouble after being trapped for so long. Keep the knife covered, or you chance letting them loose to wreak havoc."

Jerome had been staring at the canvas in Skye's hands ever since hearing her tale. He kept shaking his head and muttering as if to himself. "This is too much. But it makes sense. It must be what my ancestor was talking about last night."

"What?" Skye and Flora asked.

Jerome looked at them as if suddenly realizing they were still with him. "Sorry. I had a vision last night when I had this place staked out." He explained what he'd seen, half expecting that they'd meet his tale with disbelief. Of course, with all that had gone on, his story was a tame one.

"So you think William Phips has been trying to free the souls trapped in the knife?" Skye asked.

"Well, yes. It makes sense if he feels responsible for them being there in the first place. After all, history does say he did a turn around halfway through the trials as if realizing that the situation had gotten out of hand." He looked at them hopefully. "It makes sense that he'd want to make things right, doesn't it?"

Skye's heart ached for the little boy tone of Jerome's voice. Wanting to believe his ancestor was good and not evil. Seeking a kind of exoneration for actions taken by a man hundreds of years earlier. Poor guy. Living with guilt that wasn't his and driven to solve his mother's disappearance, he couldn't have lived a very fulfilled life. Skye laid her hand on his arm and smiled encouragingly.

"Yes, it makes total sense. The question is, what do we do about it?" Skye looked at her mom, hoping she'd have an answer.

"I guess we need to free the souls and bind the knife, which is what Sarah had been trying to do when Ann interrupted her."

"Do you know the ritual to do that?"

"No."

The single word set Jerome into frenetic motion. He ran his hands over his head and down the back of his neck as he paced the garden path. "Great, I still need to solve my mother's murder, we have a killer on the loose, some unknown entity after a knife that's pumped full of restless, dangerous souls, and no way to control the power of said knife." His glare settled on Skye's mom who nodded and wiped away a tear.

The sympathy of a moment ago dissolved in the face of Jerome's unreasoning anger. She stood and faced him. "Quit badgering my mother, you big bully. Don't you think she's been through enough? She said she didn't know the ritual. It's not her fault."

"I said I didn't know the ritual. I didn't say we couldn't find out what it is." Two pairs of eyes turned to her in disbelief. "*Faerie Enchantments and Sorcerer Magick*. The answer will be in there."

"Of course." Skye frowned. "But I have a feeling that's not the only reason we have the book. Things are going to get more complicated before they're better."

Jerome threw his hands up in the air. "Oh, isn't that good news.

Skye looked at his glowering features and giggled. She couldn't help herself. It was probably her way of releasing the tension of almost being sucked into eternity by the knife. She didn't care what the reason was, she just giggled.

He fixed the full force of his glower on her, narrowed his eyes, and slapped his hands to his hips. Skye giggled harder. Uncontrollably. Until tears rolled down her cheeks. Then she waved a hand in his direction. "You're such a tough guy."

"Am not." He pushed his chin out belligerently.

"Are so."

Jerome's lips quivered into an almost smile. "Did you just call me what I think you called me?"

"What?" Skye tried to focus on what he meant, and when she realized his meaning, she broke out into hysterical laughter. "N-no. No. Really, I don't think you're an asshole at all."

"Skye." Her mother gasped, but recognizing the much needed release of tension, she smiled. "Come on, you two, we have a knife to bind and some murders to solve."

"Now you sound like me," Jerome said.

"I could think of worse people to sound like." She shot him a smile that he returned easily.

"Well, let's get started then. And the sooner the better as far as I'm concerned." Skye clenched the knife closer, as if to protect it until they could release the souls.

"You two go ahead. I have a killer to find and it doesn't look as if this is the knife used in any of the killings, either my mother's or the more recent ones."

Jerome's voice had returned to its usual flatness and Skye felt sorry for the boy who'd grown into a man and been able to perfect such an emotionless, toneless voice over the years. Even harder to accept was the hint of despair that she barely detected when Jerome mentioned his mother. How sad.

The shrill ringing of a phone interrupted the heavy silence. Jerome grabbed his cell and barked a hello. Whatever the person at the other end said had an instant effect on him because his eyes darkened from jade-green to the forbidding green of the forest at dusk. Shadows danced and light faded in their depths. His jaw clenched, and his nostrils flared. Something was wrong. Seriously wrong. Skye subconsciously took her mother's arm and hugged her close while he snapped the phone shut.

Desperation flickered in the depths of his eyes and when he spoke, he forced the words through clenched teeth. Skye was barely able to understand what he said, but when she did, the horror shot through her like adrenaline.

CHAPTER
TWENTY-SIX

"My house is on fire. We need to go. Now." He grabbed each of them by an arm and dragged them with him to his car.

"Wait, Jerome, my Jeep's here. You go ahead and we'll meet you there."

"No. We stay together. It's safer that way." Without waiting for their agreement, he practically shoved them into the back seat of his car and jumped into the front seat.

Skye knew he was upset, but the desperation ravaging his face made little sense until she remembered.

"Chance," she whispered.

"Pardon, dear."

"Chance." Jerome volunteered from the front seat. "My dog."

"Oh."

No one spoke, each person lost in his or her own thoughts. Within minutes, they approached the turnoff for Winter Island Rd. Wisps of smoke became visible through the trees.

Sickly dread wended through Skye as Jerome cursed and made a hard turn onto the road that held both their homes. Within a minute or two, it became obvious that the fire was Jerome's house. Skye had hoped there'd been some mistake.

Orange and blue flames licked skyward, while smoke billowed like rolling waves; thick, choking, pervasive. Jerome brought the car to a stop on the road in front of his house and stared at the raging flames consuming his home and possessions. A couple of fire trucks slashed bright red and firefighters ran about everywhere.

Some soot covered, others soaking wet, but each of them looking exhausted from fighting the losing battle.

"Damn it, I can't just sit here." Jerome leaped from his car and ran to the front steps, only to have a couple of firefighters restrain him. A horrendous crash caused by the living room roof caving in resulted in increased action and shouts. Jerome realized that trying to get inside was a futile effort. He ceased his struggles and straightened his shoulders. "Did you save anyone? My dog."

The firefighter restraining Jerome shot him a look of pity and shook his head. "Sorry, no survivors, human or otherwise." His words elicited what could only have been a strangled sob from Jerome. Pain etched deep into his eyes, and Skye knew the loss was one that he'd feel for a long time. Probably forever.

The rest of the roof chose that moment to crash into a heap of burning lumber and sparking embers. The firefighters shouted and backed off, pulling their hoses and equipment with them. From a distance, they directed the water onto the fire to ensure it didn't spread any further. The smell of sodden ashes and wet wood filled the air, and Skye felt sick. Sick with grief for Jerome's loss of his home and everything he owned. Most of all, she sympathized with him for losing one of his best friends. Yes, Chance qualified as a friend. She'd seen the way Jerome watched the canine and the bond of love and trust between the two had been obvious. Man's best friend.

"Chance." Whispered with love and pain, the single word wound through the smoke and disappeared amidst the roar of fire and water.

Another realization hit and Jerome whispered, "My sculptures." The words broke her heart all over again. Years of work. Gone. How much more could a person stand before breaking?

She laid a hand on his arm, and he looked down at her. She didn't need to say the words; they shone from her eyes and emanated from her very soul. She sent comforting energy to wrap around Jerome, whose only response was to narrow his eyes and stare deeper into hers. Unrequested, unexpected, Skye gave of herself so that Jerome's pain could be lessened, even if just a little.

At first, he resisted, but Skye persisted enough that he must have figured resistance was an effort he didn't have the strength for. With a sigh, he let his barriers down. The connection between them sizzled and then flamed. The fullness of love echoed through them, bounced between them, found a home, and set down roots. For the briefest moment they were somewhere not of this world, and the only thing that mattered was each other.

The sound of a slamming door roused them to awareness of their current situation, but before the bond of energy broke, they formed another bond. One of two souls finding each other; trusting and believing in the ultimate fate of love and each other.

"Someone knows we have the knife."

Abrupt and out of place, the words shattered the shared moment. "What? Sorry, Mom, did you say something?" Skye felt warm from the inside out and had trouble concentrating. She also had trouble tearing her eyes from Jerome to focus on her mom.

"I said, someone knows we have the knife."

"You're right, Flora. Someone knows."

Skye looked at the certainty on her mother's face and the blazing determination on Jerome's.

"How do you two know that?"

"Gut instinct." He narrowed his eyes and grazed a look around the area. "This is a message directed at me and I'm worried that whoever did this will also have a message for you. Come on, we're going to your place."

Once there, they noted that everything outside her house seemed to be all right. No fires, no burning effigies hanging from a tree, no shadowy figures lurking about in the trees. Skye was relieved. She couldn't imagine losing everything the way Jerome just had. Leaving her mom in the kitchen to make tea, Skye and Jerome made the rounds upstairs, but found nothing out of place.

"Well, that's good," Skye said, as they made a check of the last room in the house, her bedroom. "Everything looks fine." "Yeah." He glanced around the room, his eyes missing no detail. Skye wished she'd straightened up earlier, because her panties and T-shirt strewn in the middle of her bed earned an arched eyebrow and a smirk from Jerome. She gave an inward groan and moved to the hallway, attempting to draw him out. Instead of following, he moved to her dresser and looked at the array of photos she kept near. She had everything from her first pony ride to her tenth-year birthday party; even the embarrassing photo of her high school graduation and the hideous ruffled, fuchsia colored dress she'd worn. In each photo—depending on who'd been snapping the shot—her parents figured prominently.

Jerome brushed his fingers over each picture, his features tight. Skye could tell nothing of his feelings from his face, but his eyes, oh, his eyes ached with longing and regret. Not knowing what to do, she could only stand in the doorway and witness the pain of someone who'd never known his father and then lost his mother so young. Someone who'd never experienced the life and love that shone through in each photo on her dresser. Her heart broke for the lost little boy that still resided inside Jerome, no matter his tough exterior.

"You're so lucky."

"I'm sorry," she whispered.

He snapped his head around. "Don't be sorry. It's not your fault. You've lived the life you were given, that's all. Just like I have."

Impulsively, she placed her hands on his chest, noting the feel of hard, sleek muscles under her palms, and kissed him. What started out as a tender act meant to console quickly escalated into a hot plundering of mouths and senses. Dizzy with the sensation wracking her body, Skye moaned. The sound of pleasure drove Jerome over the edge, and he pushed her up against the wall, his hips grinding into hers. She trembled with a desire that now burned tenfold since their bonding at the fire. She loved the feel of his lips when they claimed hers, and how his moist, probing tongue drove her crazy with need.

Aware of the fact that they were in her bedroom and her mother was downstairs making tea, Skye attempted to gain control. It wasn't easy. It felt so good to have someone who made her feel such passion. No act of sex had ever evoked such sensations, such an out of this world reeling of the senses, as a single kiss with this man. She wanted more. She needed more.

The invasive sound of a creak slammed into her mind. She knew that sound. It was the fourth step from the bottom of the staircase, which could only mean her mother was on her way up. Heck, she was almost here. With a major effort of will, she shoved Jerome away from her and, ignoring his confused frown, stepped to the other side of the room as if she'd been there all along.

"Tea's ready."

Skye wasn't sure if she welcomed her mom's interruption or not. But she knew that it wasn't over between her and Jerome. It had only just begun, and his pointed look in her direction said exactly the same thing.

"We're coming, Mom." Skye looped an arm through her mothers and the three of them moved downstairs to the kitchen.

"So everything looks all right?" Flora asked.

"For now," Jerome replied. "I don't like it, though. Having the knife in your possession makes you both prime targets. Even more so because of your ancestry."

"I still can't believe it," Skye murmured as she sipped her green tea.

"What? That you're descended from one of the witches executed during the Salem witch trials?"

"Well, yeah. Wrongly executed, I might add. How does someone live up to that legacy?"

Flora patted her arm. "We do whatever it takes to bind the knife so no one can use it for evil."

"Yes. That should put an end to everything." Jerome agreed.

"As soon as we find out how to bind the knife's powers."

"Yes. You mentioned a book called *Faerie Enchantments and Sorcerer Magick*."

She explained to a confused Jerome. "Nora, from The Magic Corner, gave us a book that she seemed sure we'd need. It looks like she was right."

"You don't mean the book she kept displayed in her showcase, do you?"

"Yep. The one and only."

He sat back in his chair and laughed. "I don't believe it. She's had offers for that book from half the practicing witches in town. I'm talking a lot of money too, and she's turned them all down. Now you tell me she gave it to you, someone who has only been in town for a few days. A stranger?"

Skye nodded. "That about covers it."

"Amazing. Simply amazing." His cell phone rang, putting an end to any further comment.

A knock on the door interrupted her musings. Her mother moved to refill the teapot. Not expecting anyone, and leery now that they had possession of the knife, Skye strode down the hall and peeked out the window before opening the door. Matthew's smiling face greeted her. Nora's comments about Matthew flew through her mind, and she hesitated. He'd seen her so she couldn't pretend not to be here. Besides, Jerome's car sat out front, making it obvious they were not only home, but had company. Pasting a smile on her face, she opened the door.

"Hi. Hope I'm not interrupting anything." He looked pointedly at Jerome's car.

"No. We just came from Jerome's. I guess you saw what happened."

"Yeah. That's too bad. I know that he and I don't see eye to eye on a lot of things, but I'd never wish something like that on him. How's he handling it?"

Skye sensed unsettled feelings masked by those innocent enough words. But then again, it could be her imagination.

She didn't know what to think about most things these days. Within a matter of no time, her understanding of her powers, her ancestry, her mother...it had all turned upside down.

"I'm doing fine." Jerome strode from the kitchen, stood beside Skye, and draped his arm across her shoulders.

Matthew noticed the intimate gesture and flushed. "Hey. I am sorry. It's a terrible thing to happen."

"Yeah, I'm sure your heart is breaking."

The two men stared at each other in an age-old battle of macho intent. Prickles of sharp anger crackled the air, yet neither of them moved. Skye shifted uncomfortably and looked from Matthew to Jerome, afraid of what might happen if she didn't stop them.

"What are you doing here, Matthew?" Even to her own ears, her voice was high and just a little breathless with anxiety.

Matthew was visibly uncomfortable under Jerome's intense gaze. Skye had a hard time imaging him as the morbidly evil kind of person it would take to commit the murders of recent years, as well as the murder of Jerome's mom. He was too eager to please, too innocuous.

"I came to see if Skye wanted to attend Chastity's funeral with me." He blinked. "I...ah...didn't know that you two..."

"She can't." Jerome spoke before Skye had a chance to remember that the burial for the young girl she'd met a few days ago was today.

"Excuse me." She glared at Jerome, put off by his high-handed assumption that he could decide for her. An awkward silence followed. Jerome set his jaw and stared at Matthew while Skye tried to wriggle out from the hand that now clenched her shoulder.

"Look, I only thought that you'd like to go, since you seemed so upset when you heard about her disappearance the other day."

Before she could answer, Jerome dragged her into the living room.

"We'll be right back." He snapped at Matthew.

Jerome slammed the door behind them, and Skye whirled about to face him. "What do you think you're doing?"

"You can't go to the funeral with him. What are you thinking?"

"Jerome, come on, it's a funeral, a public place with lots of people around."

"You don't think he's guilty, do you?"

"Let's just say that I have a hard time seeing him as an evildoer, is all. It's a role I see his mother in more easily."

"You're still not going."

"Look, I'd like to go to the funeral. I didn't know Chastity well, but..." Her chest tightened with the ache of knowing she'd seen the girl's death and not done anything to prevent it. "I owe her."

"How can you possibly owe her anything if you hardly knew her?"

He glared, waiting for her explanation. "Well?"

Skye didn't want to say the words. Speaking them would give them substance and make her responsibility that much more real. But one look at Jerome's face and she knew he wouldn't move until she told him. The words welled within her, bubbling up from the safe spot deep in the pit of her stomach where she'd pushed them upon hearing about Chastity's death. Gushing out in a garbled account of her meeting with Chastity, she told him about her vision and the conflict about whether to tell the girl what she'd seen.

It felt good to put substance to the guilt that had eaten her up over the last few days. She finished her story and fully expected Jerome to be disgusted, even upset. Instead, he cupped her cheek with his palm and a calming warmth spread through her.

"It's not your fault, Skye. Blame it on the animal who is killing these girls."

"But I saw her death. I should have warned her."

He pulled her into the circle of his arms and held her tight.

"You said you warned her before she left. What more could you have done? Think about it. You were brand new to town, knew nothing about the murders, and had only dabbled in some meditation and minor ritual spells. How could you possibly expect to have understood your vision that day? With more experience with your powers and a better grasp of the situation in town, maybe, but with what you knew, no way. It's not your fault."

Skye took comfort in his closeness, and the deep rumble of his voice echoing in her ear resting on his chest. He made sense, but it didn't stop her from wishing she could have done more to prevent Chastity's death.

"I really want to go to her funeral." Her words came out muffled because she spoke against his shirt. "Why don't you come."

"I can't. That was Samson on the phone. He wants me at the station, and I want to find out who burned my house and killed Chance."

She squeezed her arms tighter around his waist. "I'm so sorry about Chance."

"I know. I don't want you going to the funeral, at least not with Matthew."

A gentle knock on the door interrupted them. Skye's mom cleared her throat loudly. "Ahem. Can I come in?"

"Sure." Jerome stepped aside and opened the door.

"Why don't I go to the funeral with Skye and Matthew?" The sound of approaching footfalls quelled any further debate. Matthew poked his head into the living room. "Hey, I didn't mean to cause any trouble. It was just an idea. I'll go to the funeral alone."

He turned to leave, but Jerome stopped him. "No." With an obvious effort, at least to Skye, he pulled himself under control. "Sorry, Matthew, I was overstepping my bounds. You know how it is with a new love." He leaned over and kissed Skye's cheek, and she had to bite her tongue to keep from smirking at the adoring puppy look he emulated so well.

"Oh. Uh, sure. I didn't realize that you two...well, you know. So that means you're coming?"

"Yes. Give me ten minutes to get changed. Oh, is it all right if Mom comes as well?"

Matthew's smile slipped for a split second, but he recovered. "Sure. What about you, Jerome?"

"I've got to go to work."

"Too bad." A huge smile lit Matthew's face. "Don't worry, I'll take care of the women for you."

Innocent words that echoed ominously as each person considered how many ways they could interpret those words.

CHAPTER
TWENTY-SEVEN

Jerome cursed the fates and harangued himself for acting the fool. If he'd learned one thing over the years, it was that you never told a woman she couldn't do something. That was a sure-fire way to make sure she did exactly what you'd told her not to do. Women. Who could figure them out?

No matter what Skye believed, he knew with deep-down certainty that Matthew was guilty or involved with his mother's death. To satisfy his own mind, he'd made a phone call to the station and called in a couple of favors. Matthew and Verity would both be under observation by plainclothes officers using their time off to help. Jerome felt a twinge of guilt at keeping Samson out of the loop, but he didn't have time for red tape or protocol.

With that load relieved for now, he was able to take a deep breath, but as he wheeled into his parking spot at the police station, a sudden thought struck him. Shit. With all that had gone on, he'd clean forgot about Eldon. He hadn't heard from his friend all day. Considering the fact that Eldon knew everything that went on in town, and news of the fire would have made the rounds by now, it was strange not to have heard from him.

Unease snaked through his belly. He yanked his cell phone out and dialed Eldon's number. No answer, which was also strange because it was the middle of the day and Eldon was fastidious about being available during working hours. If he wasn't, he ran the risk of missing a sale or an important phone call from a client.

Something was wrong. He knew it. He'd have to check in with Samson first and then take a look over at Eldon's office.

"Hey, Jerome, sorry to hear about your house." Jaks hollered from the front desk. "Real sorry about Chance, too. I know how you loved the mutt."

The pain of loss stabbed his gut. Chance. To hide the rising tears, he waved Jaks's direction and continued to Samson's office. When he entered, he knew why he was there. No words needed to be spoken between childhood friends. The air hung thick and cloying over Jerome, while the sympathy lighting Samson's eyes lent credibility to the fact that blood on the knife had matched Jerome's mom. His blood boiled like a bitter brew, bubbling hot with the need for vengeance. With fists clenched, he made a move to leave.

"Stay. We're not done yet." Samson's tone slapped Jerome's reeling senses, and he had a hard time regaining even a small semblance of control, but he knew better than to gainsay his boss. People who did usually ended up in trouble. Not because of anything Samson did, he was too aware of the creed to do no harm. Jerome remained.

"First of all, I'm sorry about your house; more importantly, Chance. But, Jerome, there are four other murders to consider here besides your mother. I'm sorry, but that's the way of it. I can't have one of my best men running off half-cocked and doing damage to either himself or any evidence that may come from following proper procedure. No way do I want to supply a defense attorney with ammunition to get a case thrown out of court on a technicality."

"Yeah, and while we're following proper procedure, how many other people will get killed?"

Samson leaned back, a smile twitching the corner of his mouth. "Considering the fact that you have officers watching both Matthew and Verity, I doubt that will happen."

"I should have known I couldn't put one over on you."

"Yes, you should. Dammit, Jerome, I thought you trusted me."

He tried to think of a way to make Samson understand his reasoning. "It's not that, Samson."

"Then what? Tell me."

"I'll explain best as I can, but I don't know if it will make any sense."

"Try me. I'm open to anything."

"It's kind of like the connection that you and I have. Remember when we were kids, and I fell down the cliff? You came running to my rescue and brought the police, the fire trucks, and half the neighborhood. Even when I moved to Boston to live with my aunt, we always knew when the other one was in trouble or needed help. Today, when I came into your office, I didn't need to hear the words. I knew what you were telling me."

"Yeah, I know all that, but what does it have to do with the murders?"

"I have a connection like that with the killer. Granted, it's not as strong. It's more like an occasional sensation of malicious intent that invades my mind. I get glimpses into the workings of this person's mind. That's how I know that conventional police methods won't work. The evil that hangs over Salem has been here for centuries. I think the witch trials directly resulted from an archaic evil that can possess—or maybe just spellbind—people. It has a purpose, too. It wants a knife that has been imbued with the ability to wield tremendous power to the person who possesses it."

"Come on, that's a little far-fetched for even me to believe."

"Samson, a minute ago you mentioned trust. Well, now I'm asking you to trust me. Hey, you're the one who opened me up to my inner powers. Don't doubt what they're telling me. Believe me, it's going to take magic to stop this force, not proper police procedure. I can't impress upon you enough how dangerous it could be if this knife gets in the hands of whoever is doing the killing."

Samson sat stone still and stared. Jerome stared back. The silence of communication on a level beyond words carried permission, along with Samson's offer of help if necessary.

"Do what you have to and call me when it's done."

Shaking with relief, because Jerome hadn't wanted to go against Samson's wishes, but would have, he strode from the office. There was so much to do. First, he needed to find Eldon and then check on Skye and her mom.

Unease sharpened itself on his guts. Centuries of manipulations and intent had come to Salem, and the murky mantle of evil that hung over the town had taken root in the mind of either Matthew or Verity. The knife was the secret. It would draw the killer out of hiding to risk their life to possess the knife. Jerome had no doubt. It was time to end his journey of revenge that had started thirty years ago.

CHAPTER
TWENTY-EIGHT

It looked as if Eldon's office hadn't been open at all that day. Mail lay scattered on the floor where it had fallen from the slot. The newspaper sat on the sidewalk in front of the door, and no lights shone through the windows. Jerome tried to think of the last time he'd seen Eldon. Yesterday at Skye's when he and Eldon had come across Flora and Skye right after their retrieval spell. He'd received a phone call about someone wanting to look at a pink elephant he'd been trying to unload.

Great. It was a place to start. Jerome assumed that Eldon would have returned to the office to grab the keys for whatever house he was showing and maybe scribbled a note or two. If he could get inside, he could see what set of keys was missing and know where Eldon had gone.

"Jerome."

He turned to see who was hollering at him from across the road. *What the heck?* "What are you doing here, Brent? You're supposed to be at *Witches Haven*."

"I was. Hell, I've been looking all over for you to tell you that Verity's not there. The store is closed and there are no signs of life anywhere."

"That doesn't make sense." Jerome's gaze wandered to Eldon's office and back to Brent. He shivered. "It's the middle of a business day."

Brent shrugged. "I'm sorry. Maybe she's home sick or decided to go to the funeral. Do you want me to check her house?"

Jerome needed to find Eldon, but he also didn't want Verity running around without someone keeping an eye on her. It felt wrong to leave Eldon's mysterious disappearance for later, but it was also possible that there was a relation between his friend's disappearance and Verity not being at her store. "Yeah. If you don't mind, go have a look at her house, while I check the funeral to see if she's there."

"Sure, no problem." With a wave, Brent sprinted down the street.

"Hey." Jerome hollered after him. "Be careful." He wasn't sure if Brent heard his warning or not, but hoped he had. He'd hate for anything to happen to his fellow officer, especially since Brent was doing him a favor on his day off. With one last look at Eldon's dark office and a silent oath to find him no matter what, Jerome climbed into his car and sped toward the funeral home, ignoring the person he'd quite effectively cut off as he wheeled from the parking spot.

He screeched to a halt in front of Abe's Funeral Parlor, but the decided lack of any vehicles or a hearse in the parking lot or on the street quelled any hope of finding Skye and her mom here. That left the cemetery. Cursing the fates that had brought him to such a nerve-wracking day, he peeled rubber in the other direction and headed to the Old Burying Point Cemetery. As he weaved through the busy streets, he had to fight the bile that rose in his throat. The closer he came to the cemetery, the more his senses reeled and his stomach bucked. Not a good sign. He wasn't going to find them at the cemetery. He knew that as surely as he knew that everything was going to end today. One way or another.

His head throbbed and something sharp was digging into his hip. Eldon shifted. When he couldn't move, realization struck that having his hands and feet bound made movement near impossible. What the hell? It was too dark to see much. Boards covered the only visible window, but a single shaft of light filtered through the crooked boards and lent a dim haze to the room. Not enough to determine where he was.

He tried to remember what had happened. How long had he been there? Who had done this to him? Anything at all. But nothing came. The last thing he could remember, he'd been at Skye's house. He and Jerome had disturbed Skye and Flora right after their retrieval spell. Jerome had battered heads with both of them, shown them the knife, talked about that night thirty years ago, and then finally come to a hesitant trust and offer to help each other. They'd also planned to meet at the jailhouse the next morning. Had that been today? Yesterday? A week ago? Eldon had no idea of the passage of time.

A rustling in the far corner of the room set his heart to racing. Rats probably, but it sounded larger than that. It moved again, as if trying to pull free of something. Was there someone else down here with him? Jesus, he was more terrified than he'd ever been.

"Hello. Anyone there?" he whispered, almost afraid that someone just might answer him. More rustling sounded, as well as a fervent scratching sound. Before he could say anything else, the drone of voices echoed from above. Someone was here, wherever here was. Footsteps clattered down wooden stairs. The door opened and threw a shaft of blinding light into the room. Too much light to be able to see anything after the darkness he'd become used to. But he recognized the people's voices. That was when fear pierced his heart.

Damn. Double damn. The only sight to greet him at the cemetery was a worker busy shoveling dirt into a fresh grave. Chastity's, no doubt. A promising life cut short by an unconscionable act of twisted evil. Jerome's gut gave another jerk of anger.

Breathing deeply to calm himself, he sat and considered his next move. His gaze drifted across row upon row of stone markers, a long-standing reminder attesting to the fragility of life. Eerie. And sad. Jerome suddenly missed his mother more than he'd ever done. More to the point, he missed ever having the chance to get to know her. A relationship just coming into being as he matured enough to understand and relate to her. A mother and child bonding with a common interest. And then she'd been taken from him.

The gentle touch of a breeze wafted through the car window and swirled around him. Strangely enough, the breeze seemed alive with the essence of life, offering consolation and encouragement. For the briefest moment of time, the breeze formed into a hazy mist that resembled the face of the dead girl.

Chastity.

Jerome jolted upright in his seat. A feeling of peace washed over him as the specter of a dead girl offered comfort. The comfort of knowing that a person never really dies. The sure realization that his mother's spirit lived on somewhere. Chastity's presence drifted back through the window. Her absence left him feeling bereft but reassured. Just before the mist disappeared, a voice as beautiful as musical chimes in a light breeze spoke to him.

"Save them. Save them before it's too late."

His heart slammed against his chest. How could he have let his mind wander for even a minute? This was not the time to be reminiscing. Not when it seemed as if everyone he knew had gone missing. But shit, where did he start looking?

CHAPTER
TWENTY-NINE

Skye woke to the knowledge that she and her mother were in serious trouble. Her last memory was of Jerome leaving and Matthew smiling. Everything after that was blank.

Hard-packed dirt added another level of pain to her aching head, and her stiff shoulders felt like someone had wrenched them from their sockets and tied them behind her back. Pervasive darkness and the heavy mantle of evil that hung over the room did nothing to quell the fear that this basement might just end up being her coffin.

She shifted in an attempt to relieve her shoulders and bruised hip. It didn't work. As her eyes adjusted to the dark, her gaze stretched across the room, looking for her mother. "Mom. Mom, are you here?" Even though she'd kept her voice low, it reverberated loudly, bouncing from wall to wall. Skye cringed.

"Skye. Oh, thank goodness. I was so worried about you. You've been unconscious for so long."

"Oh, Mom." Relief that her mother was there faded into guilt at wishing such a horrendous situation on her own mother. "Are you all right?"

"Besides being knocked on the head and tied up, sure." "Mom, it's all my fault. I'm so sorry." A sob caught in Skye's throat as she thought about what might be in store for them.

"It's not your fault. Put that from your mind right now, young lady. We are here because of something that started long before either one of us was born. By the way, we have company. Eldon is here. And I'm guessing that's Chance whining in the corner."

"Eldon? Chance?" Skye had trouble comprehending how and why they were all in this place. She did know that Jerome would be thrilled to know that Chance still lived. At least for now. And the reason for Eldon's disappearance.

"Eldon? I guess this is why you didn't show up at the jail this morning."

"Sure is. I went to show the house I received the phone call on while I was here yesterday, and bam, someone slugged me on the noggin. Next thing I know, I woke up here. Any idea where we are?"

"Yeah. The basement of my house."

"What? Jesus, that makes a sick, twisted kind of sense. The full circle theory at its best. Question is, what happens next?"

"I don't know, but whatever it is, it won't be good for us."

"Well, hopefully, Jerome will find us soon." Eldon's voice held desperate hope.

Skye shivered. They'd probably all be dead by the time Jerome found them. Sacrificed in some sordid ritual meant to sap them of their power and grant it to someone who would use it to kill again. Panic took hold of her and set her heart to fluttering unnaturally. A bead of sweat broke out on her forehead and she struggled with the ropes binding her wrists.

"Skye." Her mother's voice reached through the fear, calming and reassuring. "We'll be fine. Jerome will find us and everything will be fine. In the meantime, we have to keep our senses about us. Do you understand?"

Skye's hammering heart slowed, and she gulped, almost choking on the deep breath of musty air she inhaled. "Sorry, you're right. We have no idea what's going on, but Jerome will find us, and we have each other as well as the knife. We have the knife, by the way."

"You found it?" Eldon almost shouted with excitement. Realizing the danger of alerting their captor to that fact, he lowered his voice to a whisper. "You found the knife?"

"Oh, yeah. We have it. For now," Skye said. "Mom, what are we going to do? We can't just hand the knife over. If we do, a lot more people will die."

"If we don't, we'll die. Guaranteed." Eldon offered his comment from the corner. "And I also guarantee that it won't be an easy death."

"Eldon, harping on the negative won't help matters any." "I know, Flora, but I've been down here a lot longer than you two. I've had the chance to envision my death in a multitude of manners."

"We will not die."

"Okay, you two, enough. We need to be constructive here, not destructive."

"What do you suggest, dear?"

"We need to free ourselves and then get out of here."

"Yeah, right."

"No, she's right, Eldon. Look, we have the power of three witches in one room. Are you telling me we can't even get ourselves free from a couple of ropes? Pretty sorry excuse for witches, if you ask me."

Chance's adamant whining seemed to confirm that statement.

"Great, since we're all in agreement, let's focus our powers on Eldon's ropes since he's been tied up the longest. Which do you prefer, Eldon, cutting or burning?"

"Cripes, ones as good as the next."

"Good, we'll focus on fire. It's a specialty of mine," Skye teased, knowing that her mother would remember her aborted attempt to light a candle on the altar when she was younger.

"Oh, yes, I'll vouch for Skye's affinity with fire."

"Fine. Fine. Let's get started. I'm tired of lying around doing nothing. I want to kick some ass."

Silence fell as they drew in their energy and focused on the task. Their three breaths became one, while their minds formed a single entity and intensified the power of three. The presence of power nullified the darkness of the room and leant a circle of light, much like an aura around the three captives. Skye felt a shift in the fabric of the room and knew that their combined effort was working.

That was when the door slammed at the top of the stairs.

The connection between the three of them snapped like a twig ground beneath the heel of an unyielding interloper. Their captor stepped into the room and shone a flashlight upon them.

"I can feel your power like an insidious bug. Don't think you can escape me. I've waited far too long to exact revenge for wrongs done long ago, as well as those not so long ago. The knife will be mine and the power will be mine. I have one phone call to make. In the meantime, if I feel your attempt to escape again, I'll slit Eldon's throat and let him bleed out in front of you."

The room fell into darkness as their captor left with the flashlight. The sound of footsteps retreated like an angel of death. Except this angel of death would be returning to finish the job later.

"Thanks, Brent. I'll meet you at *Witches Haven*. We'll break in if we have to." Jerome waited for the obligatory objection and cut Brent off before he could finish arguing. "If it'll make you feel better, check with Samson. He'll back me up." Jerome snapped his cell phone shut and turned his vehicle toward downtown. Having Verity missing did nothing for his roiling nerves. She wasn't at home, so that left the store. Any alternative didn't bode well. An insistent vibration against his hip warned him that his phone was about to ring. With a curse, he grabbed it. "Brent, I'm on my way. Can't it wait?"

"Sorry to disappoint, but this isn't Brent."

The whispering voice oozed from the phone and set Jerome's warning instincts on full alert. It was a familiar voice, obviously muffled by something held over the receiver, but he couldn't tell whether it was a man or woman speaking. He only knew that evil breathed on the other end of the phone.

Dreading the answer, he asked. "Okay. Who am I speaking with then?" The caller chuckled. But Jerome wasn't feeling very humorous and he'd run out of patience almost before the day had begun, so he snapped his phone shut. Distaste at the maliciousness he'd come in contact with touched deep in his gut and worked up to his throat. Feeling the need to throw up, he yanked his car to the side of the road, opened the window, and gulped in a lungful of fresh air.

The jarring ring of his phone sent fresh fear through him. With shaking hands, he answered. "What?"

"Never do that to me again, or I'll make sure you're very, very sorry."

The caller's voice shook with anger. Jerome smiled. Seemed he wasn't the only one riding high on emotion.

Maybe he'd gain control over the situation yet.

"Who are you, and what do you want?"

"You can't expect me to give you all the answers so easily, can you?"

"Then why are you calling me?"

"I have a special surprise for you. Oh, yes. You'll like this."

"Look, I'm busy and don't have time for this shit. Goodbye." It was an awful chance, but Jerome was so tired of playing games. It was time to make things happen. He ended the connection.

The phone rang almost immediately, and he answered.

"This is your last chance. Tell me what you want or I won't answer next time."

"I told you not to hang up on me. Now you'll be sorry."

Footsteps on wood sounded over the phone, as well as a door opening and a hollow echo. Then a sound that ripped at Jerome's heart. A solid thump. Once. Twice. But it was the familiar howl and yelping following what must have been an attack on a dog Jerome thought dead. Chance. Then voices yelling for the attack to stop. Jesus fucking Christ, he knew those voices.

He screamed into the phone. "Stop. Stop it." Anger and pain tore through him. "Just tell me what you want. I'll do anything." Desperation lent validity to his declaration, and it must have been enough to convince the caller because the attack stopped. For a second, the only sound he heard was a mournful whimper. Unabashed tears slipped from his eyes. "Chance," he whispered. "I'm so sorry."

"Well. I see we have an understanding."

"Yes."

"I thought that would end it. I've waited far too long for this day."

"Just tell me what to do." Wound tighter than his nerves could handle, Jerome forced the words through clenched teeth.

"Come to the Good house. I'm setting up a wonderful surprise for you. Oh, and don't call anyone or...well, you had a taste of what I'll do." The click of the phone signaled the caller disconnecting, but not before the sound of triumphant laughter sounded through the line.

Jerome stared at the phone and swore. Damn it. Chance hadn't died in the fire. And Eldon? His friend's unusual absence all day now made sense, as did Skye and Flora's lack of communication. Oh, man, this was not good. The phone call had left his nerves jumping and his inside twisted with fear, anger, and helplessness. Whoever had been on the other end of the phone had murdered his mother, was responsible for recent murders, and could likely kill again before the day ended if he didn't do something. He needed to get control and calm down.

Taking Samson's earlier advice, he closed his eyes, relaxed, and cleared his mind. Mentally reining in his emotions and calming his rapid heartbeat, he was able to feel tense, knotted muscles relax and let go. Heat hummed through his veins and his heart beat in time with the flow of life-giving blood through his body. Giving free rein to the spread of energy, he felt a burgeoning sense of his own innate powers raging from deep within, and it felt amazing. Surely he could handle anything. He was ready.

Breaking all speed limits, he spared no time reaching the Good house. His journey would finally end in the same place where it had begun thirty years earlier.

CHAPTER THIRTY

When he reached Skye's house, late afternoon had passed to early dusk, and the events of the day had taken their toll. Weary, hungry, and emotionally wrenched, Jerome rallied his energy and took the front steps two at a time. Now was not the time for weakness. He threw open the front door and stepped into the house.

The smell of burning candles and the cloying scent of various oils and herbs attacked his nose, while the overwhelming feel of dark magic assaulted him to the extent that he staggered. Unseen fingers probed at his skin and attempted to invade his mind, and it took all Jerome's focus to repel the force. A murky mist shot with shadows of black twisted through the hallway and into the library. No surprise there. What began in that room would end in that room. Jerome knew that as clearly as he knew, that danger beckoned him. Taking a deep breath to restore composure and strengthen his state of mind, Jerome moved with deadly intent to the library.

Only partially sure what to expect, Jerome wasn't prepared for the blast of putrid energy that hit him full on and forced the breath from his body in a gasp of disbelief and pain. He gathered his senses, clenched his teeth, and threw up a field of white light energy around himself. Protected from the unseen forces battering him, he performed a sweeping gaze around the room to make sure that no one waited to attack him physically.

With all shades and curtains shut against the fading afternoon sun, candles provided the only source of light. The many-hued flames lent shadows to a scene horribly reminiscent of the past, and his grasp on the present wavered.

Time receded into a haze of memories, and he was a scared young boy clinging to his mother's leg while she explained the approaching ritual. Soft, gentle, with a touch of huskiness, her voice soothed and reassured.

"Jerome, you need to understand the powers that flow within you. Tonight is the first step toward understanding the responsibility that comes with such a legacy." She put her arm around his shoulders and hugged him closely. The scent of lavender drifted over him and his nervousness had eased. After all, it was only a summer solstice ritual, and he had been curious about the strange feelings and sensations he'd experienced lately. His mother was there. Nothing could go wrong.

But it had. And the resulting circumstances from that night had somehow led to this night. A mournful whine and voices calling his name drew him fully back into the present. Shit. How long had his mind drifted in the past? His gaze swept the room, his police training allowing him to analyze and catalog everything in an instant.

His gut clenched at the sight of the pentagram drawn in red on the library floor. The center of the pentagram gave rise to a wooden altar laden with a silver bowl, two black candles, a deck of tarot cards, various figurines twisted into macabre shapes and near impossible sexual positions, and a sharp-edged knife.

Except for the strange figurines, the altar seemed to be set up identically to what Jerome remembered from that long ago night. Once assured that no one lurked about in the shadows, he turned his attention back to the pentagram. Drawn large enough so that the points ran almost from wall to wall, what he saw flamed him with anger and fear. Eldon, Skye, Flora, and Chance each held a position at the tip of a pentagram point, their very presence adding a living addition to the ancient symbol.

Chance whimpered a greeting. His loyal canine friend lay there panting and whining, probably exhausted and in pain from the beating Jerome had heard earlier over the phone. Tears filled his eyes and fell freely at the sight of Skye, bound and helpless. Her plight forced a growl of primal anger and possessive savagery from deep within him. Filled with fear mixed with a hint of stubbornness, her blue eyes glowed luminescent in the soft candlelight. A grimace of pain touched her face, and anger burned like acid in his stomach.

"Cripes, son, it's good to see you." Eldon's voice was strained and raspy. Jerome assumed he must have done a lot of yelling.

"Thank the fates you're here, Jerome," Flora whispered.

"Thank God I'm in time." He barely managed to choke the words out. Each one of these people, and Chance, held a place in his life and heart. So much that solving his mother's murder suddenly moved down on his list of priorities. For the first time he could remember since losing her, something held more importance to him. Saving the ones he cared about. Jerome moved toward them, but before he could take a step, the whisper of a breath warmed his neck.

"I reserved the fifth point for you."

Jerome's gut reacted to the familiar voice. There was now no doubt who was responsible for all this. Reining in his desire to smash something, Jerome turned to face the person who'd set this horrific scene and held prisoner everyone he cared about.

"Matthew." He stared into a face lit with fanatical fervor. Matthew's eyes glowed with inner madness while malevolence colored his aura dark.

Jerome mentally strengthened the white light barrier around himself. Then he noticed the gun in Matthew's hand. "I see you don't trust your powers against mine," he taunted.

Irritation flickered across Matthew's face. "You always thought you were better than me. Even that bitch who whelped you thought you were too good to associate with me."

247

Jerome almost reacted to the blasphemy of that bastard daring to talk about his mother like that, but he realized he needed to remain calm. Or they would all die. He clenched his fists and let Matthew continue.

"She refused my mother's offer for us to train together, saying that I would hold you back because your powers were pure, whereas mine were tainted. I'll never forget hearing her say that. Of course, I was supposed to be in bed at the time, but I couldn't trust my own mother to look after my best interests, so I snuck downstairs. I've hated you ever since." To emphasize his point, Matthew jabbed the gun into Jerome's side and pushed him toward the one empty pentagram point. "Now I'll have my vengeance. Against the arrogant Goods as well as you. I'll prove that my tainted power is stronger than yours."

"Come on, Matthew, none of this is his fault. Or ours. You're holding a grudge against the wrong people. Why not just let us go? We'll forget any of this ever happened." Flora pleaded.

"Not your fault." Matthew's voice screeched with anger. "Everyone here is guilty." He sneered and jabbed the gun in Jerome's direction. "Take out your handcuffs and put them on."

When Jerome hesitated, Matthew strode over, grabbed Skye's hair and pulled her into a kneeling position with the gun at her temple.

Jerome's mind raced. He couldn't let Matthew hurt Skye, but if he handcuffed himself, he'd be almost useless. Matthew clicked the hammer back on the gun. The distinct sound caused Flora to gasp. "Please do what he says, Jerome."

Frustration and helplessness tore at him as he yanked his handcuffs from his pocket and snapped them around his wrists. "Dammit, Matthew, if it's me you hate so much, let them go."

Matthew laughed, more at ease now that Jerome was incapacitated. "You don't get it. I hate all of you. This is much bigger than a rivalry that began between two boys."

"Well then, tell us what it's about so we can understand," Jerome snapped.

Without answering, Matthew shoved the gun into his waistband and moved to the altar. Skye sank back to the floor. Safe for now. Knots of tension unwound in Jerome's belly. Damn, what did this guy want? Where had all that hate come from? If Jerome could find the answer to that, he might be able to figure a way out.

Intent on arranging items on the altar, Matthew seemed distracted, maybe even dazed. A low humming rolled from his throat and the occasional sneer twisted his features. And then, with one swift movement, he grabbed a knife from the altar and advanced on Skye. Jerome made a move, but a force pressed heavy on his chest, keeping him in place. Matthew clutched the knife, white-fisted, and laughed when Skye tried to pull away from him. He snatched her arm and raised her hand. One slice of the knife across her palm caused a thin stream of blood to flow. Pulling her hand to him, Matthew smeared the blood across his chest, all the while chanting a strange, guttural language.

He repeated the same with each person there, as well as Chance. Each swath of blood, he smeared onto himself seemed to incite his chanting into a frenzied screech. Covered in blood and looking as if the hold on his sanity had slipped beyond return, Matthew moved to the altar and began to arrange the items more precisely. His attention was no longer on the prisoners.

Skye frowned and looked hopefully at Jerome. He read her thoughts as easily as if she'd spoken aloud. Now's the time to try to escape. Jerome agreed. Wriggling carefully on his butt across the floor, he moved beside Skye, turned his back to her, and struggled to loosen the ropes around her wrists, ignoring the handcuffs chafing his own.

Leaning close, she whispered, "What do I do when I'm free?"

He smiled at her encouragingly. "I have no idea. Play it by ear."

"Play it by ear? For Heaven's sake, come up with something better than that?"

He yanked at her ropes, doing a quick check to make sure Matthew hadn't come back to awareness. "We need to get out of here. Matthew's insane and not afraid to kill. Once you're free, grab the key from my front pocket, unlock my cuffs, and then untie your mom, Eldon, and Chance. If Matthew returns to any semblance of sanity, I'll keep him occupied while you guys escape."

One last tug, and Skye was free. Matthew's chanting increased.

"Look at him," Skye whispered.

Jerome couldn't believe the evidence of what was right in front of him. Pulsing with heat felt throughout the room, Matthew swayed in time to some unseen music or chant. His physical body took shape in varying degrees of density, giving way to forms that occupied nightmares. Twisted, deformed shapes. Atrocities against humanity. First, a slobbering, humpbacked reptilian creature with fangs and blood-red scales. Then, a winged beast with claw feet, strands of greasy hair, and bulging eyes. Too many shifts of form to comprehend them all, but Jerome knew that Matthew had been right. This was no rivalry started between two young boys. Matthew was nothing but a pawn for an evil as ancient as the beginning of time; the epitome of the constant battle between dark and light, monstrous and angelic, perverted, and pure.

A combined gasp of horror lent speed to Skye and Jerome. "Go. Free the others." He whispered urgently.

Skye moved while Jerome watched Matthew. His mind raced with possibilities. Even if they all got free, what then? How could they stand against whatever it was that Matthew had become? Oh, oh. It looked as if they were going to find out, because Matthew turned from the altar, his eyes glowing like red coals in the dark of the library. Unaware of Matthew's attention, Skye worked furiously at Flora's bonds. Maybe he could waylay the monster long enough and intercept any movement that Matthew might make in Skye's direction. It was a futile effort. Matthew merely laughed and flicked a hand that sent Jerome flying across the room and smashing into the desk.

Cripes, that hurt. Jerome sucked in a breath of air that jolted his bruised ribs. What now? Matthew didn't leave him in suspense for long.

"Don't bother." He sneered at Skye. Rumbling and rolling, the words slipped from his mouth in varying tones and different speeds, so the effect was of one person speaking with the cadence of many. "I no longer need physical restraints to keep you here." He shrugged. "Your fate is written, so you might as well agree."

Skye's gaze darted between Jerome and Matthew, the hope dimming with each second as she realized they were lost. She let go of her mother's half untied ropes, fixed her gaze on Matthew, and stood. "Fine. What is it you want?"

"Why, the knife, of course."

CHAPTER
THIRTY-ONE

S kye trembled. She faced Matthew, yet saw no sign of him reflected in the eyes of the creature standing before her. In fact, if she wasn't mistaken, his features still wavered in and out of solid substance. She could have sworn that it was a young woman with thin features and pinched lips looking at her, but Matthew's features returned too quickly to be sure. What she knew was that Matthew waited expectantly, but she didn't intend on handing over the knife. She couldn't. Not to this abhorrence of humankind.

She shrugged, presenting a nonchalant attitude she wasn't feeling. "I don't know what you're talking about." A lie that she regretted instantly as crippling pain shot through her. Deep into her stomach and then winding around her intestines, a pain so hot that she went numb. She fell to her knees at the same time as Jerome leaped across the room and tackled Matthew. The struggle only lasted a second before Jerome writhed on the floor in obvious pain.

Matthew stood and flicked a piece of dust from his shirt. "I said, I want the knife. You know what knife I'm talking about, and I know it's in your possession. Stop playing me for a fool."

Skye turned a pleading look to her mother, who mouthed the words, *I'm sorry*, and sent a stroke of comforting energy. Skye just shook her head. This wasn't her mother's fault any more than it was hers. Something far beyond their scope of understanding or responsibility possessed Matthew. But what to do about it? To hand over the knife would mean their deaths, she was sure, but not to hand it over would also end in their death, and then Matthew would just go searching for it himself. Why didn't he just kill them and go look for the knife? He must need them alive for something. An idea curled around her mind. She faced Matthew.

"I'll give you the knife, but you have to let the others go first."

"No," Matthew bellowed. "Everyone here must pay for their deeds."

"What deeds? Jerome is the wronged one here. It's his mother who was murdered, not yours." She shot Jerome a look of sympathy, and she wanted to make sure he was okay. He nodded at her and stood on shaky feet.

"She deserved to die. She tried to stop my mother from performing the ceremony that would have given me the power I deserve."

Flora spoke. "The knife ceremony that Verity attempted was for you?"

"Yes. You all should have died that night; sacrifices to the dark forces for bestowing the power of the knife on me." Frustrated, he clenched his fists and screamed. "Except my stupid mother had the wrong knife. Nothing went as it should have and you all lived. That is, all of you except Amanda. She recognized the verse as the one that would transfer the power of the knife to another, and she threatened to expose us to the coven. That wasn't wise. She had to die. Don't you see?"

Afraid at first that Jerome would attempt another attack, Skye looked over at him to see that the opposite was true. Tears streamed down his cheeks, and he stood silent and still. She ached for him. He'd lost both parents in his life and now had to listen to the animal who'd killed his mother explain it away so calmly. She realized how fortunate she'd been growing up with the love of both parents and how much she'd taken their love for granted. Suddenly it meant everything to her to save the ones she cared about, even if it meant she had to die. Resolved and determined, she faced Matthew.

"So, decide now. Set the others free for my life and the knife."

"No, Skye. You can't do that," her mother pleaded. "The Fates will keep us safe, but we have to stay together. Trust and believe. Eldon and I are strong, and both you and Jerome possess blood awash with light energy and old magic. You just have to believe. Whoever Matthew has become will be no match for the four of us. But we have to stick together. We have to combine our powers."

"How sweet." Matthew's tone implied anything but that sentiment. "I won't free anyone." He strode to Eldon and yanked him to his feet. "But I will thrust this knife into his gut and watch him die a horrible death unless you go get the knife for me now."

A sudden truth slammed into Skye. One of Sarah's diary entries said the knife was spell bound and only visible to a Good, or to others if held bare in the hands of a Good. She gasped and then clamped her hand over her mouth. How could she use the information to her advantage?

Eldon didn't struggle, but sensing the last minutes of his life, cried out. "No. Don't give him the knife."

"Ahhh," Matthew shouted as he plunged the knife into Eldon's belly and threw him to the floor. Pulsing with anger and twisting into distorted forms again, he advanced on Skye. "Get the knife now, or I'll kill everyone you care about." With a whimper, she ran toward the library door. She couldn't stand there and let Matthew kill everyone. She'd get the knife and figure out what to do then. Fingers curled around her ankle, and she almost screamed until she realized it was her mother.

Beckoning Skye closer, she whispered, "Remember, the person who holds the knife, controls the knife. When the time is right, unwrap it and harness the souls within."

Skye hesitated, remembering the howling melee of discontented souls, and how the distorted shadows of light and dark had drawn her to the knife; almost too far.

"It's okay, Skye. You overcame the sensations last time. You gained control once and the spirits in the knife will respect you for it."

"Go," Matthew bellowed from across the room.

She scrambled from the room and tore up the stairs to where she'd hidden the knife. She and her mother had been planning on binding it once they figured out the ceremony, so she hadn't hidden it, only shoved it into one of her drawers. Retrieving it easily enough, she ran back downstairs. Upon entering the library, she noticed that Eldon still lived. Pale-faced and in obvious pain, he wasn't bleeding as much as she would have thought. She had to think of something fast and maybe they could get help to Eldon before he died.

Matthew's eyes lit with avaricious thirst when he glimpsed the knife clutched in her hand. "Give it to me," he commanded, without taking his eyes off the canvas package.

"No." Skye moved the knife behind her back. "Let the others go first."

"Nooo." Matthew emitted an unholy screech and lunged for the knife. Skye sidestepped him and sprinted across the room. He turned to her and bared his teeth. When he spoke, a heavy accent rendered his words hard to interpret.

"Witch. Ye tormente me still."

Skye looked on, amazed as Matthew's features shifted to the feminine face she thought she'd glimpsed earlier. Even his voice rose and thinned out to sound like a girl or a young woman. Not sure what he meant, but wanting to find out more, Skye asked, "Torment you? I barely know you. What could I possibly have done to torment you?"

"Eeeiyah! Doe not speake so to me. I am named Ann Putnam, and it incites my most righteous anger to looke upon the offspring of that bitch Sarah Good." The distorted person, who was once Matthew, but now Ann, jabbed a finger at Jerome. "And ye, ye filthy offspring of a deceitful judge. Muchly did my embarrassment

CATHY WALKER

follow me through life when William Phips declared all testimony based on ghosts and specters to be false. Townspeople snickered behind me, besieging me with disdainful comments. Your ancestor with his holy decrees and court proceedings gave cause for me to apologize." She spit on the floor and glowered at Jerome. "Ye shall be most painfully put to death."

"This is impossible," Flora whispered.

Skye tended to agree with her mother, except the proof wavered before her. She noted that her mother had moved over to Eldon and pressed her sweater to his wound. He was still alive, but wouldn't be for long. Jerome had moved closer, keeping behind Matthew—Ann, who was distracted by the knife.

"She's right. It is impossible." Skye said.

"Obviously, it is possible." Matthew preened and ran his hands over his body in a feminine manner. His form wavered between man and woman. Matthew and Ann, finally remaining as Ann. "I have waited untold passing of years to revenge myself for being denied. So afflict'd have I become with a need to learn witch's ways that I made a covenant to procure the knife that Sarah has denied me. Bitch. She denied me." A horribly twisted smile curved her lips. "But she and her whelp paid. Now ye, her wretched descendants shall pay."

Skye stepped back as the apparition in front of her advanced, but the move was unnecessary. Amidst another transformation and a screeching denial, Matthew stood in front of her. All signs of Ann Putnam gone. Jeesh, this was more than weird.

"No. Vengeance is mine, not yours." Matthew castigated the absent Ann. He wheeled around and faced Jerome. "You and your mother denied me my rights as much as Sarah denied Ann hers. It felt good to plunge the knife into her stomach and watch her writhe in agony."

Anticipating Jerome's reaction, Matthew slammed him against the wall with a flick of a wrist. Skye moved toward them, but realized that keeping the knife safe was more important at that moment.

"At Mother's suggestion, we used Amanda's blood to perform a ceremony that would eventually return all of you to Salem. She thought we could find the correct knife and try again." His self-satisfied laugh grated on Skye's already frazzled nerves. "It seems she was right. Here we all are again. Too bad she couldn't have minded her own business about other things." He shrugged. "Oh, well, I'd grown tired of playing the momma's boy. Don't look so shocked. I didn't really consider her my mother, merely a vessel that gave birth to the physical body needed to hold my spirit." Sadness flitted across his face and his shoulders slumped ever so slightly. "To tell the truth, some days I am torn between two souls, not knowing which one is stronger, more ambitious, or more likely to win. It's quite tiresome."

Skye blanched. She'd held some hope that Matthew might listen to reason, but a man who would kill his own mother had to be beyond redemption. Yet, she still tried to appeal to that sliver of humanity she glimpsed. "Matthew, you don't have to do this. There are ways to enhance your abilities that don't involve murder."

"You. Do. Not. Understand." Each word spit from his lips like bullets. "Stupid, stupid woman. This is not about my powers. This is about revenge. Plain and simple. Short and sweet. Revenge." Clearly agitated and reaching the end of his patience, Matthew moved toward Skye. "The deal is that I get a physical body and my revenge, while the dark forces get the power of the knife. Now, everyone return to your place on the pentagram. It's time to begin."

No one moved. Matthew rolled his eyes. "Must we always do this the hard way?" He raised a hand, but the threat alone sent Flora and Jerome to their positions. Eldon already lay in his place, and Skye hesitated, realizing that it was time to use the knife.

She took a deep breath and surrounded herself with white light. Matthew put his hand out and asked for the knife, but Skye ignored him and focused on the sudden, overwhelming array of energy threads thrown her way. She recognized her mother's touch. Soft and pink, it was an offering of love, the one emotion that could overcome all others. Colored deep blue and gold, Jerome's touch exuded protection and strength, although the palpable veins of pink surprised and pleased her. Even Eldon sent a wavering yet encouraging thread her way; brown for stability and grounding. Surety and power flamed through her, strengthened and filled her with purpose.

Unease flickered deep in Matthew's eyes, but he advanced another step and demanded the knife. Tauntingly lifting the corner of her mouth, she held it up, cradling it in her palms. "Is this what you want?"

Desire and greed gave fire to Matthew's power, but it also weakened the tenuous hold he had on himself. Thrusting his chin forward, arching his neck, and clenching his fists, he looked to be in a battle with inner demons. The grotesque re-shaping of his facial features started again and Skye almost lost her composure, but pulsing encouragement from the others held her fast.

"So who do I give the knife to? You, Matthew, or Ann? Or maybe the dark forces would like it instead."

"Give it to me."

The high-pitched screech that rasped from Matthew sounded like a cross between a train whistle and roaring fire, while the contortions that twisted his body were unlike anything Skye could imagine. Bone crunched and skin molded into horrendous shapes as the demons within battled for control of Matthew's body. Not to mention Ann's stubbornness as she tried to exert herself into the grasping attempt for the knife.

It was time. Skye steeled herself and unfolded the canvas. Grasping the knife's hilt in her right hand, she noticed the same coldness as before, even as the breath whooshed from her chest and the voices of the lost souls assaulted her.

Screaming, demanding, wanting freedom and redemption, they danced around the library. She remembered her mother's words. The one who controls the knife controls the souls within.

Relax and breathe. And then she knew what she must do. Use the powers of everyone in the room. Grasp the knife with intent and radiate that intent to the souls of the knife.

Clenching the knife with both hands, she thrust it high above her head. Matthew screamed and leaped for her, and even though she felt him battering against her, some kind of unseen barrier kept him from reaching her. Incensed, he rammed into the barrier again, and Skye knew she had to hurry before he broke through. Combining the energy from everyone in the room, adding it to her thoughts, she formed it all into a tangible heat that she shot through her arms and into the knife. The knife tip glowed orange, darkened to red, and then burst forth with a blinding white flame that bathed the room in an otherworldly blaze.

And then the knife jumped in her hands. Afraid of losing it at first, she then realized that she'd actually gained control. The light connected to the restless souls wandering from shadows to light around the room. Drawing them together in a single pulsing stream, it shaped them and gave them purpose. Skye's purpose. Elation and hope bubbled. She had it. She controlled the souls and the knife. Smiling, she lowered the blade and aimed the tip at their captor.

"It's time to end this, Matthew."

"Nooo!" A heart-wrenching screech came out of nowhere and a figure, no more than a blur, raced across the floor and launched itself at Matthew. All hell literally broke loose.

CHAPTER THIRTY-TWO

Jerome hated being helpless. His ribs burned with each breath he took, and he thought he might have broken an arm when Matthew sent him flying against the wall. He felt battered—inside and out, and he didn't feel the elation he should have at finally discovering his mother's killer. Probably because some perverse reincarnated version of Ann Putnam now threatened everyone he cared about.

He couldn't just sit there and do nothing like an unwilling prisoner sacrificed on the tip of a pentagram point by a freak bent on a twisted sort of revenge. Damn it, he needed to help Skye. Just look at her. She was magnificent. Standing with the knife thrust high, her body arched, dark hair flowing down her back with tiny sparks of energy highlighting it, and her eyes glowing with an unnatural blue sheen. Attempting to stand, he found himself thrust back on his butt when the entire room lit into a dazzling blast of light. Instinctively, he closed his eyes and covered them with his hand.

The light faded almost instantly, and with the familiar dim candle light came a new sense of power in the air. He glanced around the room for whatever had changed. Souls, once shifting and darting about aimlessly, now formed a single shape. A triumphant glint danced across Skye's face, and he realized she had lowered the knife so it now pointed at Matthew's chest.

For the first time since entering the library, Jerome held hope that they might make it out of this situation with their lives. Flora had crept over to Chance and loosened his ropes, while Eldon had crawled across the floor and grab the gun Matthew had lost during one of his twisting contortions.

Then it happened.

And it happened so fast that Jerome barely had time to stand. Matthew's enraged scream paled in comparison to the scream of whoever had burst through the library door and leaped at him. Tumbling across the floor, Matthew and his assailant banged into the altar, the resulting crash adding to the chaos of the moment.

"How could you do that to me? Your own mother."

Verity, in a frenzied fit of temper, scratched at Matthew and slapped mindlessly at his head. Discolored, swollen, and tear-streaked, her face contorted into a mask of disbelief, while a blood-soaked stain seeped through her blouse and created a stark contrast to her usual perfect appearance.

Matthew fought back, but seemed to have reverted to human powers. He threw his arms across his face and rolled away from Verity's concentrated attack. He kicked out at her and a cracking sound preceded her falling to the ground with one leg angled awkwardly beneath her. Panting, Matthew scrambled to his feet.

"Bitch. How dare you interfere?"

Verity reached out imploringly. "I'm your mother. Everything I've ever done has been for you. I helped you hide Amanda's body. I knew you murdered those girls and told no one. It was all for you. Why did you try to kill me? I don't understand." She whimpered and slumped to the ground in obvious pain.

Regaining his composure, Matthew shrugged his shoulders back and lifted his chin. "Like I told you earlier, I don't need you anymore." He lifted a hand and thrust his fingers outwards at her. Nothing happened. Disbelieving, he tried again. Nothing. Snarling, he spun about to face Skye. "Give me the knife."

"I don't think so," Skye murmured, intent on her task.

Each second with the knife directed at Matthew seemed to sap him of strength. That was why he'd not been able to defend himself against Verity. That was why he staggered weakly toward

Skye and Jerome. Just as a backup Jerome raced over to Eldon and relieved him of the gun, giving his friend's arm an encouraging squeeze.

Chance added to the melee with his stream of barking. Grateful to be free, the canine limped over to Jerome and moved excitedly around him. Thank God he was limping only slightly and seemed to be no worse off after his beating. Rubbing Chance vigorously to reassure him, Jerome kept the gun leveled at the waning Matthew, just in case.

Matthew sank to his knees and wailed as he clawed at himself. Even after everything Jerome had seen, the scene struck him with awe. Darts of light spun around Matthew and enveloped him. Glowing light entered his nostrils, ears, and mouth, only to turn about and suck from him the very darkness that had led him from one lifetime to the next.

"No. Please. They're all over me. Sucking me dry. Stop them. I can't stand the pain." Each word sank into a swirl of unintelligible gibberish and any threat Matthew offered sank with him. No one spoke while he lay on the floor and whimpered. His eyes held no semblance of intelligence and a blob of spit hung from his lips. Broken. Beaten. A useless husk of a body.

Dragging herself across the floor, Verity fell over Matthew and sobbed. "Oh, my baby. I'll take care of you." Gently, she brushed his hair back from his forehead. "Everything I did was for you. Only you. Now you're mine forever and I'll make sure no one ever hurts you again."

Jerome shook his head and turned his attention to the others. Skye looked exhausted, and without hesitation, he wrapped his arms around her. A sob caught in her throat and she dropped the knife from bloodless hands. She was alive. They were all alive. He couldn't believe it.

The moment Skye regained some strength, he reluctantly let go of her. There were things to do. He lifted her chin with his finger and looked into her eyes. "Hey. Are you okay?"

She nodded. A tremulous smile touched her lips. "I will be. Go see to the others."

Eldon needed the most immediate attention. Flipping his cell phone from his pocket, Jerome made a 911 call and requested an ambulance. Then he called Samson.

"It's over."

"Oh. I'm assuming that everything's okay."

"I'm talking to you, so, yep, but you should be the one to come to this crime scene. I don't think anyone else would know quite what to make of it." He looked at the pentagram drawn in blood, the scattered altar items, a slobbering Matthew, the knife they could never hand over to the police, a wounded Eldon, and a slightly crazy Verity who'd likely get locked away and never see her son again despite her assurances to take care of him. No, this incident needed writing up with a lot of creative license. Samson could deal with that. Jerome was just too damn tired.

***

Epilogue

C andles washed the library in dancing hues of light and color. Celtic music played softly in the background, the bagpipes haunting and emotional, while the flute lightened the mood with its airy, smooth tones. Skye had spent all of yesterday scrubbing Matthew's pentagram into oblivion and re-varnishing the wooden floor.

She smiled at her mom and Jerome's heart about burst from his chest. Free from the tension and distrust of the last few days—not to mention some crazy, reincarnated person out for revenge, almost killing them—Skye had taken on an ethereal beauty. More sure of herself and her powers, the woman he loved had bloomed into a vivacious, energetic person he couldn't wait to know better.

"Mom, you don't look a day over thirty-five," Skye said.

"On that, we agree, daughter." A gruff voice from the doorway signaled Walter's arrival. His release from the hospital yesterday had heralded a night of celebration and Jerome still felt the after-effects of too much beer consumed, not to mention spending half the night catching the poor guy up on events he'd missed.

Walter's reaction to Jerome and his original accusations against Skye and Flora had almost led to a physical confrontation, but Flora had smoothed the way. Thank God. Even though he was older, Walter was a big man and Jerome hadn't wanted to find out who was the stronger one.

"Good morning, dear." Flora moved to kiss her husband, her gold silk robe floating about her, and her hair hanging halfway down her back in a cloud of silver.

"Hey, Dad. Glad you could make it," Skye teased.

"Humph! Are you kidding? I wouldn't miss this for anything. After all, this darned knife caused all the trouble, so the sooner we bind it, the better. That's my thought on the subject. I'm just here to make sure it gets done right this time."

Skye and Flora rolled their eyes and, with one smooth move, gave him a gentle shove that landed him on the couch beside Jerome. The two men looked at each other. Nostrils flared. Primal instincts climbed and then subsided as rational thinking intervened.

Walter nodded. "Jerome."

"Walter."

"Jeez. Men." Skye shook her head and moved to the altar beside Flora.

"Ignore them for now, dear. We have more important things to attend."

Walter raised an eyebrow and whispered to Jerome. "Hmm, more important than us? Remind me to have a heart-to-heart with you about women sometime later."

"Yes, sir. I look forward to it." From the corner of his eyes, Jerome saw Skye's mouth curve into a smile, and he had to force himself to remain serious. Her father was not the kind of person to tick off.

Walter reached over and slapped him on the knee hard enough to hurt. "Good. Good. Now, we better be quiet, Flora's giving me the evil eye."

Ignoring his stinging knee, Jerome let his hand drop beside him and fondled Chance's ears. The canine whimpered with joy and rolled over to sleep some more. The vet had given him a clean bill of health, but said Chance would need a lot of rest. Keeping one hand resting on his dog, Jerome turned his attention to the ritual.

Skye's silk robe matched Flora's exactly, except for color. Where Flora's was gold with threads of burgundy interwoven in the fabric, Skye's was sapphire with threads of jade shot through it. *It matches both our eyes*, were her words when she'd shown the robe to him that morning. Just after they'd finished making love. His face heated, and he had to shift uncomfortably as thoughts of their lovemaking, both night and morning, invaded his mind. Thank goodness the ritual had started, or Walter's questioning glare would have needed an answer. Instead, Jerome just smiled and pointed at the woman.

The music merged beautifully with the ritual, weaving and enchanting. The tune rose and fell with Skye and Flora's low chanting. Warmth and love filled the library, bringing with it a sense of oneness and belonging. Even though Walter and he were there as bystanders, Jerome felt the ensuing connection between the four of them. Family and love. What could be stronger? His throat swelled and his eyes teared up when he thought of how his mother would love to be here now. She'd love that her son had found a place to belong. A family to belong to.

He heaved a deep, quivering sigh and let go of the uncertainties that had ruled his life for thirty years. He'd found a new life amidst the shaky foundations of his old one. He watched Skye unwrap the knife from its canvas covering and hold it in her palms. A tear wound a pathway down her cheek, and he knew she was also saying goodbye to a lifetime of questioning who she was. She'd found a new relationship with her mother. Flora and Skye had talked long into the morning to settle their somewhat rocky relationship, and Flora had admitted that she'd been wrong to hold Skye back from her powers. That was like cutting someone off from his or her sight, sound, touch, smell, or taste. Skye's powers were as much a part of her being as any one of her other senses.

Walter nudged him. "Are you paying attention?"

"Yeah. Thanks."

The book, *Faerie Enchantments and Sorcerer Magick*, lay open on the desk and Flora recited a verse while Skye held the knife high above her head. They needed to free the souls before binding the knife, because once bound, the knife would trap the poor souls forever. Flora's voice increased in tempo. Each word spoken created a vacuum in the library. Strange words, reverently spoken, yet once uttered, forgotten.

Jerome struggled to understand them, but his brain was a sieve and the poem lost itself in the shadows of memory. He shrugged. Who was he to question anything?

Skye's body trembled, and the knife took on a luminescent glow. Pulsing, shimmering, it released the souls with one great shift that caused it to jump in her outstretched hands. No screeching or swirling this time. The souls were free and had a purpose. Twirling upward as if one entity, they disappeared with barely a whisper. Although, they left behind a pink aura of love that bathed the room for a moment and then dissipated, but not before each person in the room felt the thanks of the long-suffering souls.

Flora closed the book and picked up a black silk cloth, a needle, and thread. Careful not to touch the knife without the benefit of cloth between them, and with Skye moving the knife as needed, Flora wrapped and sewed the knife within the folds. Black would banish any evil from the knife as well as bind the powers of the knife from doing further harm. Once sewn shut, each of them used the palm of their hand to draw an imaginary pentagram over the knife. The proper way. Not Matthew's distorted pentagram.

Carrying the wrapped, blessed knife, Skye moved over to the hidden area behind the bookcase. They had decided to hide the treasure there for now. The house would be around for a long time and this way they could keep an eye on it until they could fill a future Good in on the details. Jerome thought he'd feel something when Skye entered the place that had held his mother's skeleton for so long, but he didn't. The pain was gone, along with the past.

She peeked out from around the bookcase. "What about the book? Should it go here as well?"

"No. I think it's safer to keep them separate. If, fates forbid, anyone finds the knife, at least they won't know the ritual to unbind it. Besides, Nora told us that the book would let us know when it was time to pass it on, so I think we should keep it handy for just that instance."

"Okay." Skye stepped from the secret place and swung the bookcase shut. With a deep sigh of satisfaction, she turned to face the others. "Well. That's that. So, now what?"

Walter jumped from the couch, as spry as if he'd never been in a coma. "Now, I say we go visit your friend, Eldon, in the hospital and then get Jerome here to give us a tour of Salem. I have seen nothing but the inside of a sick room."

Skye grinned. "That sounds like a great idea. Mom and I will get changed, then we can spend the day getting to know my new home."

Walter swung his arm across Jerome's shoulders. "Take your time, ladies. That'll give me a chance to fill this young man in on how to handle your women."

Jerome laughed. "Sir, that's a lesson I'm looking forward to learning." And he meant it with every fiber of his being.

Cradled in the soft embrace of silk and hidden within the dark recesses of a trunk in the attic, the book came to life. It began with the sparkle of white light and increased intensity as the leather binding and parchment pages shone with each color of the rainbow. If anyone had been nearby, they would have heard the thrum of ancient voices chanting in a rhyme indistinguishable as any known language.

Yellowed pages appeared at the back of the book and in a swath of uneven writing, words scratched themselves across the pages. The story of a knife forged in Avalon, given for safekeeping to the witch of Salem, and then lost in the annals of time only to be found in present-day Salem amidst a dark mist of revenge. Each detail of the story that started in a forest glade and ended in a library splayed itself across the pages.

The next action of *Faerie Enchantments and Sorcerer Magick* was to focus its energy and send out a summoning beacon. Times in Salem might seem settled for the moment, but the darkness that had fed on Ann Putnam's need for revenge and manifested in Matthew, did not rest. The face of darkness held many facets and though the knife was safe for now, the invasive nature of the forces haunting Salem had many avenues by which to achieve their twisted goals.

The beacon shot a thread of energy to one close by, and another thread traveled a distance across the land to reach another. Satisfied that both people would answer the summons, the light of the book dimmed and all became silent once again.

AFTERWORD

I hope you enjoyed reading this book and would appreciate if you could leave a review. Reviews help an author with future sales and marketing, so it's a great way to support and motivate the authors that you like. You can find me online at these places:

Website:

https://cathywalkerauthor.com
FB Author Page:

www.facebook.com/cathywalker.author

Acknowlegements

I'd like to thank Captain John A. Jodoin of the Salem Police department for having the patience to answer my many questions about police procedure and Sergeant Peter Shaffaval for showing my husband and me around the station when we dropped by for a tour. Also, thanks to Flora Tonthat of the Northey Street B&B for providing us with a place to stay and great morning sustenance to help us make it through our days of touring the town of Salem. Many thanks also to Jim Moran of Coldwell Banker Residential Brokerage in Waltham, MA. The information you provided me in regards to Salem proved very helpful.

AUTHOR BIO

Books have fueled my imagination since reading the Black Stallion series when I was younger. Never thinking that I could actually write a book, I sat down and began writing anyway. I now have multiple published books and more on the way. All of them with a theme of myths, legends, romance, or fantasy.

I am fortunate enough to live on a farm filled with animals to love and care for. Every morning my dogs, cats, goats, and horses greet me at the barnyard. Spending time with them helps motivate me to write.